C.

Mary
Magdalene

Center Point
Large Print

Also by Diana Wallis Taylor and available
from Center Point Large Print:

Martha

**This Large Print Book carries the
Seal of Approval of N.A.V.H.**

Mary Magdalene

Diana Wallis Taylor

CENTER POINT LARGE PRINT
THORNDIKE, MAINE

This Center Point Large Print edition is published
in the year 2013 by arrangement with Revell,
a division of Baker Publishing Group.

The text of this Large Print edition is unabridged.
In other aspects, this book may
vary from the original edition.
Printed in the United States of America
on permanent paper.
Set in 16-point Times New Roman type.

ISBN: 978-1-61173-573-4

Library of Congress Cataloging-in-Publication Data

Taylor, Diana Wallis, 1938–
Mary Magdalene / Diana Wallis Taylor.
pages ; cm.
ISBN 978-1-61173-573-4 (library binding : alk. paper)
1. Mary Magdalene, Saint—Fiction. 2. Women in the Bible—Fiction.
   3. Large type books. I. Title.
PS3620.A942M39 2012b
813′.6—dc23

2012018482

To women all over the world
who have been maligned,
misunderstood, and shunned,
sometimes with cause, sometimes without.
You are loved dearly by God.
It is his desire that you become
what he created you to be:
a daughter of the King.

Mary Magdalene

❧ 1 ❧

The early morning breeze lifted Mary's shawl, exposing her long dark hair, and brought with it the tangy smell of seaweed. She stood with her mother, Rachel, on the bluff overlooking the harbor of Magdala. Although it was filled with merchant ships and the sea beyond dotted with the white sails of the fishing boats, there was no sign of her father's ship. Mary was almost twelve, and teetering between child and young woman. Patience was not a virtue she embraced. With a sigh, she occupied herself by watching the seagulls dip and soar overhead. It was the fourth day they had come here to watch for him, and Mary felt surely it had to be this morning.

Her mother looked down at her. "It will be good to have your father home again."

Her father, Jared, and his brother, Zerah, built sturdy fishing boats and occasionally small merchant ships. This time Jared had combined a maiden voyage and an excursion to seek out a new source of lumber for their boats. He had been gone a month.

When a small ship rounded the point and entered the harbor, Mary danced with excitement and pulled on her mother's sleeve. "Mama, it's here. There's Abba's ship."

Her mother smiled. "Yes, Mary, I believe it is."

As the vessel approached the dock, small figures threw mooring lines to secure it.

Mary noticed her mother's eyes were moist as she looked out to sea. She knew her mother missed her father as much as she did and had tried to hide her worry. Storms on the Sea of Galilee could be fierce and dangerous for an untried ship.

With a sigh of relief, Rachel turned from the view of the sea. "Your father will need a special welcome today." She motioned to the servant who stood silently nearby. "Eliab, we are ready to go home."

The big African, over six feet tall, nodded. Women didn't venture from the house through some parts of the city without an escort. Mary heard her father say one day that their city was a melting pot for unsavory characters, brigands, and Roman soldiers on leave to watch the games in the Hippodrome. They came to drink and patronize the dark streets of the slums where the brothels flourished.

"They're blight on our city, Jared," their neighbor Samuel had commented one day. "If anything will bring the wrath of the Holy One down on us, it is those places of iniquity."

Jared nodded. "I understand, Samuel, but in a

city this size, one will find all manner of evil."

Now Rachel walked quickly and Mary ran to keep up with her. Eliab followed with long strides. Once or twice she glanced back and he smiled at her, but then his dark face became solemn again, his eyes moving back and forth, scanning their surroundings for danger.

As they walked, Mary heard the sounds of industry everywhere. Hammers sounded from the boatyards, merchants hawked their wares. With over eighty woolen mills in the city, a buzz of voices grew as workers streamed into the warehouses and factories. The scent of perfume wafted through the air from one of the stalls, mingling with the pungent odor of the day's catch spread out in the fish market. Donkeys plodded patiently up the narrow streets, laden with baskets of shells strapped on each side, on their way to the dye makers. Sheep bleated loudly as they were herded into pens, awaiting buyers for the temple sacrifices. In cages along the street of the doves, there was cooing and the fluttering of wings. Mary looked around excitedly. With Eliab next to them, she could happily take in the sights and smells all around her without fear.

She glanced back at the huge man following them and murmured to herself, "I am glad Eliab is with us."

Mary's mind churned with questions she had wanted so much to ask the last few days before her father set sail with the ship. Why the unexplained looks that passed between her parents and why had her normally cheerful mother gone about her work so quietly? Her father, who enjoyed time with his family, appeared distracted and spent long hours at the boatbuilding yard. Fear tugged at her heart, a nagging disquiet followed her like a shadow.

Uncle Zerah had come the evening before the ship sailed. A gaunt man, with a short black beard, he stalked into the house as if loath to be there. When her father was watching, Zerah was the benevolent uncle, smiling indulgently at his niece, but his smile never reached his eyes. Mary knew her uncle was not what he seemed. She was courteous to him, respectful as all children were taught to be, but stayed out of his way.

That night Zerah glowered at his brother and was barely civil to Rachel.

"Zerah, we are brothers . . . ," Jared began, as they ate. "We have the finest boatbuilding yard in Magdala. We must work together—"

"It was necessary to cut costs," Zerah murmured, aware of Rachel and Mary nearby. "You don't appreciate that I can increase our profits."

Her father leaned forward. "At the cost of our good reputation, brother?"

Zerah started to answer, then with an imperceptible nod of his head toward Rachel, looked pointedly at his brother.

Jared followed his gaze and stroked his beard. "Perhaps the garden . . . ?"

Both men rose and strode outside, her father leading the way. Her uncle's face was pinched and hard.

Mary helped her mother put things away and then went up to her bed but couldn't sleep. Voices outside in the garden drew her to the window. Her father and uncle shared an animated conversation, speaking in fierce whispers. She couldn't understand most of their words but caught snatches of the conversation. It seemed to have to do with the new merchant vessel.

"Change your ways, Zerah," Jared admonished, and turned abruptly to return to the house.

Zerah looked after him, then started for the courtyard gate. Suddenly he paused and looked up to Mary's window. His eyes narrowed when he saw her and his face clouded with anger.

The next morning as Mary helped her mother prepare the bread dough, her thoughts tumbled into a question.

"Mama, are Abba and Uncle Zerah angry with each other?"

Her mother slid the paddle with one of the loaves of bread into the clay oven and turned to her. "What made you ask that?"

Mary hung her head. "Last night they were arguing in the garden outside my window about the new ship. Abba was very angry." She told her mother what she'd seen and what little she'd heard.

"They had a disagreement about something. A problem at the shipyard. There is no need to trouble yourself about it."

Mary lifted her face. "I thought you and Abba were angry with each other. We hardly see him anymore. I was afraid."

Her mother turned and drew Mary to her. "There is no trouble between your father and me, just a problem at the shipyard that concerns him."

Mary leaned into her mother's side, relief lightening the burden she had carried. She sent a quick prayer to HaShem, the God Who Sees, and thanked him for hearing her prayers. There was nothing wrong between her parents. It was just business. Her father was a good businessman. He would solve it.

Mary swept the courtyard, looking up at every sound as she waited for her father. When her father opened the gate, she dropped the broom and ran to be gathered in his arms.

"Abba, we saw your ship come in."

"My little blossom, have you grown in the short time I've been gone?"

She giggled. "I am the same, Abba." Then she beamed up at him mischievously. "Is there something in your pocket?"

He tried to look stern, but then smiled and

produced a small, beautifully engraved leather box from the folds of his cloak.

"Oh, thank you, Abba."

"And wife . . ." He held out a lovely scarf in shades of blue and magenta and, as Rachel approached, presented it with a flourish.

"Thank you, Jared." She smiled at the scarf, but then, with a slightly anxious tone, "The voyage went well?"

"The . . . uh . . . problems we discussed were evident. I promised Demas that I would make the necessary repairs at no cost to him."

"Oh, Jared, what are you going to do?"

He gave a slight shake of his head that said they would talk later and turned to Mary. "Tell me, my little flower, what have you been up to while I have been gone? Have you done your lessons?"

"Yes, Abba, I study hard. I have learned the Hebrew alphabet. I can recite it and write it. Would you like me to show you?"

Before Jared could answer, a familiar voice called a greeting and Mary looked up with pleasure. It was her childhood friend and tutor, Nathan.

A few weeks before her father decided to sail on their new ship, he'd approached the local rabbi of the *Bet Hasefer*, the House of the Book. He sought a tutor for Mary. He wanted her to learn the Torah but knew girls were not permitted in the school. The rabbi had been indignant. "It is better that the words of the Law should be burned than that they should be given to a woman."

"What is wrong with a girl learning the Torah?" Jared had argued in vain that Mary was his only child. "I don't want her to be ignorant."

Still the rabbi refused. When her father returned home, Mary asked him what the rabbi had said. Her father, still angry, said, "He told me it is not possible, that girls should be taught the ways of a household, to tend the home and children. He suggested there was no need to trouble your mind with things best left to men." He stalked off to the garden.

Then one day Jared overheard Nathan, Mary's childhood friend and now his apprentice, talking to her about the Torah. Her father took Nathan aside and hired him to come twice a week to tutor Mary. Nathan was admonished that it was best to keep news of the lessons to himself. The young man had agreed readily and the lessons began. Though Nathan was four years older than Mary, because he had grown up with the family, her parents did not think it unseemly for them to sit together in the courtyard. Her mother continued her work, but Mary knew she kept a watchful eye on them.

Nathan greeted Jared respectfully. "Your journey went well, sir?"

"Yes. We need to make a few repairs, but she sailed well."

The young man frowned. Mary had never heard her father mention repairs to any of their boats before. Storm-damaged boats perhaps, but not new ones.

Jared nodded to the bench in the courtyard. "Perhaps the two of you would best begin your lesson." He followed Rachel into the house.

Nathan turned to Mary, his eyes twinkling. "Good morning, my little friend."

"I am getting taller, Nathan, you cannot call me little anymore." She gave him an impudent smile.

He pretended to consider her carefully. "Ah, so you are. Should I call you my big friend?"

She put her hands on her hips. "You may call me, 'my friend Mary.' "

A smile tugged at the corners of his mouth. "Very well, my friend Mary, should we get started?"

She loved having Nathan nearby. He was like the brother she never had. She happily anticipated each lesson.

Soon the two heads were close together as he shared the day's lesson from the Torah. Nathan had her review the twenty-two letters of the Hebrew alphabet, tracing them on a small tablet.

"Aleph, Beth, Gimel, Daleth—" she murmured, concentrating on the symbols.

"Well done, Mary. Soon you will be ready for

individual words. After that, we will learn whole phrases of the Torah."

She was excited to learn the Torah. She knew how important that was to her father, but it was hard to keep her lessons secret from her friends. Yet she had promised Abba, and she would keep her promise.

Suddenly she frowned. "Will HaShem be displeased that I am learning the Holy Scriptures?"

He shook his head. "I think he would be pleased that you are working so hard to know him better."

Warmth filled her heart. She would get to know HaShem better.

She glanced toward the house. "My father is upset about something. I think it has to do with Uncle Zerah."

Nathan shifted on the bench and looked uncomfortable.

She lowered her voice and spoke in a fierce whisper. "You know something."

He avoided her eyes. "I could get in trouble with your father if he knew I told you anything."

Mary leaned forward and willed her voice to remain calm. "I can keep secrets."

He sighed heavily and shrugged. "Perhaps."

"Then tell me—please."

He looked around furtively, then whispered,

"There are problems. Zerah ordered cheaper wood to build the merchant ship."

"That is not a good thing?"

"No, only good cedar should be used for the boats. We used materials of lesser quality, but your uncle did not reduce the price."

Mary frowned, trying to puzzle out what Nathan was telling her. Uncle Zerah was doing something wrong, but she didn't fully understand what it was. "My father found out what my uncle is doing?"

"Yes." He shifted his position on the bench. "I don't think I should say any more."

"My father would never do anything wrong."

"I know, Mary. The shipyard has a fine reputation and your father is known as an honest man." He shrugged. "Your uncle's actions could ruin their business."

Her eyes pooled with tears. She didn't like discord in her family. Her heart was troubled about her uncle, but there was nothing she could do. Then a thought came to her. She must pray. HaShem would help them.

"Uncle Zerah acts strangely." She looked out over the courtyard. "He is nice to me when my parents are nearby, but the look in his eyes frightens me."

Nathan opened his mouth to comment, but just then Mary's mother came toward them from the house.

"The noon meal is ready. Come and help me, Mary. Nathan, my husband invites you to join him for the meal before you return to the yard. We will have a special dinner tonight to celebrate my husband's homecoming—you and your father are also welcome to join us then." She paused, studying them both for a moment. "How are the lessons coming?"

Nathan and Mary exchanged glances. "Mary learns quickly," he said with a smile.

Mary helped her mother serve the bread, cheese, and fruit, then bowed her head as her father prayed.

"Blessed are you, LORD, our God, King of the universe, through whose word everything comes into being."

Jared glanced up at his daughter. "So now you can recite the alphabet. Can you also read the letters?" He waited expectantly. She nodded and began to recite as she had done for Nathan. Her father nodded his head. "That is good. You are teaching her well, Nathan."

Then, to Mary's surprise, her father and Nathan ate the rest of their meal in silence. Mary caught Nathan glancing at her father from time to time, a puzzled look on his face.

When the men returned to the shipyard, Rachel sent Mary to the larger garden outside the walls for some leeks and garlic for their special dinner. Eliab followed, and like a bronzed statue, stood nearby, his arms folded, while he watched her fill her basket.

As she stood up to leave, Mary was surprised to see a man leaning up against the side of a house nearby. She couldn't see his face clearly as he stood partly in the shadows, but he seemed to be watching her. She instinctively moved closer to Eliab and looked up at her protector with a question in her eyes. Eliab was also watching the stranger, his face like granite and his hand upon his knife.

2

Rachel, happy to have her husband home again, made her best dishes. The aroma of the lamb and lentil stew with coriander spread throughout the courtyard. She mixed millet with saffron, raisins, and walnuts and piled date cakes on a platter. Nathan came with his father, Beriah. Their close neighbors, Aaron, his wife Merab, Samuel, and his wife Huldah, joined them. Her uncle sent word he had unexpected plans for the evening and Mary was secretly glad. Without his presence the mood was lighthearted. Mary loved listening to the laughter and conversation that flowed as their guests dipped their bread in the stew and savored the wonderful meal. She watched her father carefully as they ate. From time to time a pensive look crossed his face.

At the end of the meal Mary bowed her head as her father intoned the prayer said after each meal.

"Blessed are you, LORD our God, master of the universe, who nourishes the whole world in goodness, with grace, kindness, and compassion. He gives bread to all flesh, for his mercy endures forever. And through his great goodness we have never lacked, nor will we lack food forever, for the sake of his great Name. For he is God, who nourishes and sustains all, and does good to all, and prepares food for all his creatures which he created. Blessed are you, LORD, who nourishes all. Amen."

Mary felt comforted as she listened to the familiar words that thanked HaShem for taking care of them and providing their food. The Holy One watched over them.

The conversation was about the voyage, and her father talked about the arrangements for a new shipment of lumber and the ports where they had unloaded the dried fish for which Magdala was known. The women served and listened and then, when the men retired to the courtyard to discuss other topics, they gathered around the table and talked of the newest child delivered in the neighborhood, who was betrothed, and who was having visitors from other towns. Mary listened eagerly as the conversation flowed around her. Though she was only eleven, she knew that in only two years her father would be arranging her own betrothal. She imagined the faces of some of the young men who lived in their immediate neighborhood and one by one mentally discarded them. Her betrothed would be handsome and a hard worker. Without thinking, she turned and found herself looking at Nathan. Sensing her glance, he looked directly back at her and to her surprise she felt a soft fluttering in her heart. She looked away quickly, hiding the strange thoughts that now excited her mind.

Their neighbors at last rose and departed to their homes after profuse thanks to Rachel for a fine dinner. Jared waved them off, and then seeing Mary watching him, absentmindedly patted her on the shoulder and turned toward the garden where he went to pray and contemplate what was on his mind. She watched him leave and sighed. There was nothing she could do to make him feel better.

Her mother gave her a platter of food to take to Eliab. He slept in a small open room Jared had built into the corner of the courtyard. It allowed him to see anyone who came to the gate.

"Thank you, mistress."

As he took the platter, she studied his face. Eliab was a strange man in many ways. When he was with their family, he was a gentle giant, but when in the role of their guardian, a warrior. She knew he had been a slave, captured by the slave traders near the African coast. He had fought in the Hippodrome. In fact, he'd fought so fiercely, her father told her, that Eliab won his freedom. As a gladiator he always had a place to sleep and food, but freedom had come with a sad price. When her father accidentally came upon him on his way home from the shipyard, he was sleeping in an alcove in the stone wall of the Hippodrome. The man's dark face was glazed with pain from a wound on his arm that was infected and festering.

Jared brought the wounded man home and her mother nursed him back to health. In gratitude for their kindness, he surprised Jared by asking to remain with their family, swearing allegiance to her father.

When Mary returned, her father and mother were talking quietly. They stopped when they saw her. Jared blew out all but the one candle that was allowed to burn on a stand in the center of the main room of the house.

"Good night, my little blossom."

"Thank you, Abba, for the little box. I shall keep my treasures in it."

He turned toward the room he shared with her mother.

Rachel reached out and brushed Mary's hair

back with one hand. "Your father has much on his mind, Mary. We need to be understanding and helpful."

She looked up at her mother's face and nodded.

"You are growing into a young woman. Before we know it, your father will be arranging a betrothal for you."

"Yes, Mama." Mary turned and climbed the stairs, aware of her mother watching her. Marriage? That was far from her mind right now, or was it?

She hung her mantle and tunic on a peg and slipped off her sandals before padding over to the window to look at the moon—a waning sliver of light in the sky. *I wonder where God lives,* she thought, as a star twinkled here and there. *And where is heaven?* The Torah told her of a God who made many rules to live by. They were part of the Mishnah. Her father said God made the laws to keep his people righteous, but no living person could keep them all. They brought the lambs and sacrifices to the Temple to purge the sins of the people. How could she, a young Jewish girl, please such a righteous and holy God? He was called the God Who Sees. Did he see her? Did he know who she was?

Clouds crept across the moon, making the night inky black, covering the city like a shroud. She looked down at the garden's mysterious shadows and a small shiver passed through her body.

Father said there was more evil in the town on the darkest of nights, and she was glad to be safe in her own room. She turned from the window, said her prayers, and snuggled down in her bed to sleep.

✸ 3 ✸

Uzza waited until he saw only the dim light of the small lamp burning in the house.

"The problem is the huge one who guards the house. If we could knock him unconscious . . ."

The smaller man, Gera, frowned. "We must think of something, Uzza. There has to be a way. The man said it would take stealth." He grinned. "We are good at that. Are we not?"

Uzza positioned himself in the shadows near the gate, while Gera tapped lightly. The noise was not enough to be heard in the house, but enough to wake the servant.

When the huge man opened the gate, he peered at them, then stood with his arms folded. "What do you want? The hour is late."

Gera spread his hands innocently. "Forgive me for disturbing you. I have just arrived in the city and have lost my way. I seek the home of Barak the potter."

"He does not live here. He is three houses down the street."

"Ah, a thousand pardons. Would you be good enough to point out the house, my friend?"

The guardian hesitated, his brows knit fiercely as he eyed the man who waited politely in front of him. Finally, with a grunt of irritation, he stepped into the street and, with his back to the gate, pointed to the potter's house.

Uzza quickly stepped out of the shadows and brought a club down on the servant's head with all his might. The guardian slumped to the ground, unconscious.

The men looked at each other smugly. Gera retrieved the ladder they'd hidden and the two men crossed the patio quickly. They slipped into the garden and looked up at the window they'd been told to look for. They positioned the ladder underneath it.

"You're smaller. You climb up, I'll hold the ladder," Uzza whispered.

When Gera reached the top, he peered through the latticework. The girl appeared to be sleeping. Small whiffling sounds emanated from her mouth. He pried the latticework loose, stopping suddenly each time he thought she might wake. In a few moments he dropped the lattice down to his accomplice. He climbed into the room, took the small vial from his belt, and moved quietly to the bed. With one quick motion, he poured the contents into the girl's open mouth. As she sputtered, he put his hand over her mouth and pressed his dagger to her throat.

"Make one sound and I will slit your throat," he growled.

The girl was wide-eyed with fright as the potion slipped down her throat, but she did not scream. Gera grabbed her arm and pulled her upright out of bed.

The potion quickly took effect and she slumped against him.

When Mary awoke, her head hurt. She was dimly aware of her surroundings. Her hands were bound with coarse rope that bit into her flesh. She gave up trying to free herself and looked around. She lay on a dirty pallet in a dingy room. The smell of perspiration and garbage assailed her nose. In the dark something ran over her foot. She gasped and tried to tuck her feet under her.

Where am I? She began to whimper with cold and fear as she realized what had happened. Someone had taken her from her home! Something had been poured into her mouth. She screwed up her face at the aftertaste that lingered on her tongue.

Why hadn't Eliab stopped them? He was their guardian. Large tears rolled down her cheeks and she leaned to wipe her face on the sleeve of her nightshift. "Oh HaShem, help me please. Send someone to find me."

She prayed quietly for several minutes, then leaned back against the wall, listening for any kind of sound that would tell her where they were keeping her. Faint street noise came from a high window that barely let in the light. She hung her head. There was nothing to do but wait. Abba would find her. He must find her. Her father would turn the town upside down looking for her when he discovered her gone.

Men's loud voices came from the next room. As she listened, they seemed to be quarreling. Her heart pounded. They were talking about her.

"What should we do with the girl? He spouts a lot, that vain peacock, but his plan better work or he'll feel my dagger."

"Have patience, Gera. It will work. The note will be delivered. The man said she is her father's only child. The father will come surely. Then we'll have our gold."

"I don't trust the man. What if he takes all the gold?"

"What if we kill the father and take the ransom money for ourselves?"

"And what about that fool who hired us?"

There was a snort of derision. "He cannot go to the authorities. What would he tell them?" Both men laughed heartily.

Mary sat back, stifling the terror that threatened

to enfold her. What were they going to do to her? Could it be a plot to hurt her father? She whimpered softly, afraid they would hear her.

"We'd better check on the girl, the potion should be wearing off soon."

Mary quickly fell on her side on the pallet, feigning sleep. The door creaked open and heavy footsteps crossed the room to where she lay. She kept her eyes shut and waited.

The footsteps retreated and the door closed again.

"She still sleeps. You gave her too much. If she dies, we lose the gold."

"I didn't give her too much. She'll sleep it off."

Furniture scraped the floor. "Let's get something to eat. The door is locked and no one will bother her."

"You go," said the other voice. "If he comes, someone needs to be here."

Footsteps moved away and faded into the distance. Mary lay quietly, but the need to relieve herself grew, as did her thirst. Should she risk calling out? Finally, her need overcame her fear.

"Is someone there?"

The door creaked open and a man stood looking at her. He was heavy and his clothes were dirty, He had a ragged beard and smelled of wine. "Awake now, are you?"

"Please, sir, I need to—"

"There's a bucket in the corner. Do what you have to do there."

She gathered her courage. "Could I have some water?"

His face showed annoyance, but he turned and went out, then came back in with a goatskin water bag. She didn't want to think what kind of water was in it but was too afraid to say anything. He cut the bonds on her wrists and handed her the bag. She drank quickly. The water tasted brackish and warm.

She returned the water bag and the man's eyes seemed to glitter in the dim light. "You're a pretty little thing. Perhaps you could be of gain to us in other ways."

She shrank back against the wall, her heart pounding. Just then a man's voice called from the other room. "Leave the girl alone. Nothing is supposed to happen to her, remember? Come, I have bread, cheese, and some wine."

The big man laughed and went out, closing the door firmly. Mary wept with relief.

A little later he brought her a piece of bread and a small piece of cheese. She hated the way he looked at her with contempt, but she was hungry and ate quickly.

"Thank you."

His eyebrows went up and he sneered. "What nice manners we have. You'd better hope your father brings the money or you won't need to worry about being hungry ever again." He put one hand on his beard. "I could get a good price for you in the slave market. A beautiful young virgin could bring much gold." His eyes narrowed as he contemplated her.

Mary whimpered, fear knotting her stomach.

He laughed, obviously enjoying her distress, and left the room with a smirk on his face. He hadn't tied up her hands again. She brushed her hair out of her eyes, fighting panic, and looked around for some means of escape. The dim room had only one small window, too high on the wall to reach. Even if she was able to climb out, what awaited her on the other side? It could be high off the ground, or the part of the city around the building could be worse for her than staying here. She shivered again from cold and fear. As she wrapped her arms around herself and rocked slowly back and forth, large tears ran down her cheeks. *Abba must find me. He must.*

The same man returned to the room yet again. He strolled over to the pallet where Mary crouched. Staring down at her with a sneer on his face, he said, "You'd better be worth the trouble we've gone to." He pretended to study her. "Yes, you would bring a good price. You don't have long to wait. When your father is out of the way, you'll be sold. The brothels pay well for such as you. You will please many men. Who knows, perhaps I may be the first."

Mary bit her lip to keep from crying out again. He left, and as he closed the door, she wept silently. If only she could think of a way to warn her father! She looked up at the glimmer of light in the window and bowed her head.

Oh HaShem, our God Who Sees, help me. Help my father and protect him so these men won't hurt him. You are my only hope.

Mary lay on the pallet, hardly able to tell day from night with the dinginess of the room. After what seemed like hours, the door was suddenly opened and the man returned. Fearing what he'd come to do, she shrank back and wrapped her arms around herself. He grabbed her by the arm and jerked her to her feet. Placing a low stool in the doorway, he forced her down on it and tied her hands behind her back. He tied her feet to the stool so she couldn't move and then, in spite of her pleading, took a rag and tied it over her mouth. She looked in front of her and saw that she faced another door across the room.

Then realization dawned. If someone came in that door, she would be the first thing they saw. The men checked their knives and glanced nervously at the door from time to time. They were expecting someone and Mary recoiled in horror as she realized who it was. Her two kidnappers talked between themselves and watched the street through a small window. When they weren't looking, she struggled against her bonds. Her heart pounded in her chest. She had to get free. She had to. She twisted her wrists against the rope until they became raw and chaffed. Finally, she slumped on the stool as she realized it was no use. There was nothing she could do.

Hot tears rolled down her cheeks. She could only watch and wait.

❄ 4 ❄

The next morning, Jared, studying a scroll from the shipyard, looked up to see his wife standing with her hands on her hips.

"Mary has still not come down. What can be keeping her?"

He frowned. "Perhaps she is ill?"

Clicking her tongue, Rachel wiped her hands on a cloth and went up the stairs. All was silent for a moment and then he heard an anguished cry. His wife rushed down the stairs, nearly stumbling in her haste to reach him.

As he rose, puzzled at her distress, Rachel flung herself into his arms. With fear and dismay, she cried, "Mary is gone."

"Gone? Gone where?"

"She is nowhere in sight. Her clothes and sandals have not been touched."

"Perhaps she went out to the garden?"

"Jared, the latticework has been torn out of the window and there was a ladder on the ground. Someone has taken her!" She began to weep.

Jared took a moment for her words to register, but before he could reply, someone knocked loudly at their gate and called his name. Torn between comforting his wife and the urgency in the man's voice, Jared rushed outside with Rachel right behind him. He glanced around for Eliab, but the big man was not in sight.

The gate was open and his neighbor Samuel was tending Eliab, who had dried blood over his face and down his neck. A huge lump had formed on his head. It took both men to get Eliab on his feet and help him inside to his bed. Jared turned to Rachel, who was clasping and unclasping her hands in distress.

"Bring water and a bowl. Eliab is hurt."

Samuel shook his head sadly. "I was on my way to the marketplace when I saw your servant lying by the gate. At first I thought he was dead, but I heard a small moan and realized he was alive. What happened here?"

Jared flung both hands in the air. "My daughter has been kidnapped! And from my very house! Someone would have had to do this to Eliab to get past him."

Eliab's eyes were red and filled with pain as he looked up at his benefactor, his voice nearly a whisper. "A knock—I—only stepped outside the gate—gave directions to—I remember nothing more."

Jared bent over the injured servant. "Someone has taken Mary, Eliab. Do not blame yourself. You could not know their intent."

As he heard the words, Eliab's eyes widened. He reached for Jared's arm and tried to rise. "I have failed you."

He was gently pushed back down by his shoulders. "No, Eliab, it must have been well planned. Rest and gather your strength. If they are holding her for ransom, we will soon know."

Rachel, her eyes red from weeping, appeared with water in a basin and began to gently wash the gash in the back of Eliab's head. "Please, Eliab, do you know anything at all?"

He moved his head slowly from side to side.

Samuel looked down at the injured man. "I will get Merab." He glanced at Jared's face. "Rachel will need someone."

He left and returned shortly with his wife, who brought a small goatskin bag of herbs. She began to make a poultice to dress the wound.

Merab put a hand on Rachel's arm. "I will stay with you. Your husband will find your daughter."

Samuel and Jared talked quietly on the other side of the courtyard away from the women who tended Eliab.

"The only reason I can think of is that they want money," growled Jared. "We can only hope someone will contact us. They must!" He pounded his fist in his palm. "If I have to turn this city upside down, I will find my daughter. May HaShem forgive me for what I do if they have harmed her in any way."

Samuel shook his head in sympathy and pulled on his beard. "This is a large city. To find her yourself would be like looking for a kernel of corn in a field. You must wait to see what the kidnapper will do."

Jared flung up a hand. "I'm to just wait here to hear from someone while my daughter is missing?"

"My friend, I understand, but what direction will you go? Where will you begin to look for her? You must wait or be like a sheep rushing in the wrong direction without the shepherd."

Jared's shoulders slumped. "You are right. What can I do?"

"Is there someone who knows the city. . . the, uh . . . parts where you and I do not venture?"

"My brother Zerah has a slave who no doubt knows the city well, but he is a worthless servant. I would get little information from him."

Samuel put a hand on his shoulder. "I will tell your brother at the shipyard and see if anyone there has any contacts that might help. You must remain here in case the kidnapper sends word."

"Thank you, my friend. We have men working in the shipyard from all walks of life. Perhaps you are right, that one could help us. It is worth a try."

As Samuel left, a strange thought crossed Jared's mind. Who would have a motive for taking his daughter except for money? The name of his brother crossed his mind, but he shook his head and dismissed it. Zerah always needed money, but even he would not stoop to such a thing.

Merab tended Eliab and Jared encouraged his wife to return to her task of mixing the dough for their daily bread. She nodded, yet her tears mixed with the flour as she worked. There was nothing Jared could do to help her.

Jared could not remain still either and began to pace the courtyard. When would they get word, if at all? Would the kidnappers just take Mary and do something else with her? The thought brought not only shock but anger. He had to believe they wanted money and would contact him. The alternative was more than he could bear.

A stone flew through the air, just missing his head, and he jumped. As he looked down at the stone, he saw there was a piece of parchment wrapped around it with a cord. He unwrapped the parchment, and as he opened it, his heart pounded in his chest.

Rachel ran to his side and plucked at his sleeve. "What does it say?"

He sighed heavily. "I am to come to a certain part of the city alone after sundown and bring money or we will never see our daughter again." Jared knew this part of the city. No righteous man or Jew went into this dark area, full of thieves, brothels, and those who hid from the law. How could he go there alone? If he carried gold, his life was worth nothing.

Rachel gasped and cried out, her voice trembling with fear. "My husband, you must not go alone. It is not safe. Eliab must go with you."

He turned to her. "It says I am to come alone. If I bring Eliab, I could jeopardize Mary's life."

There was a knock at the gate and Jared nodded to Merab, who was closer. She opened it and Zerah's slave Badri stepped carefully into the courtyard. Jared didn't like the man, but his thin body and sallow skin caused Jared to suspect Zerah didn't feed him enough.

He faced the slave, whose stance was insolent but wary. "Did your master send you?"

The slave shook his head. His eyes took in the people gathered before him and he looked back over his shoulder toward the street. "No, Esteemed One," he said, lowering his voice, "but I have many eyes and ears in the city. It is possible that I can be of service to you."

"In what way?"

Badri hesitated, then spread his hands. "One tends to think of slaves as part of the walls of the house, but we see and hear. I know of your daughter's kidnapping. Perhaps I have reasons of my own, Most Esteemed One. How would you reward one for helping you?"

Jared stepped forward, his face near Badri's. "Do you know anything about my daughter?"

"It is possible, my Lord."

"If you know where she is and had any part of this, you'll—" His face was almost inches from Badri's. "If something has happened to her, the reward you will get is a whip."

Badri's eyes did not move from Jared's face. "You judge me harshly. I had no part in anything happening to your daughter. The only reward I ask for helping you, Esteemed One, is my freedom. I wish to return to my people in Gaul. If I find your daughter, will you buy my freedom from your brother?"

Jared took a step back. His freedom? He studied Badri's face a long moment. It was a small price to pay. He finally nodded. "I shall buy your freedom—if you find my daughter and she is well."

The slave smiled, showing missing teeth. "As you say, Esteemed One, I shall see what I can learn and return to you." With a cautious glance up and down the street, he trotted down the road.

Jared turned to Eliab, who sat up and insisted he was ready to find the kidnappers. "I have suffered worse wounds at the Hippodrome," he growled.

All morning, at the slightest sound outside the gate, everyone jumped. Jared watched his wife as she served their noon meal. Her face was solemn and swollen from crying. Aaron joined Merab and soon Samuel and Huldah, who had heard the news, came to commiserate with the family.

The shadows began to cross the courtyard, and as the sunset approached, Jared became more restless. He felt like a donkey confined to the stable when it wanted to run.

He changed his clothes to his simplest tunic. The less he looked like a prosperous merchant, the better. The note had called for 3,000 shekels, and as he moved a brick from the wall of his room and reached for the box of money he kept hidden, he became angry all over again. If he had his way, they would never live to spend it. He filled a pouch and tucked it in his waistband, on the side where the bulge would be covered by his cloak. He returned to the gathering in the court-yard and prepared to wait for Badri's return.

The sun began its descent and Jared's impatience grew. The sight of his distraught wife, who now sat on a bench, comforted by Merab on one side and Huldah on the other, stirred his desire for action. If he had to comb the city single-handedly, he would find his daughter.

The evening stars began to appear and still

Badri had not returned. There was nothing Jared could do but wait and hope the slave was able to find out what they needed to know. If Badri did not return by morning, Jared decided he would gather some men and, in spite of the note's instructions, search the city himself.

Rachel, emotionally spent, had been persuaded to rest awhile. Jared spoke gently to her. "I will alert you if I hear anything." Merab lay down on a pallet nearby to be available if needed. Samuel and his wife returned home, for they had young sons to see to.

In the early hours of the morning, Jared's shoulders slumped in despair. He begrudged the bird who sang its cheerful melody in the sycamore tree. His mood was more suited to the owl that hooted in a mournful tone as it flew low over the fields hunting its dinner. In the distance there were sounds from the city, and he wondered how Mary was. Could she be hurt? Had they killed her? Where had the kidnapper taken her? He put his head in his hands. Eliab watched with him, refusing to lie down and sleep.

At first light, Jared returned to the courtyard and opened the gate for Samuel, who came to quietly wait with him. Jared's friend had run out of things to say, and now could only share the strength of his company.

Suddenly there was a soft knock and Eliab, who had stood most of the evening near the gate, waiting and listening, jerked it open. Badri slunk into the courtyard, glancing behind him as if he'd been followed.

He bowed low to Jared. "Esteemed One, there is a possibility that I know where your daughter is being held prisoner. A friend, on an errand for his master, saw two men carry someone into a certain house. He believes it was a young girl, but he could not be sure."

"How many men did he see?"

"Two. Very bad men, Esteemed One. They are well known. They would not hesitate to—" The slave spread his hands leaving the other possibility up to Jared's imagination.

Suddenly Eliab, who stood nearby, stepped up and put his large hand under Badri's chin, almost lifting him up by his neck. "If you do not speak the truth, you will soon feel my dagger between your ribs."

The slave sputtered, choking from the grip. "I—speak—truth."

Eliab removed his hand and Badri nearly collapsed on the ground, his eyes glittering with anger.

Jared turned the situation over in his mind. If he and Eliab went in by themselves, it could be dangerous. In the slums of Magdala, there were those who would rob and kill without asking questions. Eliab was a strong and fierce fighter, but he'd been wounded. If there were more than just the two men, even he couldn't fight alone. He hated the thought of involving Roman soldiers, but his men at the shipyard were not fighters. Would the soldiers care if the daughter of an upstanding citizen of Magdala had been kidnapped —especially if the man was a Jew? The soldiers who were on leave came to Magdala for the brothels and to get drunk. Jared shook his head. Involving the soldiers would only make it worse.

Just then there was a commotion outside the gate and Nathan burst in the courtyard. "Peace be upon this house." With him was a man Jared had never seen. He looked like a gladiator, solidly built. Nathan's father, Beriah, was behind them, along with Amos, a tall carpenter from the shipyard.

Beriah spoke up. "We have come to help you find your daughter. Word has come to us of your plight."

"I'm grateful, but I do not wish to put you in danger. Nathan, you are young for this."

Nathan drew himself up. "I am sixteen and a man in the eyes of the Law. You need all the help you can get."

Beriah turned to Jared. "You cannot go alone, sir, in some parts of the city, even with Eliab. You have treated us well and helped our families. We will go with you."

Nathan took a step forward and the look of

44

determination in his eyes told Jared and his father that he would not stay behind.

Jared appraised each of the men in turn. They were sturdy men, armed with swords and daggers. Nathan pointed to the well-built man who stood silently next to him. "This is Levi, a friend of mine. He is no stranger to a battle and a good man to have at your back."

Levi and Eliab silently contemplated each other. There seemed to be a brief glimmer of recognition between them, and Jared wondered if they had both fought in the Hippodrome.

He was touched by these men who stood ready to brave danger to save his daughter. They were right. He and Eliab could not go alone. Five strong men were better than two. As he glanced again at Nathan, he saw him in a different light. Gone was the young boy Jared had hired years ago as an apprentice. Nathan was indeed a man.

"Thank you, my friends. I am grateful." He turned to Badri. "Lead the way to my daughter."

The slave's smugness disappeared when the other men arrived. His face clouded and he became sullen. His eyes darted from one man to the other. "Too many men will cause suspicion, Esteemed One. It is better just two of us go."

Jared studied the slave with a sense of unrest. Something seemed wrong here, but he couldn't decide what it was. "We will all go, but when we reach the place Mary is being held, Eliab and the rest of you must stay back unless I need you."

Badri shrugged and jerked his head toward the gate. "This way."

The men stayed close together, and however he felt inside, Jared appeared to walk confidently through the back streets of Magdala, following Badri. Rough-looking men sat in alleyways and darkened wineshops. A Roman soldier staggered out of a building as a woman held him up. They paused and stared at the newcomers for a moment but went on their way. Men and women stopped and watched them, the men with hooded eyes. The smell of rotting food and trash almost made Jared gag as he tried to hold his breath. His heart beat hard against his ribs.

Badri kept looking back nervously at them. When they had gone deep into the roughest part of the city, the slave stopped and pointed. "It is that house."

They looked at a building made of large flat bricks with many cracks where vines worked their way up. The front door was weathered and cracked. As they approached, an emaciated dog dragged itself from the gutter and growled at them before slinking off into a side street.

Jared felt their every move was being watched. One or two men nearby observed them and started to rise, fingering their knives, but Eliab stared them down and they shrugged and backed away.

When Jared turned to question Badri, he was

nowhere in sight. He had melted into the crowd. Was it a trap?

With bravado he scarcely felt, he put up a hand indicating the others were to wait.

"If anything happens, rush the door and find Mary."

He approached the door and entered slowly. Muffled sounds across the room drew his eyes. Mary! She was tied to a stool. He started forward eagerly, filled with joy to find her alive. She was moving her head from side to side and her eyes were wide with fright. He would soon have that rag off her mouth.

So intent was Jared to get to Mary that he did not see the men hiding behind the door. In an instant, something hard hit his back. As the darkness closed in, Jared realized too late that he'd been stabbed.

❈ 5 ❈

Mary's eyes were wide with fright as she stared helplessly at her father. He lay motionless on the floor, blood seeping from his wound. The small man, Gera, turned her father over and found the bag of gold.

Unable to cry out, she made small whimpering sounds. Uzza turned toward her, a sneer on his face, the knife still in his hand. She looked from her father's still body to his assailant. Was her father dead? Would they take her somewhere else as the big man had threatened and sell her? Would he kill her as he'd killed her father? Her body shook with terror.

Before Uzza could reach her, Eliab burst through the doorway. He nearly stumbled over her father. A cry of rage rose in his throat and in two great strides he reached Uzza and grabbed him by the throat. Eliab raised his knife. Gera, like a monkey, slipped quickly past the two men and ran for his life.

At that moment, Jared groaned. Startled, Eliab looked down and his grip on Uzza loosened. The man wrenched himself away from Eliab's grasp and bolted out the doorway.

Nathan dashed into the room. "Two men ran out. Are you all right?"

Eliab had moved to Mary and was cutting her ropes with his knife. "The master lives. Help me with the young mistress."

Beriah and the other men reached the doorway behind Nathan just as Eliab was pulling the gag from Mary's mouth.

Nathan looked toward the doorway and cried out, "We must go after them!"

Beriah put a restraining hand on his shoulder.

"Let them go, my son, we won't find them now. We have other matters to attend to."

After the gag was removed from her mouth, Mary sobbed hysterically. "Abba, Abba, they've killed him."

As she tried to stand, Nathan rushed over to her. She fell against him, and he held her as she wept.

"Mary, it is all right," Nathan murmured soothingly. "Your father lives. We will take you both home."

Mary knew her face was dirty and her hair matted. She felt shamed in front of these men, even though they'd come to rescue her.

Nathan gently wrapped his cloak around her frail body and lifted her in his strong arms. She put her head on his shoulder and, for the first time in many hours, felt safe.

Eliab gently lifted Jared.

Amos put a hand on Nathan's shoulder. "The girl is unharmed?"

"I believe so. I'll carry her home."

Beriah nodded to Eliab. "How badly is he wounded?"

"He has lost much blood, but he still breathes," Eliab murmured.

Levi gripped his sword. "We let them get away, but the Most High will avenge their deeds."

Mary closed her eyes, feeling her face wet with her tears. *HaShem*, she prayed silently, *help us get safely home.*

Levi shook his head. "He should have let us go in with him. Those sons of a camel driver would not have escaped our swords."

Eliab stood up, holding Jared's limp body as he would a child. He started out the door. "Come, we must get him home quickly. The wound is bad."

With Eliab carrying Jared and Nathan carrying Mary, the rescuers moved through the city. Beriah and Amos led the way while Levi, sword drawn, guarded the rear. Mary glanced fearfully from Nathan's shoulder at the crowd that watched them with insolent glances. She clutched Nathan, her heart beating erratically. No one stepped forward to challenge them.

When they reached the house, Mary's mother put a fist to her mouth as Nathan carried Mary into the courtyard. "Mary! You've found her." Then she saw Eliab carrying Jared. "Oh, oh, is he . . . is he . . . ?"

"He lives, mistress."

Nathan gently put Mary down and they followed Eliab, who gently put Jared on his bed. Rachel sent Amos to bring Merab. Word had already gone through the neighborhood, and in a short time the healer hurried in the courtyard with her goatskin bag. Rachel led her in to examine Jared's wound.

Eliab stood silently with Mary and Nathan, waiting the healer's word on Jared's condition.

Beriah, Levi, and Amos waited in the court-yard.

Merab looked up at Rachel. "It is clean. I don't believe any serious organs were touched. I will make a poultice to stop the flow of blood."

Eliab would not move from the room, his dark eyes never left Jared's face.

Nathan went out to tell the men what the healer had said.

Mary listened to her father moaning and watched Merab give him a potion to make him sleep.

Rachel tenderly touched Mary's face. "You are both safe. For that I give praise to the Most High God, blessed be his name."

Mary hung back in the house, aware of her appearance, as her mother went outside and put a hand on Nathan's shoulder. "Thank you, Nathan. I shall be forever grateful to you." She turned to Amos and Levi. "Thank you all, for the return of my family."

Beriah nodded. "It is good they are safe, dear lady."

Nathan stepped back, his face suddenly crimson. He caught sight of Mary, and with a tear-streaked face, she thanked him with her eyes. He smiled back at her and then, with his father and the other men, left the courtyard.

Once in her own room, all Mary wanted to do was cry. The stress of her last hours had built up a torrent inside. Her mother knelt to embrace her and murmured over and over, "You are safe now. You are safe now."

Rachel and Huldah helped Mary out of her dirty garment. The two women washed her and slipped a clean shift over her head. Rachel gently combed Mary's matted hair.

"I'm glad she will be all right." Huldah smiled down at Mary and put a hand on Rachel's shoulder. Mary's mother covered the hand with her own.

"Thank you," Mary whispered, as Huldah nodded and slipped out of the room, leaving Rachel alone with her only child.

Mary shivered. "Abba found me, Mama. I knew he would. I prayed very hard. They hurt him." She began to weep again. "Is he dead? Is Abba dead?"

Her mother stroked her hair. "No, child, he is not dead. He will recover." Her mother's face became serious. "They did not hurt you, Mary—in any way?"

She understood what her mother was asking and shook her head. "No, but I was afraid. One of the men kept saying terrible things." She shivered, remembering. "He kept talking about selling me to a brothel—" The man's words flooded into her mind and terror overwhelmed her. "Hold me, Mama! Hold me!"

Rachel let out a cry of outrage. "My poor child." She wrapped her arms around Mary. "Did you hear anything that would tell us why they took you?"

"Only that they were waiting to be paid gold." Mary whimpered. "Mama, they took me so my father would come. I think they were supposed to hurt him."

"They did indeed hurt him. He was wounded, but he will live. We will find out who did this. Rest, child, you are safe now."

Mary shrank against her mother and looked toward the window. "But what if they come back?"

"The men who took you are gone. They will not bother you again."

Shivering, Mary bit her lip. "Will you stay with me, Mama? Please don't leave me alone." She began to whimper again and large tears rolled down her cheeks.

Rachel brought a low stool to the side of the bed and sat down, and stroking Mary's forehead gently, she assured her, "I will stay. Go to sleep."

And Mary slept, fitfully, hearing the man's cruel words as her mind played the terrible scenario of her kidnapping again.

❋ 6 ❋

The weeks passed and intermittent nightmares filled her dreams. Once again Mary was in the dingy room, the foul-smelling man leaning over her. She heard his mocking laughter echoing in her mind. Strange people gathered around, laughing hideously as she tried to find a way out of the circle. Just when they were grabbing her, she woke up, drenched in perspiration, head pounding. Her mother would rush up the stairs and find Mary with her arms around her knees, rocking back and forth, whimpering in fear. Many times she could not go to sleep without one of her parents nearby.

During the day Mary felt normal and did the tasks expected of her but found herself jumping at every unexpected noise. One breezy afternoon, shadows that moved in the courtyard with a gust of wind filled her with terror.

Eliab watched her, his eyes full of sadness, and he was overly suspicious now of any stranger at the gate. She knew he blamed himself for her ordeal.

She tried going to the market with her mother as usual, but the very sight of a strange man looking at her reduced her to tears and the fear nearly choked her. Eliab could not go with her mother to the market and still guard Mary at home, so she was left with Merab or Huldah, who watched her like hovering angels.

One evening, when Samuel and Huldah joined her parents in the courtyard, Mary quietly bore Samuel's looks of pity.

"The child is changed," he whispered to her father.

"If I ever find the men who did this, they will rue the day they were born." Jared pounded his fist in his hand. "An innocent child, but she still suffers—nightmares and fits of weeping. Rachel and I have tried to assure her she is safe, but to no avail." He put his head in his hands.

Samuel laid a hand on his shoulder. "You have cause to be angry, my friend, but is it not best left with the Holy One? Is it not written, 'Only if you forgive others will God forgive you'?"

Jared shook his head slowly. "So speaks the Torah, Samuel, but it is easier to read than to put into practice. The change in Mary breaks my heart. It is difficult not to be angry with those responsible." He sighed heavily. "I thought she would be past this by now."

Mary hung her head as she stood in the house and listened. She wanted to be better and prayed earnestly to the God Who Sees, but the shadows came at night, filling her room with nameless terror. How could she make them go away? It grieved her to see her parents suffer for her actions, yet something gripped her that made her feel powerless.

Day by day as she went about her tasks, her mother touched her tenderly and gave her a word of comfort, even as Mary saw the agony in her eyes.

Her father had kept his word and bought Badri's freedom. Jared was surprised at his brother's lack of resistance and commented on this to her mother one day as he was looking over the accounts from the shipyard.

"Zerah is subdued. At least there is no more talk about cutting costs at the shipyard."

"He is a strange man indeed, my husband. If I didn't know he was your brother, I would not believe you were related."

Jared sighed. "He was not always like this, as you remember. It was the death of Hadassah and the child that changed him."

Rachel sank down on the cushion next to him. "I miss her. I remember how happy she was about the baby, so sure it would be a son for Zerah. That poor, tiny thing, born too soon. I know Merab did all she could, but she couldn't save either one of them."

"One cannot question the will of the Holy One, dear wife. He gives and takes away, blessed be his holy name. If only Zerah would seek an end to the bitterness. He has carried it for too long."

"You did not become bitter, Jared."

"I must confess there were hard thoughts for a time when our own sons did not live."

"Yet the Holy One in his mercy has given us Mary."

Jared smiled at her. "Yes, a beautiful child." Then his face sobered. "If only we knew how to help her."

Mary watched and listened from the stairs where she could hide quietly away from her room and the shadows that plagued her. She knew her mother had lost two babies before her time—two little brothers who'd been stillborn. Then her mother had miraculously carried Mary to full term, but after her birth, to her parents' sorrow, there were no more children. Sometimes Mary wished for brothers and sisters, knowing she was the focus of her parents' anxiety.

In desperation her father brought in two doctors, who tried their skills, one bleeding her and the other using potions, but nothing changed.

One night as her parents sat by her bed, her mother put a cool cloth on Mary's forehead. "How do you feel?"

Before Mary could stop it, a harsh sound erupted from her mouth and she began to laugh hysterically. Rachel pulled the cloth away quickly and her fist went to her mouth as she cried out. "It is HaSatan, the evil one!"

They held her down as she thrashed about, and as she finally drifted into an exhausted sleep, she heard them weep together. "What has happened to our dear child?"

The next day, her parents took her to the synagogue to consult the local rabbi about an exorcism. The rabbi listened carefully and studied Mary.

"Gather a minyan, we must have a quorum of ten men to proceed. We will gather here tomorrow."

Mary waited at home, holding her breath at the thought of being free from her torments. Her father went out to speak to neighbors and men from the boatyard. All who knew him were anxious to help, and the time was set for noon the next day.

As the sun rose higher in the sky, Mary walked with her parents, full of conflicting emotions. Fear of what was to come and what would happen in front of these men, hope that it would work and wondering if she would be healed. Neighbors stopped to watch them pass, and Mary kept her head down, choking back her fear.

When they reached the synagogue, she was seated on a small stool in the center of the group and shrank within herself at the idea of being the object of the proceedings.

The rabbi carried a shofar, the ram's horn, to the circle and instructed the minion to recite Psalm 91 three times. Mary listened to the ebb and flow of their voices as they recited the familiar words:

> He who dwells in the secret place of Elyon,
>   the Most High
> Shall abide under the shadow of Shaddai,
>   the Almighty.
> I will say of the LORD, "He is my refuge
>   and my fortress;
> My God, in him I will trust."
> Surely he shall deliver you from the snare
>   of the fowler
> And from the perilous pestilence.
> He shall cover you with his feathers,
> And under his wings you shall take refuge;
> His truth shall be your shield and buckler.
> You shall not be afraid of the terror by
>   night . . .

The terror by night? Would she truly be free of the nightmares that haunted the dark hours?

> Nor of the destruction that lays waste at
>   noonday . . .

No more spells? Dizziness? Seizures? With growing hope, she listened to the words as they washed over her.

A thousand may fall at your side,
And ten thousand at your right hand;
But it shall not come near you.
Only with your eyes shall you look
And see the reward of the wicked.
Because you have made Yahweh, the Lord
　who is my refuge,
Even the Most High, your dwelling place,
No evil shall befall you,
Nor shall any plague come near your
　dwelling;
For he shall give his angels charge over you,
To keep you in all your ways.
In their hands they shall bear you up,
Lest you dash your foot against a stone . . .

Had she not made the Most High her God? How then could this evil befall her? Perhaps now the Most High would send his angels to watch over her.

The words hummed like bees in the room and she struggled against the conflicting noise in her head that captured her thoughts. Forcing her mind to listen to the words of the psalm, she closed her eyes . . .

Because he has set his love upon me,
Therefore I will deliver him;
I will set him on high, because he has
　known my name.

He shall call upon me, and I will answer
  him;
I will be with him in trouble;
I will deliver him and honor him,
With long life I will satisfy him,
And show him my salvation.

God promised to deliver David, honor him, and grant him a long life. Were the words meant for her, a simple Jewish girl of Magdala? As the words were repeated, she prayed silently for them to be true of her also.

When the psalm had been repeated fervently three times, Mary was nearly startled out of her skin when the rabbi blew on the shofar. She opened her eyes wide and looked around at the men circling her. Their eyes were closed in prayer.

Then the rabbi began to intone a curse:

"We have set a ban against you, spirit, a divorce writ has come down to us from heaven . . . Hear it and depart from the house and dwelling of this young woman . . . I adjure you by the Strong One of Abraham, by the Rock of Isaac, by the Shaddai of Jacob, by Yah, his name . . . I adjure you to turn away from Mary, daughter of Jared ben Jacob. This divorce degree and writ and letter of separation, sent through holy angels . . . the Hosts of fire in the spheres . . ."

The rabbi went on reciting the ritual to drive the spirit out, but Mary felt the same. She continued to pray quietly for HaShem to help her. Then, in the midst of the din of voices, from not only the rabbi but the turmoil in her head, there was a sudden calmness in her spirit, and it was as if soft words were whispered in her ear—*It is not yet time, beloved. Trust me.*

Had HaShem truly spoken to her? She wondered at the words, but in an instant she knew in her heart that the healing would not come today. Tempered with her disappointment, and what she knew would be the disappointment of her father and his friends, was the sudden knowledge that the Most High would heal her, in his own appointed time.

The headache came swiftly, the forerunner of a seizure, and her father, recognizing the signs of what was to come, stepped quickly to her side, holding her in his strong arms as tears ran freely down his cheeks.

The men he'd brought shook their heads and one by one put a hand on his shoulder as they left the synagogue to return to their occupations.

Mary, seeing through a dull haze, knew the rabbi was standing near.

"Take your daughter home, Jared. The Most High has not chosen to answer our pleas in your daughter's behalf."

Jared picked Mary up and carried her outside where her mother waited.

"Jared?"

He shook his head and kept walking, even though people stopped to stare at them and comment among themselves. He looked straight ahead, as did Rachel.

The next few weeks were strangely quiet with no further manifestation. Encouraged, Mary begged her father to allow her lessons with Nathan to continue. He reluctantly agreed and Mary was overjoyed. She missed her friend more than she realized. Nathan's broad smile told her he also was glad to be sharing the Scriptures with her again.

When Mary had passed her twelfth birthday, she became "a daughter of the commandment." Her parents marked the occasion quietly and her father spoke to her of the future. He made sure that she understood that this meant she must now accept her religious responsibilities as an adult.

They'd had a reprieve from the forces that afflicted her and her father had patted her on the shoulder, his voice hopeful. "Perhaps the worst is behind us now."

At the age of thirteen, the time of women came upon her and Mary felt her body changing as she passed into young womanhood. Curves began to replace the sturdy body of a child.

By the time she was fourteen, Mary had learned to read the Shema in Hebrew and knew the

Mishnah. She loved talking about God's laws and how they applied to her people.

This particular afternoon she and Nathan were discussing the story of creation in one of the scrolls he had given her.

When a blinding headache cancelled their study time, Mary tried to apologize, but Nathan only looked earnestly at her, his face serious. There was no pity in his eyes, only warmth.

"Mary, you are made in the image of the Holy One, blessed be his name. He knows your suffering and while we don't understand it, he has a purpose for all he does. I believe he will heal you one day."

As Nathan tried to comfort her with his words, Mary grasped at the hope he implied. HaShem knew her, and after that moment in the synagogue, she could only trust that he would heal her in his own time. But when was that?

The next time Nathan came, they were reading the Torah, God's instructions to his people, when suddenly one of her headaches attacked with a vengeance, the blinding pain swept over her, and she put her hands to her head in a futile gesture to stop it.

"No, no, I want to continue," she cried to no avail, fearful Nathan might end their lesson.

He jumped up and fetched her mother, and together they held Mary as the first seizure struck, causing her arms and body to become rigid.

When she had calmed and the seizure had run its course, she saw her mother shake her head sadly at Nathan. He nodded, gathered the scrolls, and walked out of the courtyard, his shoulders slumped. Her mother helped her to bed to rest, putting cold cloths on her forehead to ease the pain of the headache.

That night her father came to her, his face grave. "I have decided to tell Nathan to discontinue the lessons."

"But Abba," she argued, "I am doing better, am I not?" Her eyes searched her father's face for any sign of relenting.

"No, Mary. This is final. Not until you are well."

He walked away and a tear rolled down her cheek. Her mother, who had been waiting nearby, knelt and tenderly wiped Mary's tears with a cloth.

"It is for the best, Mary."

The next time Nathan came to the house, it was to deliver the scrolls from his father concerning the shipyard. He visited briefly with Mary, looking over his shoulder lest her mother or father shoo him away, then slipped out the gate.

She had waited eagerly for him and felt a sense of sadness when he left. He was her best friend.

That night, sitting on the steps, she listened to her parents.

"It is just as well, Jared," Rachel told her husband quietly. "Nathan is eighteen, an age when our young men are considering marriage. Mary is fourteen. It is not proper for him to be alone with her."

Jared looked up at her, nodding at the truth of her words.

"Our Mary is indeed growing up. Perhaps I should consider looking into a betrothal for her."

"Perhaps another year, my husband. To see if she is better?"

Mary's father sighed heavily and nodded his head. "Perhaps."

They sat silently for a moment, but Mary knew the same thought was heavy on all their hearts. Who would marry a girl with her illness?

When Nathan came the following week, bringing the accounts, he also brought Mary a copy of the Hallel, from the Psalms. She quietly put it away in her room to read later.

Her father had acquired the first eight chapters of the book of Leviticus in the hopes that Mary would be able to continue to learn the Torah. One day she watched her father finger the scrolls thoughtfully, then shake his head and quietly place them back on the shelf. Her heart was heavy, feeling the burden of his disappointment.

Mary's mother had dark circles under her eyes from lack of sleep. Lately the enemy had caused her to be summoned in the middle of the night as Mary cried out and thrashed about in her bed, battling with her unseen foe.

When all was quiet for any period of time, the reprieve from the seizures gave her parents hope—yet always, the dark shadows that plagued her would return unexpectedly and the torment repeated itself.

For her parents' sake, she stifled her fears and convinced her mother she was able to go to the market again. Rachel, delighted that Mary seemed better, allowed her to choose the foods to purchase for their table. With their fierce protector, Eliab, stalking closely behind, Mary felt she could manage.

As they walked home, young men stopped to watch her go by. Huldah had confided to her mother that Mary was considered the prettiest girl in their neighborhood. It was rumored that this one or that one would like to ask for her in marriage, and Jared prepared himself to deal with a suitor. Yet though her beauty caused heads to turn, the rumors of the strange events at the home of Jared were whispered from household to household.

One fateful day at the marketplace, Mary was reaching for a cluster of grapes, when she suddenly glanced up and gasped. Fear jolted her body as she glimpsed the face of the man who had held her captive in that dark, dirty room. He stood near the edge of the crowd, insolent, and sneering at her. She would never forget his ugly face and the fact he had stabbed her father. The choking fear cut off her breath and she sank to the ground, pointing into the crowd, her demeanor reduced to that of a whimpering child. Nearby a few children began to chant, "Mad Mary, Mad Mary!"

Eliab's face filled with rage as he saw the man he'd almost killed when they rescued Mary. He would have plunged into the crowd, but Rachel grabbed his arm. "Mary. Take care of Mary."

Eliab glanced around them one more time, but the man had disappeared into the crowd. He gently lifted Mary and carried her home as Rachel hurried to keep up with him.

Days turned into weeks, then months, as the patterns repeated themselves over and over in Mary's body.

One day, as Samuel sat with Jared in the courtyard, Mary, now fifteen, had served them cups of wine and then went to the storage room. There she lingered, listening to their conversation.

"What is the talk of the neighborhood, my brother?" her father said.

Samuel cleared his throat and pulled on his beard. "Mary is indeed a beautiful young woman—"

"But there are rumors?"

"It is her strange spells of illness that they fear, my friend. What father wants to betroth his son to a young woman who has these things happen?"

Jared's shoulders slumped. "I know."

"What will you do?"

"I decided to send word to the home of cousins in Hebron. They have a son who is ten years older than Mary." He shrugged. "I have suggested the joining of our families."

"Have you told them of the problem?"

"No. Mary has been better for some time now and I feel that a mature husband would be able to handle the situation. I want Mary provided for when I am no longer here."

Mary nearly cried out. Who was this cousin? An unknown cousin from Hebron was to be her husband?

Samuel raised his eyebrows. "You are going somewhere?"

"My health is not good, my friend."

Fear stabbed at Mary's heart. Her father had some coughing spells, but he seemed well. Perhaps he was just tired.

Samuel pulled on his beard again and nodded his head slowly. "Perhaps that is a good solution to the problem. When will the cousin arrive?"

"I have not had word back yet, but I am expecting to hear any time."

Mary listened with a growing sense of alarm. She would have to leave her home and her parents. She didn't want to go to Hebron. She sank down on the floor of the storage room, her fist in her mouth to keep from crying out, and waited in silence for Samuel to leave. To her relief, her father saw him to the gate and they both had their backs to her so she was able to slip out of the storage room and enter the house without being seen.

She hurried up to her room and flung herself on her bed. Marriage was expected and her father had the right to arrange a betrothal for her. She should have been happy, but there was only an ache inside. She could not go to her mother, for she would have to confess listening to her father's conversation. Great sobs wrenched her body as she gave in to her despair.

❋ 7 ❋

Several weeks went by before a passing merchant delivered the word from Hebron that Jared waited for. Mary watched her father read the scroll and her heart felt like a millstone in her chest. Her father turned to see her watching him.

He approached her with a confident smile. "My little flower, I have good news for you." His tone was cheerful, too cheerful. "You will soon be a bride. I have arranged a marriage for you to Asa, the son of my cousin Abirim from Hebron." He watched her face.

What choice did she have? "That is good, Father."

Ignoring her lack of enthusiasm, Jared went on, "Asa will be in Magdala in two months, following the celebration of Hanukkah, and will call on the family to arrange the betrothal. He looks forward to uniting our families."

She thought a moment. "How old is this son?"

"He is older than you by ten years, but comes from a good family."

"Will I have to live in Hebron? But Abba, must I leave Magdala?"

"There is more good news, daughter. He wishes to learn the boatbuilding business. You will remain here." Jared raised one eyebrow. "No doubt the reputation of our boats has reached Hebron."

Jared sighed deeply and looked away from her. When he turned to her again, his face was somber. "If I should die, Mary, you cannot run the business. Neither you nor your mother are a match for Zerah. As your husband, Asa can work with him, since he would take over my share of the business."

Mary knew her father spoke the truth. She couldn't work with her uncle and the men of the shipyard would not abide a woman telling them what to do.

"You would be well taken care of, Mary, and also your mother."

His comment struck her to the heart. What was

he saying? "Abba, you will be with us for a long time, won't you?" She leaned against his broad chest, apprehensive about this stranger who would be her husband, but unable to bear hurting her father who only sought her best interests.

She looked up at her father's face and wondered how she had failed to notice the shadows under his eyes. He began to cough and she stepped back. The cough that plagued him from time to time now deepened. As she stood by helplessly, watching her father struggle, it occurred to her that he was also coming home earlier each day from the shipyard.

Was that why Zerah joined them more often for dinner and walked in the garden with Abba? Her uncle's old animosity had abated, and now as they spoke quietly together, their faces were grave. When her father was home, her mother seemed to covertly watch him. Was something wrong?

Jared went in to rest and Mary picked up her broom and began to sweep the courtyard, her mind in a whirl of thoughts.

As the time drew near for the cousin to arrive, her apprehension grew. Under the law she had the right to refuse her father's choice. Yet it seemed so important to him to have her settled in marriage. How could she object? She knew about the rumors and that her chances of marrying someone from their neighborhood were slim, if any. If she wanted to marry at all, she must accept this stranger.

Later that day, Nathan came by to deliver the weekly accounts from the shipyard his father, Beriah, had carefully prepared. He usually spoke with her a short time. Though the lessons had ended, Nathan was always her friend, always encouraging. She wondered what he thought of the rumors about her in the village, but he never mentioned them.

As he touched the mezuzah at the doorpost and uttered the prayer, Mary was sitting quietly on a bench in the courtyard. She'd glanced up briefly, noting his presence, but now her eyes focused listlessly on the small tinkling fountain that Jared had installed years before.

Aware of Nathan standing quietly, watching her, she looked up again.

"What makes your face so sad today, Mary?"

She gave a slight shrug of her shoulders. "Have you not heard? A cousin is coming from Hebron and we are to be betrothed."

Nathan's face changed. His smile froze as a brief shadow of anger crossed his handsome features. "So there is no one in Magdala? He must look clear to Hebron to find a groom for the most beautiful maiden in the city?"

She was taken by surprise. Nathan was angry with her father? Her eyes took in his stance and the set of his jaw. Where was the boy she'd known for so long? Standing before her was a man, his body honed and tanned from working outside in the shipyard. His rich auburn hair fell across one eyebrow and his dark eyes flashed. As he stood staring at her in the afternoon shadows, she tried to understand why he was angry at her news.

Nathan turned abruptly and started for the house. "I will give these scrolls to your father."

She stared after him, speechless for a long moment, and a new thought crept its way into her consciousness. There was something more than indignation in his manner. She had not thought of Nathan as more than a friend, and these thoughts startled her. Suddenly Mary sat up taller. He was jealous! Did Nathan care for her? How could she have been so unaware? Her heart beat a little faster at this new knowledge. She let the thoughts play around in her head, remembering how he looked at her. Then she examined her own feelings. The lift in her spirits when he came, the peaceful pleasure of being with him when they studied together. She was always so comfortable with him. She loved the way he laughed at small things, she loved . . . and the realization came.

As the sun poured its warmth down on her, the wonderful thoughts rose to the surface. Nathan.

Then her shoulders slumped. What was she to do? Her father had already promised her to someone else. The betrothal documents hadn't been signed. Perhaps there was still time to call it off. Yet she had never disobeyed her father. How could she tell him all his hopes for her were not hers? She struggled to contain her emotions as she rose, composed herself, and went into the house to begin helping her mother with the evening meal. No one must know of her feelings for Nathan. It was too late.

She followed him with her eyes, but Nathan did not look at her when he left. Was their friendship now at an end? A sick feeling filled the pit of her stomach.

Two months had passed since the letter from her father's cousin Abirim had come. With a heavy heart and emotional turmoil, Mary struggled with violent headaches that nearly immobilized her as the household prepared for Hanukkah. Mary had usually placed the menorah in a prominent place where others passing their house could see it. This year her mother had to do this.

When Mary at last felt some relief, she forced herself to seem cheerful as she helped her mother make the *latkes,* the special seasonal potato pancakes, and the *bimuelos,* Jewish fritters filled with the traditional jelly that she loved. The special cheeses they had made earlier were waiting in the stone crock.

She pressed her hands to her temples to stop the pain in her head and tried to take part in their family ceremonies.

Her father recited the prayer for the lighting of the candles. As he thanked the Most High God for the miracles and wonders, for the redemption of Israel, through the haze in her mind, she listened to the first words of the Thirtieth Psalm . . . *I will extol you, O LORD, for you have lifted me up, and have not let my foes rejoice over me. O LORD, my God, I cried out to you, and you healed me . . .*

HaShem had not healed her, but she clung to the hope of the words whispered in her ear at the time of the exorcism. She must somehow manage until it was the time HaShem had set for her.

That night she tossed and turned, hearing noises in her head and strange voices. In spite of her resolve, she begged HaShem to heal her with tears of supplication, but there was no respite. By morning she was weary and listless from lack of sleep.

Mary had always loved Hanukkah, but this year she was troubled by the thought that not long after it was over she would be betrothed, to a stranger. Thoughts of Nathan drifted in and out of her mind when she least expected them, and she struggled to put them away.

When it was nearly sunset the first day of Hanukkah, her father lit the *shamash*, the guard candle from which the other candles were lit. Then, starting on the left, he lit one candle each night. They burned for at least half an hour after the darkness came and then were gently blown out for the next night. Each night her father lit an extra candle, so there were two, then three, then four, until the last night, all the candles on each side of the shamash were brightly lit. Mary dutifully thanked her father for the gold coins he gave her each night of Hanukkah. She put them in the leather box he had given her for her birthday two years before.

As he went on with the rest of the Thirtieth Psalm, Mary listened to the words and questions filled her mind. When would HaShem heal her? He had kept her alive when she was kidnapped and brought those to help her. Why did he choose not to heal her at this time? Was he angry with her? She had wept, night after night, and the heaviness pressed down on her soul like a huge weight. Would there be a morning again when she would wake up and smile, full of joy at the new day?

She kept her thoughts to herself, missing Nathan and their friendship. She had always been able to tell him what she thought about things and he would understand. Now he stayed away and her heart ached.

She determined to put on a happy face and not spoil this celebration season for her parents. Yet, as much as she tried to console herself that she would soon be a bride, the thoughts of that event only made her unhappy. What would her betrothed look like? She faced his eminent arrival with a dejected spirit and resignation.

❈ 8 ❈

Sometimes Mary thought back about the kidnapping. Her father did not wish to discuss it. When she asked questions, he told her it was best left in the past. Yet her mind would not shut them out. She could still see the face of the man in that dingy room and breathe the lingering odor that had come from his unwashed body as he stood before her and talked of selling her to a brothel. Her horror as her father was stabbed and left for dead. And why was she kidnapped?

Pondering these questions, Mary went to Eliab one quiet Sabbath afternoon. He sat by his shelter, staring off into space. She was surprised she hadn't noticed how the lines in his ebony face had deepened, and his hair was more gray than black. Eliab was getting older. Years before, he'd told her stories of the past, how he was taken from his home as a young man in Africa, forced to fight in the Hippodrome, sustaining many wounds. She never tired of hearing how her father had found him and brought him home, nursing him back to health.

Now, as she saw the wistful look on his face, it made their valiant protector appear vulnerable. She made a noise so as not to startle him, and he looked up at her, a slow smile crossing his dark, weathered face.

"Eliab, you've told me many stories, but not about the kidnapping. How did my father find me?"

He sighed. "The slave who used to belong to your uncle led us to the house."

She sat down quickly next to him on the bench. "What can you tell me that you saw?"

"There is little to tell, mistress. We followed your uncle's slave to a dark part of the city. It was a very bad place. I wished to go into the house with your father, but he insisted I remain with the others. I should have disobeyed."

"You could not know what would happen, Eliab."

"No, but I would have taken the knife for him."

"You saved his life."

"Perhaps. I owe him my own life and was glad to be able to repay the debt." He lifted his face and his eyes had a faraway look in them.

"What are you thinking about, Eliab?"

He smiled wistfully. "My thoughts are of my own country. I have not seen my family in many years. I do not know if any of them are alive after the raid of the slave traders, but I wish to know."

She frowned. "Would you leave us, Eliab?"

He turned his head and gave her a sad smile. "It is not yet time."

"How will you know when it is time?"

He looked off in the distance again. "I will know."

She watched him begin work on a small carving and knew he would not answer any more questions. With a small sigh, she returned to the house.

The next day, two strangers appeared at their gate. Mary looked up from preparing some vegetables as Eliab confronted them to find out what they wanted.

"I am Asa, son of Abirim, and future son-in-law of your master, and this is my traveling companion, Jonah."

Eliab opened the gate and with a hand waved them toward a low bench as Mary hurried into the house.

"Mama, I think the cousin from Hebron is here."

Rachel wiped her hands and nodded. "Go and prepare yourself. Put on your best tunic. I will send Eliab for your father."

Her mother offered the two young men some

fruit and wine to refresh themselves as Mary hurried to do as she was told. When she was ready, she waited inside the doorway to be summoned.

In a short time, Jared came puffing into the courtyard with Eliab right behind him. He welcomed Asa and his friend to their home. Mary peeked out at her future betrothed as the three men sat in the courtyard under the sycamore tree and talked. He was tall and thin and seldom smiled. He was all business, asking about the shipyard and listening intently as her father described it to him. Finally, almost as an afterthought, he asked about Mary. His friend sat silently beside him, glancing about with a disdainful look on his face.

Her mother called her and Mary stepped forward to meet this man who was to be her husband. She kept her head down respectfully.

Jared waved a hand toward her. "This is my daughter, Mary. She is the treasure of my heart."

Mary glanced up as the eyes of the two young men flicked over her appreciatively. "She is indeed lovely, cousin. I shall be an eager bridegroom and look forward to a wedding. When shall we arrange the betrothal?"

Mary looked down at the ground. Something in his eyes disturbed her. What was it? The lines in his face were more around his mouth than his eyes.

The house had been decorated and her mother gathered the ingredients to prepare her best dishes for the betrothal ceremony. She would serve fried sardines with capers, pomegranates and poached apricots in honey syrup, goat stew with squash and olives, and fresh bread. Mary's father was jubilant and told her mother no expense was to be spared for the betrothal of their only daughter.

Mary was told the ceremony would take place two days hence, to give Asa and his friend time to rest from their journey. This was enough time also to notify neighbors and friends of the joyous occasion.

As the men reclined around the low table for the evening meal, Mary and her mother served them, then, at a nod from her mother, both women retired to the house, leaving the men to discuss the betrothal.

Mary's father was not one to delay an issue. He stroked his beard as he studied his prospective son-in-law and asked the question that was on his mind. "You are twenty-five, my son. How is it you have not married sooner?"

Asa shrugged and a small sneer crossed his face. "I married, but she was not, uh, suitable. I divorced her and sent her back to her parents."

Jared was startled and the question "why" was

on the tip of his tongue. With great restraint, he remained silent. There was more to this young man and he would find out what he needed to know in his own way. Asa spoke as though it was a trivial matter.

If Mary were deemed unsuitable, would he send her back to them in disgrace? Would this young man understand what she needed? Anxiety caused his heart to beat faster. Could he picture Mary with this arrogant young man? Had he been too hasty to find her a husband?

Mary came with more wine but kept her eyes lowered near Asa. Once as her father looked up, her anguished eyes met his. He looked away.

Asa smiled. "Shall we make arrangements for the ceremony as agreed?"

Jared was not a devious man, and he resolved to apprise Asa of Mary's illness as carefully as he could. How would the young man respond?

When the evening prayer had been spoken over the meal, Jared rose slowly from his place. "Asa, there is something I wish to discuss with you. Will you come with me to the garden?"

"Ah yes, the dowry?" Asa quickly followed Jared to the garden.

When Jared was sure they were out of range for Mary or Rachel to hear, he cleared his throat. "There is something you must know about my daughter—"

"She is not a virgin?" Asa interrupted, frowning.

With a touch of irritation, Jared shook his head. "She is a virgin and well-protected by her family." He hesitated. "There was an incident a couple of years ago that affected Mary."

"What sort of an incident?" Asa folded his arms and his stance was wary.

"She was kidnapped and held for ransom."

Asa's eyes grew wide. "Kidnapped? Did they harm her in any way?"

"No, they did not harm her, they only wanted gold. We were able to find and free her, but I was wounded and they got away with the gold. While Mary was unharmed in a physical way, it was a very . . . difficult thing for her to experience. She was only a child and terrified. She still, uh, has nightmares and is, shall we say, extremely fearful in the night seasons."

Asa shrugged. "It has been my experience that all young women are fearful in the night seasons."

For a moment Jared wondered how many women Asa was speaking of, but ignored the implication. "You speak of the moments between a husband and wife?"

Asa gave him a knowing glance. "Perhaps." He looked about the garden. "I have some business to attend to, uh, for my father. My friend and I will return later?"

Jared started to speak but could not frame the

words that came to mind. His apprehension was forming a knot in his stomach. It was a strange request to make of the bride's parents, for Jared had assumed Asa would spend more time with the family to get to know each other before the betrothal ceremony. However, the young man must obey his father.

He drew himself up and regarded Asa sternly. "The evening meal will be at sundown. We shall expect you then."

When the two young men had gone, Jared sat on a stone bench in the courtyard and contemplated the situation. What had he done? He only meant to protect Mary and make sure someone would take care of her. Now what was he to do? If he called off the betrothal, he would lose face with his cousin and perhaps never have a son-in-law or grandchildren. Should he have traveled to Hebron to meet with his cousin and examine the young man before rashly sending for him?

He shook his head. The young man was here and there was no turning back.

The evening meal was prepared and Mary and her parents waited for Asa and Jonah to return. When at last they came in the gate, Asa appeared wary. He greeted her parents but watched Mary's every move with narrowed eyes. From time to time he and Jonah whispered to each other.

As she served the bread, Mary glanced their way and felt her hands trembling. Her head began to ache. *Not now,* she prayed silently, beginning to panic, *not now.* She felt a tingling sensation and a sour taste in her mouth. To her intense embarrass-ment, her body began to twitch as the seizure intensified.

Her mother recognized the symptoms. "Jared!" She grasped Mary's arm as her father instantly responded. They quickly moved Mary into another room and lowered her onto some cushions. Mary had a brief glimpse of Asa, wide-eyed, observing her with a look of horror on his face.

When Jared returned to the low table, Asa faced him, eyes flashing.

"Then it is true? When I mentioned my bride-to-be's name at the inn, they told us she is called Mad Mary. And you would have me take a sick woman to wife?" His shrill voice rose with every word. His friend Jonah sat back, his arms folded, a smug look on his face.

Jared's eyes also flashed in anger. "She is not mad. We do not know the cause of the seizures. No one knows. In between them she is perfectly normal."

"And children? What would happen to a child if she had one of these fits? You have not told me the whole of this. I do not wish to be saddled with a sick wife."

Jared rose, his voice surprisingly calm. "I see. And what is your decision then?"

Asa stood also. "I do not wish to go through with the betrothal. She is a beautiful woman, but there are other women available who do not have your daughter's . . . problem."

"Very well. I respect your decision. I thought a family member would understand. I won't keep you, cousin. You will no doubt wish to return to Hebron as soon as possible."

Rachel approached them quietly. "Mary has recovered. She is sleeping."

Asa looked from one to the other. Jared knew if Asa and his friend insisted on remaining, the family was duty bound by the laws of hospitality to continue to honor his wishes.

After a moment's thought, the young man gathered his things. His discomfort was obvious as he bowed and gave them perfunctory words of gratitude for their hospitality.

"There is an inn we passed on the way into the city," he mumbled. "I'm sure we can find accommodations there. It is on the road back to Hebron."

"One moment." Jared entered the house and returned quickly, pressing a small pouch of coins into the young man's hand. "It is for your journey. It is the least I can do for the trouble we have put you to. I send my regrets to your father, and may HaShem give you a wife more worthy of your desires."

Asa took the pouch, a puzzled look on his face. It was, under the circumstances, a generous gesture. With a shrug, he nodded his thanks and tucked the pouch in his belt.

When the gate had closed behind the disgruntled suitor and his friend, Jared turned to his wife with a sigh of relief. "He has gone, and may HaShem forgive me, but I am glad."

Tears pooled in Rachel's eyes. "It is just as well, my husband, for I was not pleased with him either." She sighed. "Now what will we do?"

Jared drew her to him, shaking his head. "That, dear wife, we must leave with the Holy One, blessed be his name."

❧ 9 ❧

To Mary's sorrow and embarrassment, it didn't take long for word to filter through the neighborhood that the betrothal would not take place. Neighbors came to sympathize with Jared and Rachel.

"The young man was not suitable."

"You will find a more worthy young man, Jared."

"How could you know—good riddance I say."

"You are well rid of him. The Holy One, blessed be his name, will bring another suitor."

Yet as they spoke words deemed to be a comfort, Mary knew they would return home shaking their heads. No one wanted to marry a young woman afflicted with nightmares and strange seizures.

On the other hand, Mary was elated. She would not have to marry that pompous young man who undressed her with his eyes. The thought of being married to him had terrified her, and with the respite came another time of reprieve from her physical symptoms.

When his relief at Asa's refusal and departure abated, Jared was filled with remorse.

"Is our only child to remain a virgin the rest of her life?" he cried to Rachel. "Are there to be no grandchildren for our old age?"

With heavy heart Mary resigned herself to living the rest of her life as an unmarried woman—a disgrace to her parents. If her parents became infirm, would she be able to care for them, need-ing help herself?

Jared took himself off to the boatyard to deal with his customers, but couldn't help wonder what his friends were really thinking. They would never embarrass him by voicing opinions in his presence, and he didn't want their pity. Day by day as he wrestled with his thoughts, Jared gradually became aware of a new serenity about Mary. She went about her chores with a peaceful spirit. What miracle was this? Had she been healed by HaShem at last? He shook his head in puzzlement.

To Mary's delight, Nathan returned, not only to bring the financial scrolls from his father, but to tentatively resume his friendship with her.

Jared watched their faces one day as they talked and a slow realization began to grow. The warmth between the two young people was almost tangible.

He called Mary to him after Nathan had gone. "Child, what is this I see between you and Nathan?"

Mary hung her head but not before he saw the light in her eyes. "He is glad, Abba, that I am not going to marry Asa."

"And why is he glad?" Jared reached out with one finger and tipped her face up so she must look at him.

"He cares for me, Abba." Her eyes searched his face for his reaction.

Jared's eyebrows went up. Why had he not seen this? Had he been so distraught with his own affairs and feelings that this had been going on under his nose?

"I see," was all he said, but a plan came to mind. He contemplated his daughter, his eyes narrowed. "Thank you for telling me, daughter, I shall think on this."

Mary looked at him strangely, but when he said nothing more, she reluctantly returned to sweeping the courtyard.

Jared hurried from the house to the shipyard. There was something he must know and right away.

He found Nathan using a plane on the side of one of their fishing boats to smooth the wood. He wore no shirt and sweat beaded on his bare back. Jared noted the muscles in his arms and smiled to himself. A strong man, a healthy man; how had he not seen what a worthy young man this was?

Nathan became aware of Jared's presence and seemed surprised to find his employer studying him. "Is there something I can do for you, sir?"

"I wish to talk with you, Nathan. Come, sit under that tree with me." Jared gestured with one arm.

As they sat in the shade, Jared thought about how he might approach the matter on his heart. Finally, he decided to just speak the truth. "When you were last at our home, I observed you speaking with my daughter. There is something between you?"

Nathan's face was guarded. "I confess that I was not unhappy that she is not to marry the cousin from Hebron."

Jared leaned forward and repeated the question he'd asked his daughter. "And why is that?"

Nathan hesitated but evidently decided that he would also be honest. "Because I have always loved Mary."

"And why did you not speak to me of this?"

Nathan waved a hand. "I was about to have my father approach you for Mary's hand when I received news of her imminent betrothal. It was too late."

There was one more thing Jared had to know. "You are not put off by her illness?"

"I understand Mary. I could live with that. I would do everything in my power to see her healed."

Jared could scarcely believe his ears. Was there hope for Mary after all? "And now that the cousin has departed?"

The young man's face was earnest now. "I still wish to make her my wife. That is, if you would agree."

Jared stroked his beard. "And Mary's feelings for you?"

"I believe they are returned."

Joy leaped in Jared's heart. Mary would at last have a husband who loved her and would take care of her. The Holy One had answered his prayers.

He smiled and clapped Nathan on the shoulder. "You have answered my concerns, Nathan, and considering what you have told me, I will agree to the marriage."

Now it was Nathan's face that lit up with joy. "You will agree?"

"Yes."

Nathan jumped up and raised both arms to heaven. "Thanks be to HaShem! Thank you!"

Jared smiled to himself and rose slowly. "I will return home and approach my daughter. It is her decision to make. If she says yes, we will arrange the betrothal ceremony."

Nathan's eyes shone with joy. "I will look forward to it."

When Jared reached his home, he nodded to Mary and went into the house to speak with Rachel. He glanced outside to make sure Mary was occupied and spoke in low tones. "Wife, there is a solution to our problem with Mary."

"A solution? To what problem, her illness?"

He put up a hand for her to lower her voice. "The problem of marriage. I have a husband for her."

Rachel rolled her eyes. "Now, who have you sent for? It will end the same as the matter with your cousin."

Jared allowed himself a pleased smile as he delivered his momentous news. "It is Nathan. He loves our daughter and now that the other betrothal is off, he wants to marry her." He ended the last words on a triumphant note.

Rachel stared at him. "So it has taken you this

long to see what anyone with eyes can see for themselves?"

"You knew? Why did you not say anything?"

She put a hand on his arm and looked up at him fondly. "You had already sent for your cousin. What good would it do?"

He sighed and sank down on a cushion. "Is the father always the last to know what is going on under his very nose?"

"You were doing what you thought best, dear husband. I understood that. Mary loves you and didn't want to disappoint you."

He thought a moment and then rose slowly. "I have been remiss. I shall speak to Mary immediately." His eyes twinkled. "It appears you will have a betrothal feast to prepare for after all."

As her father approached her with purpose in his step, Mary looked up. Now what did he have in mind?

"It seems a matter has come to my attention that needs to be resolved immediately."

Mary regarded him warily and waited.

"It seems a certain young man feels very strongly about my daughter and wants to marry her. Would you be agreeable?"

A slow warmth radiated in her heart. "A certain young man—?" As he stood there beaming at her, the truth began to dawn. She knew. "Nathan? Oh Abba, is it Nathan?"

He nodded, smiling, and was almost bowled over as she threw herself at him in an exuberant embrace.

When Mary and Nathan agreed, her father set the wedding for the fall, in the month of Sivan when the boatbuilding began to slow down for the winter. Nathan's position in the shipyard would be changed. He would be family and needed to learn the business side of building the boats.

Mary knew Nathan was well-liked among the men and they respected his father, Beriah, who took care of the accounting. Nathan confessed to her that some were apprehensive about the marriage, aware of the problems the family had with her illness, but they all knew it was a love match. In spite of whatever apprehensions they felt about his bride-to-be, they boisterously congratulated him.

❧ 10 ❧

Zerah stood with his arms folded, his face a mask when Jared announced the betrothal.

"What foolishness is this, brother? How can you be so sure this will work?"

Jared shrugged. "He loves her, and though he knows of Mary's illness, he is willing to marry her."

A slight sneer crossed Zerah's face. "Are you sure it is your daughter and not the boatbuilding business he is marrying?"

"Do you underestimate my ability to judge in this situation, Zerah?"

His brother put up both hands in protest. "Surely not, Jared, I merely hope that you have looked at all sides of this matter."

"The betrothal documents are signed and it is arranged. I do not think I have made a mistake. He is a fine young man and an honorable son-in-law."

Zerah started to speak but seemed to think better of it and closed his mouth.

"He already knows much of the financial part of the business through Beriah. I would have you teach him the process of ordering the materials for the ships. Since he has worked here, he already knows how we build the boats."

Zerah sighed heavily. "Very well, brother. I shall accept your decision. It will be as you wish. We will start tomorrow."

Jared was pleased. He had anticipated an argument from Zerah over Nathan's new status. It would be hard for his brother to treat Nathan differently, having been his employer for several years. Instead Zerah had agreed. He agreed with most things these days, especially since Mary's kidnapping ordeal. Thoughts crossed Jared's mind from time to time in regard to the kidnapping, but he dismissed them. Zerah would not have done such a thing. They were family.

With a sense of well-being, he went out to watch their latest fishing boat under construction.

Like expert cabinetwork, the hull of the fishing boat was a tightly joined shell of cedar. The workers carefully carved the opening in the mortise and fitted the tenon joint in the opening. He watched them fit these joints that became the ribs of the ship and pound in the dowels that held them in place.

It always pleased him to watch his men build a boat. His craftsmen carefully formed and fitted each hull. Since this was a fishing boat, it was only twenty-seven feet long and seven and a half feet wide, big enough for at least fifteen men. The sides were almost four and a half feet high, enough to protect the fishermen in a rough sea. He'd only lost two boats on the water over the years, a record for fishing boats in the area. He looked out toward the Sea of Galilee and sighed. Those who built the boats and those who went out on the waters of the sea were both aware of the unpredictable winds that swept down from the mountains. The winds caused sudden fierce storms that could catch fishermen unawares.

Another fishing boat was in its final stages, and he went over to inspect as the men smeared the outside of the hull with pitch to preserve the wood. Next they would cover the hull up to the waterline with a layer of tar-impregnated fabric, and finally nail a thin sheathing of lead over it all. Jared watched them work and smiled with pleasure.

He became aware of someone nearby and turned to see Nathan watching the boatbuilding process also.

"Ah, will you miss working in the yard, my son?"

"In a way, sir. I liked working outside and seeing the boats come together under our hands."

Jared nodded. When he was young and first working with Zerah in the boatyard under their father, he too liked to work on the boats. He remembered the sense of satisfaction that he too felt as each boat was completed.

A severe coughing spell interrupted his thoughts.

He wrapped his arms around his middle, bending over in pain. He quickly pulled out a cloth he kept to cover his mouth. He hoped Nathan did not see the touch of red as he hastily tucked it back in the folds of his clothing.

"Sir, are you all right?" Nathan helped him over to a bench where Jared eased himself down gingerly.

"It will pass, my son. It will pass." Jared took a deep breath as the coughing eased. He ignored the pain as he focused on Nathan's face. "Zerah will begin tomorrow teaching you about the ordering of materials. It is one of the most important parts of our business. A poorly built boat is a danger to its owner in a storm—that's why it is worth the expense to use the finest cedar and pine."

Nathan shrugged slightly. "That is why you are so successful, sir, you build a good boat and the fishermen know it."

Jared studied his future son-in-law and liked what he saw—a handsome young man of integrity and humor, with a good head on his shoulders. He would father sons and make his daughter happy. It was all a father could ask for. Yet there were things Nathan must know, things Jared had known for some time.

"Come for the evening meal and we will talk."

Nathan still watched Jared with concern. "If you

will forgive me, sir, my father has invited guests this evening and I promised to be there."

One more day wouldn't matter. "It is well that you join your father. Come tomorrow night."

Nathan smiled. "I would be most honored to join you tomorrow. You are sure you are all right?"

"Yes, yes, be on your way. I will see you tomorrow evening." He rose and waved a hand at the young man.

As Jared watched Nathan walk away, he knew Mary would be disappointed that he would not join them for dinner. The two young people could hardly keep their eyes off one another. With all the fussing going on at his home with preparations and sewing, he almost wished he'd made the wedding date earlier. His quiet household was buzzing with small gatherings of women, each with advice on how the wedding should go, what Mary should wear, and what food to be prepared. With a sigh he squared his shoulders and headed home. Tomorrow was soon enough to share with his future son-in-law what he must finally know.

❈ 11 ❈

In the quiet of the night, Rachel held her husband and comforted him. Jared had kept no secrets from her, and he knew she had anxiously watched the coughing spells increase over time. It was not a good sign. Jared dutifully swallowed potions Merab brought to the house to ease the pain, but gradually even the potions gave him no respite.

"Perhaps we should move up the wedding, Rachel," he said at last. "Yet I do not wish to alarm Mary. It would cast a shadow on the festivities."

Rachel wept. "I have prayed to the Holy One, blessed be his name, day after day. Perhaps he will hear and have mercy on you."

He patted her shoulder gently. "Are not all things in his hand? It is his will that must be done."

"Oh Jared, what will I do without you? You are my strength."

"The Holy One must be your strength, dear wife. He has brought Nathan to care for our Mary and he will be a good son-in-law to you. You will not be left alone." He gave her a weak smile. "Perhaps soon there will be grandchildren to occupy your time."

She looked up at the moonlight sending its silvery light through the window. "That would be more than I could ask for."

Jared shifted his position. "Do you think she is better?"

"The headaches are not as severe and she has only had two seizures this last month."

"And the nightmares? Have they abated?"

She sighed. "They are better, not as frequent."

Rachel turned to him, her eyes anxiously searching his face. "Do you think Nathan truly understands what he is going to have to live with?"

He was quiet a long moment. "I am going to have a long talk with him. I pray that he does. It is all the hope we have."

Rachel laid her head on his shoulder and he could feel her shudder as she sobbed quietly. He held her close, whispering soft words of comfort in her ear.

Nathan arrived before the sun had even set, eager to join them. Mary was joyful, her eyes alight with love for him. Soon they would be married and both anxiously awaited their wedding day.

Mary and her mother made a bitter herb salad with garlic, watercress, fresh mint, grapes, and walnut pieces. Mary carefully tossed the salad with mustard seeds, wine vinegar, and olive oil. A garbanzo bean puree was mixed with cumin, and a lamb and lentil stew with garlic, onions, ground pepper, and fresh coriander simmered in the pot. With almost every meal Rachel seemed to be outdoing herself. Mary's mother diligently shared the secrets of using her herbs with Mary, in preparation for her becoming the woman of the household in Nathan's home. Since Nathan's mother died when he was ten, Beriah hired a woman to come tend his house and cook for them. Now Mary would do the cooking and she wanted to be able to prepare the dishes she'd grown up with.

She smiled to herself, anticipating having her own home and being a wife to Nathan. The little fears of her illness were brushed away. Surely they would eventually recede. HaShem had given her this wonderful happiness. He would heal her.

She helped her mother serve the meal, and as their eyes caught, Nathan's love seemed to flow over her like a warm breeze.

Jared kept up the conversation with Nathan as they discussed the growth of the boatbuilding yard over the past years.

Nathan listened attentively, but when Jared paused to dip his bread, he looked his future father-in-law in the eyes. "And Zerah? Will he accept my new role in the business?"

Jared paused, hand in midair to his mouth. "He

has no choice. You are family and it is a family business. Zerah seems gruff, but he was not always that way. He will work with you. It is in his best interests."

Mary replenished dishes and moved about the dining area. She saw a brief moment of concern on her mother's face, but when Mary's eyebrows lifted in question, Rachel put on a bland look and busied herself with the cooking pot.

Her father had looked up and given her mother a slight shake of the head. What did it mean? Her mother picked up a platter and, after gathering some of the food on it, went over to take Eliab his dinner.

When the meal was ended, her father wiped his mouth carefully and looked across at Nathan. "The evening is fair. Let us go into the garden."

Mary looked after them as they left and a small sense of unease brushed across her heart.

Her father seemed to have much on his mind these days. Perhaps it was the responsibility of showing Nathan his new role in the boatyard. That must be it. She picked up a platter and knelt at the table to await her mother's return and their own dinner.

Jared strolled quietly in the garden, his hands behind his back as he considered how to approach Nathan with what was on his heart.

"You are feeling better, sir?"

"Yes, at the moment. There is something I must tell you, Nathan, for it is time you knew."

Nathan frowned and stopped walking. "Is it about the marriage?"

"No, my son, it is about me and the coughing spells you have observed."

"You are ill." It was not a question.

"Yes. I have used every means at my disposal, but the potions have not worked. The pain increases and—"

"You have been spitting up blood."

Jared turned sharply to face him. "Yes. I didn't know you saw."

Nathan's face showed compassion as he spoke. "Do you fear not being here for our wedding?"

"You are perceptive. I believe I will see you and Mary become husband and wife, but my time is in the hands of the Holy One, blessed be his name. He alone determines the moment I must be gathered to my fathers."

"Praise be to God that he has carried you so far."

Jared bowed his head to acknowledge Nathan's words, but he knew he must speak the things that troubled him.

"Nathan, I am grateful to you for not only loving my Mary but for your understanding of what troubles her. You have glimpsed her seizures and it has not dismayed you nor caused you to turn away. What you must know is that from time to time, the nightmares continue. She awakens, crying out and perspiring. The forces of the evil one plague her. She also suffers from severe headaches, and those you have seldom seen. Is your love for my daughter able to overcome such obstacles to a marriage?"

The young man was thoughtful for a moment but then nodded his head. "Whatever forces trouble Mary, we will face them together. I will find some way to make her well. I give you my word on that."

Jared's shoulders slumped in relief. "Your words bring hope to a father's heart. I only felt you must know the truth of what you are facing in marriage to my daughter. May the Holy One, blessed be his name, shed his mercy on the covenant between us."

❋ 12 ❋

It had been a long night. Mary awakened to find herself on the floor by her bed and didn't know how she got there. Then the blinding pain began. She put her hands to her head and prayed with all her might. *Oh HaShem, protect me on this day of all days. Please help me. I cannot go to Nathan like this. Oh Holy One, blessed be your name, I cannot get through the wedding. I don't want to shame my parents. Please, help me.*

To her joy, the pain began to lift, and in a few moments she felt almost herself. Rejoicing, she dressed simply and hurried downstairs.

Her mother turned from the table where she was cutting fruit and stood quietly. "You are well this morning?" It was the question she asked nearly every morning, but this time it had even more significance.

"I am well, Mama. The pain started but it is gone."

Her mother's face registered relief.

Mary helped her mother with the bread and took date cakes from the stone crocks to arrange on the tables.

There was much to do and her mother kept her busy, with a multitude of tasks, sweeping the courtyard, and anything else she could find for her to do. Men from her father's boatyard came early and set up extra tables in the courtyard.

At last the family dressed in their finest to meet their guests. As the neighbors began to arrive, some of the women brought tambourines and lutes to play.

Even though they had avoided her in her illness, Mary asked two friends she had known from childhood to attend her. They had met at the well and the two young women would not commit themselves. Mary was unsure they would even come. It saddened her, but she understood. Her problems frightened them. She met them occasionally in the village, and they spoke a few words, but then hurried off, almost glad to get away.

To Mary's surprise and relief, her friends Hushim and Prisca did come. They entered the courtyard with their parents, their manner apprehensive. Seeing Mary smiling and appearing well, they seemed encouraged and stepped forward.

"We came to help you with your wedding."

Prisca nodded. "We are truly glad for you, Mary, truly."

It added to Mary's happiness and she felt her heart would burst. "Thank you for coming. I'm so glad you are here to share this day with me."

She welcomed them with an embrace and they went with her to dress for the wedding.

The sun had broken out and the day promised to be a warm one. Garlands woven from the Palestine daisy that bloomed prolifically in the fall cascaded from the walls and were draped around the courtyard for a festive look. The tables were laden with food as each woman in the neighbor-hood contributed her special dish.

Mary's friends helped her into her tunic of fine white linen embroidered with leaves and tiny blue flowers. A band of wedding coins representing her dowry was placed on her head, along with a soft veil of silk. On top of that, Prisca and Hushim wound a small wreath.

They could already hear the musicians her father had hired begin to play in the courtyard, the soft plunking of the lutes, joined by a drummer and the sound of the tambourine.

Mary looked up through her veil and watched her mother when Rachel did not know anyone was looking. The overwhelming sadness Mary saw in her mother's face startled her. Was she upset at seeing her daughter married and off to another home? Then she saw the object of her mother's gaze—Abba. A dart of fear touched Mary's heart. Her father had been coughing more lately, but her mother had assured her Merab's potions were helping. Were they? Lost in her thoughts, Mary was aware of someone nudging her.

"Mary," Hushim whispered, "Nathan is at the gate."

Mary rose and slowly walked to her father's side.

"You are most beautiful, my blossom. May your day be happy in every way."

"Thank you, Abba."

She took his arm as they entered the courtyard where Nathan and his friends waited with torches to escort them through the streets. They agreed to return to Mary's home for the canopy and wedding feast, for Nathan's family home was too small for his father to host it.

Nathan lifted Mary's veil, exclaimed what a treasure he'd found, and then just before he lowered the veil, he winked at her and they smiled at each other.

The whole neighborhood entered the joyous procession; it seemed that all who knew the family wished them well. Hushim and Prisca carried small clay lamps filled with oil and others carried torches. Mary caught a few anxious looks on faces as they passed, but good wishes were called out from the crowd.

As they passed down one street, a little boy peered at Mary and turned to his mother. "Is that really Mad Mary, Mama?" The mother hastily moved back in the crowd out of sight.

Mary the mad woman, Mary the wild woman, Mad Mary. What other names did they call her behind her back? She lifted her chin, keeping a smile on her face as she kept walking by Nathan's side. He pressed her closer to him, keeping her arm in his. She knew he'd heard the words also.

When at last they returned with their following to Mary's home, the wedding was held under the canopy. In spite of her happiness, the words of the rabbi were almost a blur. She answered, and dutifully circled Nathan seven times according to tradition. She moved almost as if in a dream. Her heart beat faster as she thought of the time when they would be alone. She prayed HaShem would help her to get through this night's festivities and be well.

She thought of the talk she'd had with her mother the night before. Rachel sat on the edge of her bed. Taking Mary's hand, she gently told her more details about the physical love she would share with Nathan, the things she would need to know as a bride. Mary did not fear her wedding night, but feared more any outbreak of her illness that would mar her wedding day and the marriage bed she would share with Nathan.

When at last her mother had gone, Mary lay awake a long time, wondering what the future would hold. Could she bear children? Would her affliction continue? How long would Nathan be patient? She seemed to hear conflicting voices in her head and willed them away. Eventually she fell into a deep sleep, her mind filled with strange dreams and faces and then, in the morning, found herself on the floor.

Her reverie was broken as Nathan led her to their special chairs. They sat happily as friends and neighbors began to present their wedding gifts: chickens, a bag of flour, pottery bowls and platters, pillows filled with down feathers for their bed, spices, woven cloths, and candles.

Nathan's father presented them with a beautifully carved wooden menorah. "May the Holy One, blessed be his name, bless your marriage. Welcome to our family, Mary."

She smiled up at him. He was a kind man and she resolved to be a good daughter-in-law and give him no cause to regret having her in their home. Yet, as soon as the thoughts passed through her mind, she feared she couldn't keep that resolve if her illness continued. Did he know about the nightmares? Would he be as patient as her parents had been?

"Thank you, Father Beriah. I will do my best."

When at last most of the wedding guests had gone, Mary said goodbye to her parents. There were tears in Rachel's eyes as she embraced her daughter and wished them well. Her father had trouble controlling his emotions as he clasped Nathan on the shoulder and blessed them.

Beriah held the torch high to light the way as Mary walked to the home of her new husband. Their previous housekeeper had married again and moved away. Mary wondered what they had done about the new woman, a widow named

Rizpah, who now tended their home. She had been there a year, doing the household tasks and preparing simple meals. Would she still be at the house or had Beriah let her go?

To Mary's disappointment, Rizpah was indeed still at Nathan's home, bustling about. She stopped and eyed Mary coldly as they entered the small yard.

Beriah seemed surprised to find her there. "Rizpah, the hour is late. Is there something I can do for you?"

She almost simpered. "I just wanted things to be ready for you and Nathan when you came with his new wife."

"That was kind of you, but let me see you safely to your home."

Rizpah wrapped a shawl around her shoulders. "I will be here in the morning at the usual time."

Nathan stepped forward. "Rizpah, you have been a blessing to both of us for the last year, but I hope you understand that my wife will now take over the duties of running the household."

The words "If she is able?" were spoken before the woman thought.

Beriah glanced at his son's face and quickly repeated, "Let me see you home." He took her arm and steered her toward the gate.

Mary had been to Nathan's home only once before with her father and it was definitely not anything like her own home. It was much smaller and all the cooking area was outside in the tiny courtyard, but she felt a sense of possession. This was her home now and she would be the mistress of it.

Nathan led her into the house to the room his father had occupied. It had been prepared with flowers and warm rugs. Beriah had moved his pallet to the main room where he had insisted he would sleep from now on. At least they had a little privacy.

Nathan lifted her veil, and as he helped her from the wedding garments, she felt strangely calm and happy. This was what she wanted, to be Nathan's wife, and HaShem had given him to her. Nathan blew out the candle and took her in his arms. Then, as a bird sang softly outside in the darkness, calling to his mate, they discovered the joy of becoming one.

❧ 13 ❧

The crowing of a rooster in a neighbor's yard awakened her. Mary turned her head on her pillow and found Nathan watching her with a smile on his face.

"Good morning, wife. Did you sleep well?"

Thinking of the night before, she felt the heat flood her face as she answered softly, "Yes, husband, I slept well."

Suddenly they heard someone moving around in the small courtyard, making more noise than was necessary. It had to be Rizpah. They rose and quickly dressed. With a sigh, Mary realized she was going to have to deal with Rizpah again this morning.

The older woman was busy grinding dry corn for the bread. She glanced up at Mary with a brief nod and just as quickly dismissed her.

Nathan started to say something to Rizpah, but Mary gave him a quick shake of her head. This was something she needed to handle herself.

Nathan seemed relieved and almost anxious to get away to avoid the conflict. "I will be back for the noon meal, Mary." She could hear him mutter almost under his breath, "Mazeltov." *Good luck.*

When he had gone, Mary turned to the older woman with what she hoped was a sincere but firm voice. "Good morning, Rizpah. You are early. It is good of you to help for a while. What ingredients will you put into the bread dough?"

Rizpah seemed startled, obviously expecting a different reaction. "The usual—maize, wheat flour, and a little oil and water."

"Well, that will be fine for today. Tomorrow we will add millet, a small amount of lentils, and fava beans, ground up. Also we'll use some barley grits and crushed coriander seeds. It makes very moist bread." Mary turned away, calling over her shoulder, "I'm going to inspect the storeroom to see what provisions we need from the market."

Feeling she'd won the first round, she resisted the urge to gloat. This was probably not the last clash she would have with Rizpah, but she allowed herself a little smile of triumph.

A short time later there was a knock at the gate and Eliab stood waiting. "Your mother wishes me to ask if I may escort you to the market-place."

She gave him a grateful smile. The storeroom had been practically empty, and there were foods and spices her mother always used that she wanted to purchase. Nathan had entrusted her with a small bag of coins for the household.

"Thank you, Eliab, I was wondering how I would be able to get the things I need."

Rizpah appeared at her elbow. Her lips pursed. "I will go to the marketplace for you." If it had been said kindly, Mary might have relented, but observing the faint sneer on the other woman's face, she became determined. Did the woman think she was incapable of handling even something as simple as this?

"I am able to shop for my household, Rizpah, but thank you for the offer. I'm sure you have many things to do."

The woman pursed her lips, then grumbled, "I've always gone to the market for this family."

Mary took a deep breath, biting back the words that sprang to her tongue. "I understand, but I am mistress of this house now and will attend to those duties."

There was a flash of anger in Rizpah's eyes, but she turned away and grabbed the broom, sweeping furiously.

Eliab kept his usual solemn face, but a smile twitched at the corners of his mouth. "Come, mistress, let us go."

Mary covered herself with her mantle and, without a backward look at Rizpah, went with Eliab.

The market was busy. They passed by the beggars sitting in the dust near the entrance to the street, laborers loitering by the main square waiting to be hired, and turned into the street of the spice vendors. Along the narrow street were the voices of buyers and merchants haggling over goods. Mary lifted her head, savoring the variety of smells coming from the open market—fish, produce, and perfumes. Lambs bleated loudly from the small confines of their pens as they awaited buyers on their way to the Temple in Jerusalem to present sacrifices.

Eliab walked with her to the stalls of the various merchants. Determined to do things properly, she chose a small amount of goat meat and some squash and olives for one of her favorite dishes. She would show Nathan and his father that she could not only feed them but feed them well. As she moved about making other purchases, she turned over the problem of Rizpah in her mind. She knew she had to be strong or the woman would take over. She couldn't show herself weak in any area to the older woman. Perhaps she could persuade Nathan's father to let her go. She felt well and strong. As she reached for a pomegranate, she wondered if perhaps the worst was over.

She handed her purchases to Eliab to carry and started home with her head held high.

It was almost two weeks before the nightmares struck her again. She woke up sobbing in the middle of the night with Nathan's arms around her.

"It's all right, Mary, it's all right," he crooned as he rocked her.

She looked up and saw her father-in-law standing in the doorway, concern and apprehension written on his face, and she flushed with mortifi-cation. When the episode passed, Beriah returned to his bed and Mary and Nathan lay back down again.

Tears ran down her cheeks. "Oh Nathan, I'd hoped they were gone."

He smoothed her hair with his hand and kissed her. "We will face it together, Mary. Don't be afraid. Whatever happens, I will be here."

"You are here in the night, Nathan, but what about the days? What if something happens while you and your father are gone?"

He hesitated. "That is why Rizpah is still here."

"She doesn't like me, Nathan. She lets me know in every way that I am not suitable as a wife."

He chuckled. "I think you have things well in hand, my love." Then he became serious. "Until we find a cure for the seizures, you cannot be alone, Mary. That was the agreement I made with your father."

She should have known that was why the woman was still here, but she wished there was someone she felt more comfortable with.

She moved toward him, seeking comfort, and he kissed her softly, then more urgently until he met her need with his own.

• • •

The next morning, over Mary's protests, Nathan took her to the local rabbi. He questioned her and shook his head, stating bluntly, "She has been here before and the ceremony was not successful."

Nathan's shoulders fell. "What are we to do?"

"Your only hope is to take her to the Temple in Jerusalem. Perhaps the high priest can help her."

Mary turned to Nathan. "If I went through the exorcism here and it was no use, how can the high priest help me? We would make a trip for nothing."

As they walked away, Mary sensed Nathan's disappointment. She wanted to please him. Perhaps HaShem would have mercy on her and this time she would be healed. How could she not try—for the sake of their marriage?

She put a hand on his arm. "If you wish to travel to Jerusalem, Nathan, I will go."

His eyes lit up with hope. "I only want you to be healed. It is nearly the time of Shavuot when I must travel with my father to Jerusalem. Your father must go also. Your mother can travel with us."

She looked up at him with love and tenderness. "Then I will be all right."

As they walked, frightening thoughts assailed her mind. What if she had an attack on the way? It would take three to four days to reach Jerusalem.

Could she do this? She must. It was the only hope she had.

Preparations were made as Nathan, Jared, and the other Israelite men living in Magdala began the journey to Jerusalem where every male of the family that was of age was required to go for Shavuot. It was a day to celebrate the giving of the Torah, the instructions of God to Israel. One of the three pilgrimages all men of Israel were required to make to the Temple in their holy city of Jerusalem. Rizpah was left to tend the house of Beriah, and Eliab remained at the home of Mary's parents.

Mary looked around, relieved that she and her mother were not the only women who would travel with the group. Nathan brought a donkey for Mary to travel on, but she preferred to walk. Instead Jared was persuaded to ride. His drawn face indicated his discomfort, but he insisted he was fine.

Rachel and Nathan walked on either side of him for support and Mary walked beside her father-in-law. Beriah never mentioned the episodes at their home and for that Mary was grateful to him. She felt his concern, and knew he observed her thoughtfully from time to time. He had not spoken to Nathan that she knew of, but it was only a matter of time.

They camped along the road for three nights and walked as far as they could by day. To

Rachel's delight, Jared's spirits seemed to improve as well as his strength. Merab sent herbs with Rachel to be steeped in his tea. Mary was hopeful that he would make the journey without incident, and prayed for him as well as herself. So far no signs of her illness manifested itself. She walked with a lighter heart, enjoying the flowers in the fields and along the roads and listening to the birdsongs around her.

Mary's mother brought four loaves of bread, two for Jared to sacrifice as a celebration from the wheat harvest and two for her brother-in-law, Zerah, though he seemed scarcely grateful. Mary proudly provided bread from her own household for Nathan. Ahead of the group, a team of oxen plodded on, carrying baskets filled by each household with the fruit and bread offerings that symbolized the words of Moses to their ancestors:

"For the LORD your God is bringing you into a good land . . . of wheat and barley and grapevines and figs and pomegranates: a land of olives and honey."

Each of the farmers selected the best of their crops as they ripened and tied a reed around them to indicate they were to be set aside. Mary had helped wind the garlands of flowers around the horns of the oxen that had been gilded for the journey. Joy permeated the travelers, for as they passed through each of the cities and towns, people came out and accompanied them for a short distance with the music of flutes and tambourines.

Mary had never been to Jerusalem and her first sight of the Holy City filled her with a sense of excitement. The Temple seemed like an enormous giant overseeing the city, its walls blazing white in the afternoon sun.

The sense of joyfulness even, for a time, lightened the countenance of her uncle Zerah, who seemed to scowl less as the days went by. Mary's father and the other men in their company looked forward with glad faces to celebrating the giving of the Torah at Mount Sinai, when the Israelites became a nation committed to serving God. She thought of the stories her father had told her, and as she gazed at the Temple, the words of the Shema, God's commandments to the Israelites, came to mind once again—

"Hear, O Israel, the Lord our God, the Lord is one! You shall love the Lord your God with all your heart, with all your soul and with all your strength. And these words which I command you today shall be in your heart. You shall teach them diligently to your children, and shall talk of them when you sit in your house, when you walk by the way, when you lie down and when you rise up . . ."

Even though she had not been allowed to attend Hebrew School, her father had made sure she was taught the Torah, God's word to them. She looked affectionately at Nathan, thinking of all the times he had come to give her lessons. She was an able homemaker, thanks to her mother, but knew more of the Law than most women, thanks to her father and Nathan.

Mary and her mother, along with Zerah and another family, settled at a local inn where the women would wait patiently while the men of their households performed their duties in the Temple. The women occupied themselves making preparations with the innkeeper to serve the traditional foods required on the Feast of Shavuot. They had brought cheeses with them and date cakes but purchased milk and other foods in the marketplace.

The first evening, Jared, as the leader, read to them from the Book of Ruth. He solemnly intoned to his attentive audience that it was believed King David was born and died on Shavuot.

The celebrations ended, and the next morning Mary waited with a sense of apprehension for Nathan to take her to the Temple. She walked with her father and Nathan from the inn to the Temple, where Jared had arranged the meeting with the high priest. They had been told the great man was a master of the mysticisms of the Talmud.

Mary was brought into a small room where the sight of the tall, imposing figure of the high priest filled her with dread. What would he do to her? He had gathered a group of the other priests in the Temple. She sensed power emanating from this man as he studied her, and if Nathan had not been behind her giving her support, she would have turned and run from the room.

"We shall see the enemy flee from this daughter of Israel." The high priest looked around as if daring anyone to contradict him. The other priests nodded in agreement.

Mary was placed on a small stool and bowed her head submissively as the high priest began his incantations. In a loud voice he recited the Ninety-first Psalm as the Rabbi in Magdala had done, but also Psalms 10 and 121. An involuntary shudder passed through her as she waited for the unknown to happen.

When the Psalms had been spoken, the high priest began to speak strange words about divorce. She began to panic. Was he advocating that Nathan should divorce her?

Then she listened more carefully. It was the same divorce degree pronounced against the evil forces that plagued her by the rabbi in Magdala.

"A divorce writ has come down to us from Heaven against you . . . under the ban . . . hear and depart from this daughter of Israel. You shall not again afflict her, either in a dream by night or slumber by day, and I adjure you to turn away from this afflicted one. This divorce writ and letter of separation . . . sent through holy angels . . ."

He went on and on for what seemed an endless period of time. It was as if he enjoyed the sound of his own voice.

Mary waited, and when he was at last silent, she was aware the men were all watching her for some sign or response. The silence was overwhelming. No one spoke and she cautiously looked up. In her head she heard faint laughter and wondered if a seizure was imminent.

"Have you sensed a change, daughter of Israel?" The high priest was peering at her, his face stern and terrifying.

She did not feel anything had changed but feared saying so. "Thank you for your words," she said cautiously. "I am sure that I will be better now."

Nathan helped her to her feet, and as the other priests watched her, she felt like a worm being examined by a circle of crows. All she wanted was for Nathan to take her away from this frightening place. Nathan thanked the high priest and handed him a small pouch, which Mary realized contained gold coins. It must have come from her father, for she knew they did not have a gift like that to give.

The high priest looked pleased as he tucked the pouch in his belt and smiled at her magnanimously. "You shall be free from this time on."

She nodded, not daring to speak again, and followed Nathan from the Temple.

When they were outside, Nathan turned to her, his eyes alight with love. "I know you shall be free now, Mary. The high priest is a powerful man. To have him pray for you is all I hoped for. Surely the forces of the evil one cannot stand against such a man."

Mary smiled at his optimism, but she knew the forces that had afflicted her for so long. However powerful the high priest, were they indeed intimidated and forced to flee by the words of one man?

✵ 14 ✺

To the delight of Mary and her mother, a small miracle occurred. Jared began to get better. His coughing subsided and he stopped spitting up blood. Mary felt their prayers for him had been heard and rejoiced. Her father had been granted a small reprieve by the Most High God, blessed be his name.

Mary felt it was a sign that she would also get better. She and Nathan had come from the exorcism at the Temple with high hopes. Mary did not suffer the headaches and seizures or even the nightmares on the way home. She could hardly contain herself. Was there a chance now that she would feel normal? Would HaShem also enable her to bear a child? Each month that had gone by had seen her hopes dashed, but now she had reason to hope again. She could only pray that the enemy was not just lying in wait to strike again.

On the last evening, before they reached Magdala, Mary listened from her tent as her father, Nathan, and the other men sat around the campfire, deep in discussion.

"The Roman soldiers who come to Magdala cause nothing but trouble, patronizing the brothels."

"There are fights on the streets of the city between drunken soldiers. Innocent civilians have been injured."

Jared spoke up. "The Hippodrome brings them. Gladiators fighting, animals and bloodshed, will it never end?"

She recognized the voice of her uncle Zerah, who growled, "What can we do about it? We cannot fight the taxes, nor prevent the soldiers from coming. If we interfere, we are likely to get run through with a sword."

There was silence for a few moments.

She knew Nathan. He would wait until the older men had spoken before commenting. At last she heard his voice. "That man who was crucified on one of their crossbeams outside the city when we left? A shopkeeper told me he was arrested for stealing from a soldier while he lay drunk in the streets. The man was hungry and took only enough for some bread."

There were murmurs of outrage among the other men.

Beriah snorted. "A more fiendish means of torture and death could not be found—to suffocate in the sun when the pain in their arms no longer allows the poor victim to raise himself up for breath."

Her father spoke again over the murmuring. "The man committed a crime for which he was punished, but I feel the penalty was excessive."

As Mary listened to the men's conversation, a chill went through her body. She had seen a man crucified once. Her mother had tried to get her to look away, but as a child she had stared at the poor man hanging there with heavy nails driven through his wrists and feet. What human being deserved to die that way?

She listened again as her uncle changed the subject. "At least we have work. The boatyard is doing well."

"That is true," Nathan said. "The reputation of our boats is well known."

There was no comment from Zerah, but Mary wondered what he was thinking. He had given in to Nathan becoming a part of the family and thus part of their business, but she sensed he was still not happy about it. There was something so sad about him. She tried to remember what he was like before her aunt and the baby had died, but it was so long ago, and she'd been so young, she had to take her mother's word that he had indeed been different then.

She lay down and covered herself with her cloak, waiting for Nathan to return to their tent. At last she heard his footsteps and in a moment he lay down beside her.

"What were you talking about?"

He chuckled. "I knew you were listening. We talked about things that men discuss, my curious wife."

He sounded stern, yet she could sense him smiling in the darkness. She waited. He would tell her, he always did.

"It was of the Messiah to come. Samuel was reminded of Judas of Galilee who rose up in the days of the census, claiming to be the Messiah, but when he perished, his followers fell away. With the stranglehold Rome has on our people, we agreed it would be a good time for the Messiah to make his appearance."

He placed an arm across her. "There are some who feel talking of anything regarding religion is out of place for a woman."

"But why? You have taught me many things from the Torah."

"Yes, but not openly, Mary." He sighed. "They worship many gods, these Romans, and do not understand the God we worship. We are careful

130

not to make comments while at the Temple. The Romans have spies everywhere. One does not criticize Caesar."

Mary pushed herself up on one elbow as she whispered back fiercely, "My father is wise. He would not do that."

There was a murmur from another tent nearby and Nathan pulled her gently back down beside him. "We are disturbing those who want to sleep."

She pulled her cloak about her. Nathan had added his cloak to their covering. In only a few moments he was asleep.

Mary smiled at the ease of his slumber and continued to stare into the night, thinking about the things the men had spoken about. What would the Messiah be like when he came? Would he come in her lifetime?

At last, her eyes heavy, she moved closer to Nathan's warm body and slept.

Ignoring Rizpah's protests, Mary went to the market by herself, two days after they returned, feeling that she did not need Eliab or Rizpah to go with her. She felt free and alive. It was a glorious morning and as she walked she heard the sounds of the sparrows calling to one another among the bushes. Her heart lifted as she looked at the first figs ripening plump and juicy on the trees and noted the grapes were nearly ready for harvest. She purchased what she needed and lingered at the leather shop, examining a pair of sandals. She needed a new pair but did not have enough of her household money to purchase them this day. In spite of the merchant's persuasive pleas, she would have to talk to Nathan about them first. She turned away from the merchant's stall and was walking toward home, feeling pleased with her outing, when she felt the familiar signs of a seizure coming on. She looked around anxiously for someone to help her. Her basket fell to the ground as she put her hands to her head to stop the voices that plagued her. She cried out and just as she was slipping into unconsciousness, she felt strong arms lifting her. It was the last she remembered until she woke up at home. Nathan was sitting beside her. She looked up only to see his face dark with anger. Nathan had never been angry with her before, and she cowed back against the cushion.

"Mary, you are never to go to the marketplace, or anywhere else, alone. Do you understand? Eliab came to the gate and Rizpah told him you had gone to the market. What would you have done if he had not gone to find you? You would be unconscious or worse along the road. What possessed you to go alone?"

Her voice sounded small in her ears. "I thought I was well enough."

His face softened. "It was too soon to tell, beloved. Please do not frighten me again like that. I can deal with it when I'm here, but how can you manage if you are by yourself?"

"I will not go alone again, I promise," she answered meekly and looked up at him with large tears running down her cheeks.

He fell on his knees and gathered her to him. "I could not bear it if I lost you. When Rizpah came to the boatyard to tell me I was needed at home, I feared the worst. From now on, either Rizpah or Eliab must go with you."

She nodded against his shoulder. "It will be as you wish, Nathan."

He kissed her and sat back. "I must return to work, there is an order of lumber coming in on one of the ships and I must go with Zerah to check the inventory. I will return later. Are you sure you are all right now?"

She nodded again, not trusting herself to speak. She had been so foolish. As she rose slowly, Nathan helped her up and she walked with him to the gate.

"Take care, beloved," he murmured and left.

Mary turned to see Rizpah watching her with a smug look on her face.

"Thank you, Rizpah, for sending Eliab."

The older woman shrugged. "He watches over you from a distance. Like a hawk, he is."

She should have known that her mother or father would have him keep an eye on her. She began to prepare the vegetables for a bitter herb salad, rinsing and drying the watercress and young dandelion greens she had gathered the day before and kept cool in the storeroom. She put Rizpah to work toasting and grinding the mustard seeds and gathering fresh dill and some grapes. She must concentrate on preparing the evening meal. Yet, she felt so tired, so worn out with lack of sleep. Each time the seizures came, and the nightmares that broke the night seasons, she felt strength ebb from her. What was she to do?

That evening when the meal was over and Beriah had seen Rizpah home, Mary lay in Nathan's arms with tears in her eyes.

"How can you stay with me, Nathan? I am weary from my illness and you are going without sleep also. This is no life for you." She broke away and sat up, her eyes searching his face. Lack of sleep was affecting him also. Fatigue showed in lines on his face. "Divorce me, Nathan. It is your only hope of a normal life." She put her face in her hands. "I cannot even give you children."

He pulled her down to him and held her fiercely. "I will not do that, Mary. There must be some way to set you free. I will find it. There must be someone who can help you. I don't want a divorce and you are dearer to me than children. Rest, beloved, we will face this together . . . always, together."

She sighed heavily. What more could she say?

She lay against the cushions and tears ran down her cheeks.

Nathan wiped them away gently. "Sleep, beloved, I am here. I shall always be here."

In time she heard the soft sounds of his breathing as sleep overtook him. She looked toward the window. An owl flew into the sycamore tree, calling out to his mate. A gentle peace settled over her and she thought of the voice she had heard in the Temple, saying, "It is not yet time." What did it mean? With questions in her mind, she slept at last and didn't wake up until morning.

As the months of her first year of marriage went by, it amazed Mary that Rizpah was on her best behavior and solicitous of her when Beriah and Nathan were around, but when they were gone, Mary felt her contempt. She did what she was asked but many times ignored Mary as though she had not heard her. Mary's complaints to Nathan went unheeded.

This morning she sat on a bench in the small courtyard. She'd had a particularly difficult night, and it was all she could do to try to put her thoughts together. The lack of sleep at night made it more difficult to be rational in the daytime.

She saw Rizpah watching her with a curious look on her face. Finally the woman's eyes narrowed and she asked, "How do you know when the spells are going to come upon you?"

Mary thought for a moment and sighed. "My head begins to hurt and I feel a tingling in my body. Then I know a seizure is near."

Rizpah shook her head. "It is the evil one who has possessed you. You have been to the rabbi and even to the high priest in Jerusalem. What good has it done you? You will never be free. You trouble this household with your sickness and your husband waits and hopes in vain. HaShem has cursed you. There will be no children."

Taken back with the vehemence behind Rizpah's words, Mary could only stare at her. The words hung in the air, proclaiming aloud what Mary had thought herself so many times. She turned away and went into the house, weeping silently. Rizpah wished to marry Beriah. Mary had discerned that earlier in their relationship. With Mary in the household, there was no need for Beriah to have anyone look after him. *Nathan must divorce me,* Mary thought bitterly. *Rizpah is right. I cannot give him children. Perhaps HaShem has truly turned away from me.*

She had to get away from the house and the woman's constant condemnation. Gathering her shawl, she glared at Rizpah, daring her to follow as she left the courtyard.

"I am going to the home of my parents," she tossed over her shoulder and left before Rizpah could respond.

She walked quickly, covering her face so no one would recognize her. It was difficult to go out in public, even with Eliab, for the whispers grew louder as she passed—"There goes Mad Mary, the crazy woman. How does her husband stay with her? I hear she is cursed for she bears no children". . . on and on the words swirled around her like bees buzzing around a hive.

When she entered the gate, Eliab, who had been carving a small animal out of wood, stood quickly and watched her silently as she walked into the house. Rachel had seen her and hurried to her side.

"Mary, is something wrong?" She guided Mary to a bench in the shade and sat down beside her. "What has happened?"

"Why does he stay with me?" Mary cried in despair. "He must be weary and so am I. He will not set himself free from me. He says he does not care if we have children. I don't believe him. I've seen him with the children of our neighbors and he loves them. It would be better if I were to die. He would be free of me and this interminable illness!"

"Mary, do not talk like this. Nathan loves you. He understood when you were married what he would have to deal with."

"But why am I not cured? The rabbi prayed for me, the high priest said all those words over me, yet nothing happened. Nothing has changed.

What am I to do? I can't go on like this. With everything else, I must endure Rizpah's scorn day after day. She hates me."

Rachel looked surprised. "Nathan tells me only good things about Rizpah, how she looks after you and worries about you."

Mary waved a hand. "Only when they are present. She wishes to be the wife of Beriah and resents me. When no one is there but the two of us, she barely speaks to me. She tells me I am cursed by HaShem and I am troubling the household."

Her mother sat back. "Are you sure? You are not just imagining things because you are tired?"

"No, it has been going on since the day I came to the household as a new bride. She has made her feelings for me clear."

Rachel was thoughtful for a while. "I will speak to your father. It is possible that he can persuade Nathan to choose another companion for you. I will not have my daughter suffer under that woman's cruel words."

Mary sighed with relief. She could not bear to think of having to put up with Rizpah another day.

She rose and turned toward the gate. "I will await word from Father."

Eliab was still standing by his shelter. As she approached him, he smiled at her. "You are well today, mistress?"

"Yes, Eliab." She glanced back at her mother watching her. She wanted to ask Eliab about her father, for her mother would not talk about it. She would not be able to ask today either.

Eliab held out the small figure he had been carving.

She looked up at his dark face and beamed. "Thank you, Eliab. I shall treasure this. It's beautiful." She turned the animal over in her hand, noting the find details of his workmanship.

"Take care, mistress."

Suddenly her heart felt lighter and she walked back to her home holding the little carving tightly. Perhaps someday she would have a child to give it to. She looked down at the figure and wondered why he had chosen to give her this animal. Maybe it signified what she was to him, a lamb.

✺ 15 ✺

Three years passed and there was no change. No child grew within her, and little by little she'd been forced to give up her household duties. She just couldn't manage.

This morning Mary sat in the shade of the sycamore tree, her flowing hair disheveled, for she could not bear the touch of a brush to her head. Her eyes were red from lack of sleep. The dull pain in her head seemed to roll on and on in ceaseless waves. She couldn't open her eyes, for the blinding sunlight only made the pain worse.

Mary was grateful for the gentle hands and soothing voice of Keturah, a young widow Huldah found for them to take the place of Rizpah. There was a distinct difference in the household when Rizpah left, which was soothing to Mary. Fortunately Rachel had persuaded Jared to talk to Nathan. Thinking Mary had exaggerated the situation, Nathan returned to the house in the middle of the day out of curiosity and lingered outside the gate, to see what he could see and hear.

It was unfortunate for Rizpah, who chose that moment to vent her frustration on Mary.

"You are a useless woman. You cannot even take care of your own household. I can't imagine what kind of a wife you are to a fine young man like Nathan. This would have been my home had you not interfered and turned them away from me—" She was halted in midsentence as Nathan stormed in the gate.

"Leave this house and do not return, ever!" he thundered at her as she fled from the terrible anger in his face.

She covered her head with her hands as she left, as though fearful he would strike her. Her mouth worked, but she could find no words. Mary knew Nathan had heard the abusive words Rizpah said to her.

Mary began to weep in relief and he wrapped his arms around her. "You shall not endure that woman another moment, beloved. I shall find someone else for you, someone who has a kinder spirit."

"Oh, Nathan. How can you keep loving me? I didn't like Rizpah, but her words were true. What use am I?"

"You are dear to me, wife of my heart. I want no other. HaShem will hear our prayers, and in his own time, I believe he will heal you."

Huldah and Rachel alternated staying with Mary, but Huldah wasted no time seeking Rizpah's replacement. She told Nathan and Mary that she knew of a young woman, recently widowed, who needed a means of support. She had no family nearby.

"She is a worthy young woman, but she has a child, a little boy not even a year old. Would that be a problem?"

Nathan frowned. "I'm not sure if that would be a good choice." He glanced at Mary. "It might be difficult for a child."

Mary put a hand on his arm. "I would welcome a child nearby. Couldn't we meet her and see how it works out?"

He smiled down at her. "All right, if you wish, beloved. Let her come for one week and then I will decide."

She knew Nathan was apprehensive about how a child would react to one of her seizures. Mary agreed that if it proved difficult, they would find someone else.

Nathan's fears were laid to rest the first time Mary saw the baby. Keturah trustingly placed him in Mary's arms.

"His name is Mishma," Keturah said softly.

When the baby looked up at Mary and smiled, she turned to Nathan, her heart in her eyes, and what could he do? He shrugged helplessly and Keturah joined their family.

This morning Mishma watched her from across the small courtyard where he was playing with a little wooden cart. He came over to Mary and put a pudgy hand on her knee, looking up into her face. She tried to smile at him, but the pain in her head was a distraction. He patted her arm and settled himself down quietly with his toy, just keeping her company. It was as if he understood she needed comfort.

So Keturah learned what to do when Mary had a seizure and put cold cloths on her head when Mary's headaches struck without warning. Somehow with her presence, peace settled on the house of Beriah.

One day, not long after Keturah came, Mary sat with her, pulling the wool from the spindle into thread for the loom.

"What happened to your husband, Keturah? I was told he died."

Keturah looked down at the ground. "It was an accident. He struck his head on a stone."

"How terrible. Did he stumble?"

"He had too much wine."

Little by little Mary learned that Keturah's husband had been an abusive man, taking his temper out on his young wife. She'd almost lost the baby in one incident. When he died, she learned the house was not hers but a cousin's and she had to leave. A neighbor had temporarily taken her. The neighbor was a friend of Huldah's.

Mary persisted. "How did you happen to marry him?"

Keturah looked up and gave a slight shrug. "I was a plain girl and my parents were afraid they would not be able to find a husband for me. When Zadok made the offer, that was that. I didn't meet him until my wedding day."

"Oh, Keturah, I'm so sorry." Mary stopped twirling the spindle. "You are not plain. When you smile, your face is beautiful."

A little color tinted Keturah's cheeks and she bowed her head again.

"Was there no one in the family to take you in or become your kinsman redeemer?"

"I did not wish to stay, and there was no one who wished to marry me."

Mary put her hand on Keturah's. "Then we are fortunate that you came to us."

Keturah raised her eyes to Mary's and they were shining.

When she was able, Mary helped prepare meals, but she had not gone to the market for a long time. Her mother went for her with Eliab and Keturah stayed at the house with Mary. Rachel came more often to help, and as they settled into a routine, the months passed.

This morning Keturah had prepared a simple breakfast for Nathan and Beriah, and the men had gone to the boatyard to work, Beriah to his bookkeeping and Nathan to oversee the finishing touches on one of the boats. Mary was proud of how Nathan was doing at the boatyard. He had learned the best source of lumber and the amounts needed each month. But working with her uncle had been difficult. He'd gone with Zerah on one of the merchant vessels to purchase wood and managed to maintain his composure in the face of Zerah's unreasonable animosity. His frustration had mounted until, finally, in exasperation, he told Mary he was going back to work on the boats, the part he loved to do most. Mary could only pray he and her uncle could work together in a more congenial way.

Mary watched Mishma play with the wooden lamb Eliab had carved years before. She had seen him look longingly at it one day and on an impulse put it in his small outstretched hands. He kept it with him at all times and even slept with it.

Each day Keturah brought Mary the cup of strong liquid made from special plants, and Mary would reach for it eagerly. When Merab first brought the herbal mixture, she told Nathan it would help ease the pain of the headaches. Mary was grateful for the comfort, but it never seemed to be enough. As each dose increased, it seemed to take more and more to achieve the same peaceful effect and keep the pain at bay. Little by little she'd come to depend upon the medicine to get through the day. She learned it was her father who had suggested it. Dealing with pain himself when his own sickness returned, he knew the relief it brought.

Nathan was at first baffled by Mary's behavior. Her times of illness hadn't changed, but he would come home to find her in a dreamlike state, speaking strangely. Gradually he began to understand what was happening and who had instigated the potion. In anger he went to Jared to confront him.

"Now along with everything else, must I also live with this? What possessed you to suggest that Merab give her that mindless herb?"

Jared regarded his son-in-law and shook his head slowly. "Who but one who has endured pain and felt the only relief open to me could know the relief I wanted Mary to feel. You have done what you could, but nothing has changed. The exorcism didn't work. I could not bear to see her suffer so."

Torn between respect for his father-in-law and desperation, Nathan flung up a hand and sat down suddenly on the bench in Jared's courtyard. "At least she was still the Mary I knew. Now this strange woman greets me at the end of the day, her words jumbled, her appearance unkempt—" Nathan put his head in his hands.

The silence was overwhelming to Nathan, and when at last he looked up at Jared, he was startled to see the older man clutching his chest, his face wracked with pain.

"Sir, are you all right? The illness has returned then?"

Jared's reply was cut off by a bout of heavy coughing. He grabbed a cloth from his belt and held it to his mouth. As he struggled to catch his breath, Nathan helped him to the bench.

The spasm subsided and Jared breathed heavily. He lifted sorrowful eyes to Nathan. "It has returned, and this time I'll have no reprieve. As to Mary, forgive me if you can. Perhaps if you begin to dilute the amount Mary is taking, you can stop the drug. The aftereffect is terrible to endure, but if you feel you must do this, I understand your fear. She is my only child and I could not bear to see her suffer so. Each year it seems to increase and I have no answers."

Nathan's shoulders sagged. "Nor do I."

The two men sat quietly together, each with their own thoughts, and at last Nathan stood up to leave. There was nothing more he could say. What would happen if Mary lessened the potion? As Jared had said, the only thing he could do was try. Whatever it took, he wanted his Mary back.

Rachel arrived at her usual time to help Keturah bathe Mary and dress her for the day. Keturah put some fruit on the table. Mary stared at it as her mother urged her to eat.

She looked up at her mother through a haze.

The days seemed to speed by, and at times it was hard to distinguish one from another. She knew this was her mother, but she could not recall the woman's name. Then she looked away across the courtyard and wondered at the sycamore tree that seemed to move in strange ways, though there was no wind. She shook her head trying to clear the fog that dominated her days.

"Mama . . ." The word rose up from the agony that filled her being.

Rachel started to speak soothingly to her, but they were interrupted by a commotion at the gate.

Eliab called out, "Mistress, come quickly. It is the master."

"Keturah, bring Mary."

Keturah grabbed Mishma's hand as Rachel put a heavy shawl over Mary. Keturah took Mary's arm and the women hurried her through the streets behind Eliab. They had no sooner entered the courtyard when Zerah burst in behind them, followed by Beriah, Nathan, and Amos, who were carrying Jared. The front of his tunic was covered with blood and he was unconscious.

Mary was quickly settled in the shade with Keturah and Mishma.

"I will prepare his bed," cried Rachel as she hurried into the house.

Mary stirred. Something was wrong. The realization that it was her father penetrated the haze of her mind. "What is wrong with my father, Keturah?"

"I don't know, Mary. I think he is ill."

"Please, I want to see him."

Keturah hesitated, but admonished Mishma to wait there for her.

Eliab stepped forward. "I will watch the child." He looked toward the house, his face drawn, and then he squatted down by the little boy as they examined a trail of ants, crossing in the dirt.

Keturah helped Mary up and, with a hand on her elbow, led her into the house.

Mary fell on her knees by her father's bed. "Abba! Abba!" It was the cry of a lost child, and Mary realized it was her own voice.

Rachel looked down at her husband and struggled to hold back tears. "So it has returned, and with a vengeance. I was afraid it was only a matter of time before the blood came again." She turned to Keturah. "Get a basin of water and cloths."

Nathan put a hand on Mary's shoulder briefly, in comfort, and then turned toward the door. "I will call Merab."

Mary's mind clouded over again and she sat watching the drama in front of her with almost a detached air.

Zerah stood nearby and took a step forward, looking down at his brother. "He collapsed in the boatyard, spitting up blood."

Keturah returned with the basin. Rachel dipped

a cloth in the water and wrung it out, then gently washed the blood from her husband's face and beard.

Mary looked up at her father-in-law and recognized sadness. Why was he sad? She mentally shook her head and for a moment the shadows abated. Beriah's gaze went from Jared to Mary. He slowly shook his head and then motioned to Amos to follow him outside.

Pray. Mary remained on her knees and the words formed in her mind. She needed the strength of HaShem to be of help to her mother. She prayed with all her strength as her father's face went in and out of focus.

Rachel looked up at Mary's uncle. "He has been more weary lately, Zerah." She sighed. "I didn't want to think he was ill again, just tired. He kept telling me he was well."

Zerah's gaze rested on Nathan, who had returned with Merab. "We have work to do. Rachel will let us know if we are needed. Jared must rest." His tone of voice was that of one talking to someone inferior, and Mary looked at her husband, waiting for his response.

He ignored Zerah and turned to Mary's mother. "Mother Rachel, is there anything further we can do for you?"

She shook her head. "I will watch over him. If there is a change, we will let you know. Thank you, Nathan."

Nathan touched Mary on her arm and she looked up. "Stay here with your mother. She needs you right now." He walked past Zerah, ignoring the man's dark countenance.

Mary watched her uncle storm out of the house, muttering curses.

Her prayers were heard as HaShem granted Mary a miraculous reprieve from her drugged state. Her father lived for three days, with Mary, Rachel, and Merab taking turns watching over him and ministering to his needs. Nathan and Zerah came and went as often as they could, and when Rachel realized the end was near, she sent Eliab to bring them right away. The other men from the boatyard came also, and Mary heard the murmur of their voices as they waited in the courtyard.

Zerah's haughty attitude for once was not in evidence. He stood near his brother and Mary saw tears gathering in his eyes.

Jared looked up at him and spoke haltingly. "I pray you will find peace, my brother. Let the Most High, blessed be his name, heal the wounds you bear. I trust my family into your care."

Zerah nodded, and it was a moment before he could speak. "You have dealt well with me, brother. I will care for your family."

A slight smile appeared on Jared's face. "And Nathan . . . ?"

A heavy sigh. "I will deal fairly with him. You have my word."

Mary held her father's hand as he turned his head toward her. "My little flower, I go to my fathers and to our Most High God, blessed be his name. I can go in peace, for you and your mother are in good hands."

"Abba, I cannot bear it. Don't leave us." Large tears spilled from her eyes and ran unchecked down her cheeks.

Jared then spoke to her mother. "Rachel, my heart, you have been a good wife to me, and beloved. Be strong now, for Mary's sake and your own."

Mary's mother wept quietly, bowing her head.

Mary gazed down at her father's face. He closed his eyes and a soft rattle sounded in his chest. Then there was silence. When they realized he was gone, the anguished cries from Mary, her mother, and the other women echoed from the house as they poured out their grief. The sound rose over the wall and carried to the surrounding neighborhood, as everyone within hearing knew Jared, the boatbuilder, the beloved husband and father, was dead.

❖ 16 ❖

Mary struggled through the hazy, disjointed days in a stupor. At times it was as though she was outside of her body looking in. She studied her hands as though they didn't belong to her. Who was she? What was she doing in this room? Was it day or night? It all seemed the same. When she felt herself rational for a short while, the realization of the death of her father sat like a stone on her chest and she cried out in grief. Why couldn't she herself have been the one who died? She was useless to everyone, especially Nathan. The forces that drove her caused her to shrink back from him when he tried to touch her. The sadness in his eyes haunted her.

This morning Nathan had railed at her. "No more! I don't know what Merab gives you, but no more! I'd rather have you as you were before than this ghost of a woman who spends her days like this."

He'd stormed out and slammed the gate behind him. Merab had not come again to her, and now, as the effects of the potion were beginning to wear off, she felt her skin crawl. The walls seemed to move like shadows and the voices in her head taunted her, and she fell to her knees rocking back and forth. Would no one help her?

Suddenly Eliab, Nathan, and her mother were beside her. Eliab held a clay bowl, and as Mary wretched, Nathan spoke in soothing tones.

"I'm here, beloved. I am with you."

To her surprise the voices were silent. This time she did not push Nathan away. He wrapped his arms around her and rocked her as one would a small child.

Eliab's deep voice whispered in her ear. "It will pass, mistress. It will pass. This is the beginning, but you will be well soon."

Then Eliab spoke somberly. "I have seen this before. Many at the Hippodrome resorted to this potion. It helped them to overcome their fears. Not every man who fought in the ring was a brave man. Like me, they were slaves, groomed to fight to please the screaming crowds." There was a bitter note to his voice.

"How long will it take?" Nathan asked.

"It is hard to say, young master, but it will be hard on her."

Rachel sighed. "Her father only sought to help her. I begged him not to do it, but I did not prevail."

"I am her husband," Nathan cried out. "She lives under my roof. He had no right. See how she suffers, even more than she did without it."

Rachel wiped Mary's face with a cool cloth. "I'm so sorry, Nathan."

"I told Merab she is never to give it to her again, or she will be forbidden to enter our home."

Mary felt her body begin to shake with chills and Nathan wrapped his cloak around her.

She heard the pleading note in her mother's voice. "Can we bring her outside where it is warm?"

Nathan sighed. "She has escaped before, into the town."

Eliab stepped forward. "I will watch over her, young master."

Then her mother's voice. "Oh Eliab, what would we do without you?"

Nathan slowly stood up, prepared to carry his wife, but Eliab nodded to him and gathered Mary in his great arms, carrying her easily from the room.

When they were in the courtyard, Keturah stood up from stirring the stew and watched her with wary eyes. Mishma also watched her from a distance. His young face held puzzlement and a new emotion, fear.

"Will she run away again?"

Eliab folded his strong arms. "I will watch her."

Rachel brought a small bunch of grapes and gave one to Mary. She tasted the sweetness and moved it around in her mouth. Rachel gave her another one and she ate that too. Then her sides began to cramp and she bent over, wrapping her arms around her body and moaning.

Nathan knelt before her. "If I could take this from you, I would, beloved."

She looked up at him, his face blurred by her tears, "I want to die. I want to die. Please, let me die."

Eliab knelt down so his eyes were level with hers. "You will not die, mistress. You will feel like that, but you will not die. When it has passed through your body, you will be better."

Then she fainted. She didn't remember being carried back to their room. She vaguely heard Nathan whisper his love and felt a rug being gently tucked around her. Her mind swirled down into a vortex of darkness and she heard a small child whimpering in fear. Was it Mishma? No, the voice was her own.

Nathan sat on the cushion after the evening meal. Eliab stood outside Mary's door and Rachel had taken him his dinner. Keturah quietly gathered the platters and began to wipe them with a cloth.

Beriah sat shivah, the week of mourning, with the family upon the death of Jared. Since Jared had no son to mourn him and say *Kaddish*, the prayer for the dead, Nathan had taken the part of a son. Through all this, Beriah said little. During the ordeal with Mary, he'd remained silent. Now, throughout the evening meal he had been thoughtful, and Nathan looked up to find his father studying him from time to time. Beriah

156

waited until Keturah had left them to settle Mishma for the night and Rachel had returned to her home with Eliab.

Then, into the silence, he spoke his heart. "My son, the time has come for you to make a decision. I wish to marry again, and I cannot bring a wife into this situation. You have my heart and I feel deeply for all that your wife is going through, but I am getting older. I desire peace in my household. Mary needs the care of her mother, and Rachel is now alone. You must either send Mary away to the house of Jared, or go with her."

Nathan hung his head. "It has been difficult for you, I know. You have been patient with Mary, and I understand. You should not have to be without comfort because of my wife. Who is your chosen?"

"A widow by the name of Beulah. She was married to a friend of mine in Capernaum for many years and is lonely, as I am. She has consented to marry me, but cannot bring herself to enter the situation as it stands in my home."

Nathan knew his father had traveled to Capernaum many times, but felt it was for the boatyard and had not thought to ask the reason for his trips. His father was right. He could not bring a wife into their home with Mary's condition affecting their lives.

"I will speak to Rachel this day, Father. If she is agreeable, we will return to Jared's home." He gave his father a searching look and then smiled. "You have kept your secret well."

The look of relief on his father's face touched Nathan's heart.

Keturah gathered Mary's clothes and few belongings and bundled them up. She led Mishma and Eliab carried Mary's things. Nathan gathered Mary up in his arms, and when she whimpered and asked where they were going, Nathan just held her tightly and murmured, "We're going home, Mary."

Nathan realized it was a wise decision when he saw how relieved Rachel was to have her daughter near to care for. It would help both of them deal with their grief.

Keturah and Mishma moved with them and Nathan was pleased how quickly they all settled into a routine. Rachel did most of the cooking, with Keturah's help, sometimes with Mary's, when she was able. Without grandchildren of her own, Rachel gave her heart to Mishma, who returned the affection.

By now Nathan had taken over Jared's part of the business, with Zerah's reluctant agreement. Nathan was now a full partner and refused to be manipulated. Zerah still came to the house to have dinner with them once in a while at Rachel's insistence, and grudgingly admitted how well Nathan managed at the boatyard.

A few weeks later, in a simple ceremony, Nathan's father married Beulah, a woman with an ample waist and a gentle nature. He knew his new stepmother would be good for his father as soon as he met her.

❈ 17 ❈

Nathan stood in the boatyard, savoring the signs of spring in the air. The storms of winter had passed and his men were hard at work on three different boats. The smell of fresh-cut wood and resin filled the air. As he spoke to one of the men, he felt a stab of irritation that Zerah had left the yard early—again. He knew Mary's uncle was headed for his favorite wineshop. Zerah had become even more moody lately and seemed to spend a great deal of time away, yet there appeared to be little Nathan could do about it.

His attention was caught by three strangers who entered the yard, looking around at the boats. Nathan sensed they were related from their similarity of appearance. One younger man was a big, brash fellow, his dark hair barely contained by the headband he wore. The other, younger man was pleasant of face and seemed content to merely watch the proceedings.

Nathan stepped forward with a smile. "Good morning, my friends, can I be of help to you?"

The older man nodded. "I am called Zebedee, and these are my two sons, James and John. We are in need of a new fishing boat. One of ours was severely damaged in a recent storm. I was told to ask for a man named Jared. His reputation is well known."

Nathan spread his hands. "It is with regret that I must inform you that Jared, my father-in-law, died three years ago. I am Nathan and I would be happy to assist you in any way. Will you join me in the shade for some refreshments?"

Zebedee stroked his beard that was nearly white with streaks of gray. "I see. Perhaps we can still do business." His piercing eyes beneath heavy brows looked deep into Nathan's.

"My father-in-law's brother, my partner, is out of town, but I also handle the sale of the boats."

Zebedee nodded but did not reply.

James eyed the pitcher Daniel, Nathan's young helper, had brought. "A poor man's refreshment," he muttered.

Nathan smiled. "Perhaps a cup of wine?"

Zebedee tilted his head. "If you could spare some wine, it would be gratefully received, but do not trouble yourself. We will have the milk."

Nathan kept his face placid, but went to get a bottle of wine from the storage room, then poured it generously into their cups. As they refreshed themselves, Nathan waited patiently, knowing they would discuss business in their own time.

"Tell me, sir, what is the news from Capernaum?" Nathan settled himself and leaned forward to listen.

"All is well, but for a strange man baptizing in the Jordan River. His name is John, a teacher of sorts, dressed in camel skins. It is thought he is possibly Essene, from the desert. He baptizes those who come to him in the river."

Nathan leaned forward. "Is he a prophet?"

The son called John shrugged. "He says he is preparing the way for one to come."

"The Messiah?"

Zebedee looked away toward the hills. "It is a strange thought. We have looked for the Messiah from generation to generation, yet here is a man who says that the One who sent him to baptize with water told him to look for the man on whom we see the Spirit descending. He will be the One."

There was a huff from James. "Words in the wind. Who can believe a wild man who rants as he does?"

John spoke up. "What if what he says is true, James? No one knows the time of the Messiah's coming, why not now?"

James gave him a scowl of dismissal.

Nathan was intrigued. "I would see this strange man."

Zebedee glanced at his sons. "It is good that you scoff. I would not have my sons running off to follow some madman." He turned back to Nathan. "If he is still there when you deliver the boat, you shall have your chance."

At last Zebedee inquired as to the price of one of the fishing boats nearing completion in the yard. The three men strolled over to watch the work in process. They walked around slowly and Zebedee's eyes missed nothing of the careful construction. He nodded to his sons and Nathan was sure he'd made a sale.

Nathan named the price and Zebedee appeared to be shocked. "We are but poor fishermen, such a price is more than we can consider."

And so as the bargaining process began, Nathan enjoyed the banter and the haggling, for thus it was so in his part of the world. A buyer would never consider purchasing an item at the merchant's first price.

When at last a price had been agreed on, Zebedee still maintained the air of a man who had been duped into paying more than the boat was worth, but the documents were drawn up by Beriah and signed by Zebedee. The nearly completed boats in the yard were already destined for new owners, so Nathan agreed to deliver

Zebedee's boat in two months' time to the harbor at Capernaum. Zebedee handed Nathan a bag of coins containing half the purchase price of the boat, the other half to be paid when their boat was delivered.

Zebedee looked at him shrewdly. "You drive a good bargain. We will look for you in sixty days."

When they had gone, Nathan allowed himself a pleased smile. In Zerah's place he had sold a boat and collected half the price. It would ensure more work for their crew. He turned to his father. "Do you think you have a good place to put this?" He handed him the bag of coins.

Beriah beamed. "I do indeed. It shall be quite safe."

Knowing Zerah's penchant for spending money from the boatyard, Nathan and his father had conspired to make a place in the storeroom, behind some bricks, to safeguard Nathan's portion. Zerah was ever in need of funds, and money seemed to disappear whenever he was aware it existed. With the safety of the business in mind, Nathan felt it was necessary to protect some of their income.

Beriah took the pouch. "You have done well, my son. I will see to this." They smiled at each other in mutual understanding.

Nathan started home with mixed emotions. Perhaps today would be one of Mary's good days. He never knew what to expect when he returned at the end of the day. Would he find her greeting him, her eyes alight with love, or would he find her sitting in the courtyard, eyes glazed in pain, unaware he was even there? He thought he knew what he was taking on when they married, but did he? Young and full of love and hope, he'd been convinced that he could find a cure for Mary, picturing children on his knee and a loving household to come home to.

Seven years had passed since their marriage and Mary was no better. Now twenty-three, she had still borne no children. Perhaps HaShem in his mercy had closed her womb. She could not attend events in their neighborhood. Mary was afraid of something happening, and in turn, people were wary when around her. They considered her possessed by the evil one, and Nathan believed it too. She could not even go to synagogue on Shabbat. He made the annual trips to Jerusalem with his father and other men on the three holy days set aside by the Most High, blessed be his name, but Mary remained at home. Friends had tried to persuade him to divorce her and let her mother take care of her. *You are wasting your life,* they said. *Marry again and you can have children.* The thoughts echoed in his head and there were days when he was tempted to do just that. From time to time Mary begged him to divorce her so he could have a normal home life.

Then there were the days when Mary seemed well and his love for her rose up, obliterating any other thoughts. He held her in his arms and knew her sweetness. How could he leave her?

He cried out to the Most High God once again to hear his prayer. As he looked up, the sun was setting in a hazy glow of orange and gold, and suddenly a sense of peace flooded his heart. Someday he would find the way to help Mary. As long as they loved each other, there was still hope. With a lighter step, he hurried home.

18

Rachel lay on her bed, her eyes bright with fever. The loss of Jared five years before and the constant care of Mary were taking their toll on her strength. Mary helped Keturah put cold cloths on her mother's brow and would not leave her side. Alternating between feeling normal and whimpering in a corner like a small child, Mary tried to sort out the confusion in her mind. For once, her mother, who had been so strong and caring, could not help her.

Her mother's good heart may have been her

undoing, for Rachel had gone to the home of a neighbor to help nurse the mother and three small children who were ill with fever. Two of the children died and the mother hung on to life by a thread. Two days later, as Rachel was preparing to go to the home again, she fell to the floor of their house and was helped to bed by Keturah.

"Dear lady, you are tired. Rest yourself."

Mary watched from where she sat in the shade. Her mother was ill? She tried to process the thought. Her mother was never ill. She was always there when Mary needed her. Mary stood up, struggled for balance, and shuffled into the house.

Seeing her mother's face, red with fever, she found herself struggling for breath as terror constricted her heart. She had lost her father. She could not bear to lose her mother also. She would not leave her mother's side in spite of Nathan's pleading for her to rest. Huldah came to help. Keturah was now fearful for Mishma. At least at eight, he was at Hebrew school most of the day.

Nathan tried to gently draw Mary away so the other women could minister to her mother, but she turned on him like a wild woman.

"Leave me alone! Don't touch me!" she screamed at him, her eyes wide like a wild thing.

Hearing the screeching voice, Nathan stared at

her and then turned on his heel and rushed out, leaving her in Huldah's care.

"Now, Mary, sit here by your mother and be a good daughter. She needs you to be calm. You do want to help her, don't you?"

Mary nodded and slowly sat back down. Now she sat, rocking herself and staring at the still figure in the bed. She tried to stifle the whimpers that slipped out from time to time.

Huldah told Keturah to stay away and keep Mishma as far away from Rachel as possible so they would not catch the fever. Keturah was only too eager to comply. Merab tended Rachel also, allowing Huldah to return home from time to time to see to her family. They took turns staying through the night. Merab was herself weary from tending so many who were sick as the fever tore a tragic swath through the homes in their community.

Two days passed as Mary slept fitfully, hardly aware of those who came and went from the room. She was even oblivious of Nathan who tried again to speak to her and was ignored. When conscious, her eyes never left the face of her mother. She listened to the raspy breathing and watched her mother's chest slowly move up and down.

Though Huldah whispered to Merab, Mary understood the words. "If she makes it through this night, she has a chance."

Merab sighed. "I've seen the signs so many times. I fear her body is too worn down to resist. Taking care of Mary all these years has made her an old woman before her time. Then when she lost Jared . . ." The woman moved away and Mary couldn't understand their words anymore. She reached down and took her mother's hand as if she could will her back to health. Rachel's hands were so cold.

When Huldah came back in with fresh water to put cold cloths on Rachel's face and brow, she paused in the doorway. She stood there a moment and then turned on her heel and hurried out.

A short time later, Mary was aware of Nathan squatting next to her and looking into her face. "Beloved, Huldah has brought me sad news. Your mother has gone to join your father. You must come with me."

Mary turned and stared at him, hearing the words but not comprehending. "I don't want to leave her. She is better, I know it." She put her head down on her mother's breast and with a start realized her mother's chest was not moving. Rachel was not breathing at all.

Nathan sighed and, with a strong arm around her shoulders, lifted her up. As he forcibly tried to lead her away, she struggled with him. "No, I want to stay."

"Huldah and Merab will take care of your

mother. Come, beloved, come out in the sunshine and sit with me."

Finally the thoughts and words connected in her mind. Her mother was dead. As Nathan eased her down onto the bench by the fountain, she wrapped her arms around herself and began to moan and rock back and forth.

"Mama, Mama, Mama," she whimpered over and over, until the whimpered words became a wail of grief.

Nathan looked up as Huldah and Merab passed him with preparations for Rachel's body. Huldah paused a moment, her dark eyes full of compassion. The question hung in the air unspoken, What will you do now? Jared was gone, Rachel was gone, and Mary was slipping more and more into madness. Now that her mother was gone, what would they do?

Nathan put his face in his hands and wept.

19

Zerah sat in his usual place, a dark corner of the wineshop where he could watch those passing by. He knew he had work to do at the boatyard, but he resented how Nathan had stepped so quickly into Jared's place. Those who came from Magdala to buy boats liked the young man's cheerful manner and asked for him. "Nathan should defer to me. I am the elder," he grumbled to himself. Yet even as the thoughts struck like darts, Zerah knew Nathan had retained a respectful attitude around him. He could not find fault with Nathan's work either. He smiled to himself. Perhaps there was still a way to get rid of Nathan and have the business to himself. He would have no trouble with his niece. As sick as Mary was, perhaps she would not live long anyway.

The thoughts of the kidnapping plagued his mind. Was he to blame for Mary's illness? She had not been like this before the kidnapping. Anger rose up as he realized how he'd been tricked by the kidnappers. He'd gotten none of the bag of gold coins. Those sons of a camel driver had escaped with all of it, and his brother had nearly been murdered. He'd tried in several ways to find the men, but thieves take care of their own and no information was given him, despite an offered bribe of money.

Zerah leaned back against the wall, thinking—he had a young partner challenging his knowledge of the business; a niece, known throughout the town as "Mad Mary"; and his brother and his sister-in-law were dead. He wallowed in his self-pity and continued to allow the merchant to refill his wine cup.

As the sun set and the shadows crept up the walls of the street, he became aware of the merchant standing by his side.

"My friend, perhaps it is time to return to your home. The shadows come and thieves are about. It is not safe for you to remain here."

A shot of anger rose. He would allow no one to tell him what to do. But just as quickly came the realization that Tubal was a source of much information and a trusted friend. Zerah couldn't afford to offend him. Rising slowly with Tubal's help, he straightened himself and began to walk unsteadily toward the door. Lost in his thoughts of revenge, he did not see the Roman soldier staggering down the street toward him. In a moment they collided and the soldier reached for his sword.

"Jewish pig! You would accost a Roman soldier? I'll cut you down where you stand!"

The soldier stood over him, reeking of wine and weaving back and forth. His eyes were bloodshot and blood was running from a scrape on his arm.

Zerah sank to his knees, shaking with fear, knowing his life was about to end. With sudden clarity he realized the position his bitterness and jealousy had put him in. He had nothing but a dagger to defend himself with and that was no match for the Roman broadsword. He closed his eyes, unable even to speak or beg for his life, and waited for the end to come. He could only cry out in his heart, *Oh Most Holy One, blessed be your name, save me!*

Through the haze of his thoughts, he heard the voice of Tubal. "Ah, Linus, my Roman friend, you are hurt. Turn into my shop and let me tend your wound. I have fresh wine from the coast."

The sword wavered as the unsteady soldier listened to Tubal through a drunken haze. Zerah fell to the ground and prostrated himself, remaining motionless. Perhaps the soldier would think him already dead.

Tubal's voice came again, wheedling. "See, you have done away with the man. We will get rid of the body for you. Come, let me refresh you."

With great effort, the soldier resheathed his sword, and with a curse and a sharp kick that struck Zerah in the ribs, he allowed Tubal to draw him into the wineshop. As Zerah listened to their footsteps move away on the stone floor, he tried to think what to do. Then someone leaned down and whispered fiercely in his ear,

"Get up, you fool, while you have the chance. He is not looking this way. If you are lucky, when he sobers up, he won't remember the incident."

Zerah got up carefully, feeling the sharp pain of his bruised ribs. Tubal was tending to the soldier, who had his back to the entrance. He didn't need to be told twice. Holding his side against the pain, he ran.

Amazed that he had reached his home without being accosted or robbed, Zerah made his way painfully into the courtyard. His servants, Saffira and Jokim, a husband and wife who cared for his home, hurried to him and helped him to his bed. Saffira bound up his side. It was not the first time he'd come home after too much wine, but he had not come home injured before. They shook their heads and left him to sleep it off.

Zerah woke in the morning to the smell of bread baking in the clay oven. It made his mouth water. He'd thought only of bread as a means to assuage his hunger to go on to better things, but now it soothed him. He lay quietly, contemplating what had happened. He had almost been killed. The realization brought fresh tremors of fear. Then he thought of the frantic prayer he had prayed to HaShem. Had his prayer been heard? He should have been dead, run through with the soldier's sword, and yet here he was, safe and alive in his own home. What miracle had caused the Holy One to spare his worthless life? He didn't deserve to live. He was a wretched man who had sinned greatly. In his mind he cringed as he recalled Mary's bedraggled state and the torment she had suffered over the years from that episode. He could no longer push the knowledge to the back of his mind of his guilt for her mental state. How could he ignore what he had done? His foolish actions and the bungling of the kidnapping years ago had contributed to Mary's illness.

As he sat up, wincing, the face of Mary, groaning in pain from the headaches, morphed into the face of another woman. Her dark, flowing tresses damp with perspiration, her face contorted in the agony of childbirth. Her eyes that had been filled with love for him, now glazed with pain. Her life was ebbing away and he could do nothing. He put his head in his hands. Hadassah. How he had loved her. The ache in his heart was almost unbearable as he remembered the last moments he held her in his arms, crying out to HaShem to spare her life. His tiny son, born early and not yet ready to enter the world, had been buried only hours before. As Hadassah slumped lifeless, his anger rose against God. They loved each other. They had looked forward to a long life together, children and grandchildren. Now she was taken from him and his bitterness against their God consumed him.

How worthless his life had been these past years, full of himself and his wants. He had gone through the motions in the synagogue, but his heart was far from worship. Now Zerah saw himself as he was, and he shrank back in shame. Why had the Most High, blessed be his name, seen fit to spare his life? He sank to his knees, begging for forgiveness, pouring out his heart to his God. And the cleansing came. He looked up toward the heavens, tears flowing freely down his cheeks, and finally, to his amazement, gentle waves of peace washed over his soul. He raised his arms in thankfulness.

How long he had been on his knees, Zerah didn't know, but when he opened his eyes, he heard a flock of sparrows in the olive trees nearby chattering to one another. He rose to his feet, feeling more alive than he had since before Hadassah died. He washed his face in a basin of water and put on fresh clothing. HaShem had given him another chance and he would not waste it.

As Zerah stepped from the house, Saffira and Jokim eyed him warily. They knew he was given to moods and watched to see what he would do.

"Ah, a good morning to you both. Is that good bread ready yet? I find I am famished."

Saffira's mouth opened and then closed again. She raised her eyebrows toward Jokim, who stood as if in suspended motion with an armload of wood for the fire.

"It will be out of the oven in moments, sir." She set a platter of ripe figs in front of him and began to slice a round of goat cheese. "You are feeling well this morning?"

He heard the curiosity behind her words. "I am well, Saffira. More so than I have been in a long time. Tell me, what am I paying you and Jokim?"

She named the sum, omitting the fact that it was paltry for the work they did.

"I must increase that, starting today. You should be paid fairly for your work."

Saffira stared at him, her eyes wide with disbelief.

He chuckled. "No, I have not lost my mind." He looked up at the sky, where the gold and pink of sunrise was giving way to the deep blue of morning, and stroked his beard. "Perhaps I have instead found it," he said softly.

❊ 20 ❊

The eyes looking back at him were not Mary's. Strange sounds came out of her mouth and she sank to her knees. "Leave me alone," she growled.

Hearing the guttural voice, Nathan backed against the wall, his heart pounding in his chest. This was the worst he'd seen her. He wanted to cry out to the Most High, "I cannot take this anymore. It is too much." Day after day, month after month, year after year, the woman he'd loved was no longer. Instead he lived with a sick woman who resembled a crone more than the beautiful woman he married. In spite of Keturah's constant care and help, their household had become a place to dread at the end of the day. He slipped out of the room and bolted the door behind him. After her mother's death, he'd had to resort to locking Mary in her room for her own safety. In spite of Eliab's watchful eyes, she had craftily escaped a couple of times, wandering through the market-place and tearing at her hair. If it were not for the faithful Eliab bringing her back home, he didn't know how she would end up.

Nathan moved slowly down the stairs. How long would they have Eliab? Keturah could not handle her alone anymore and even young Mishma cowered away from Mary now.

Nathan passed Eliab, who sat as he did these days, his back to the wall in the sun, staring off into the distance. He was getting older and his hair was nearly white. As Nathan observed him, he wondered if the former gladiator was thinking of his home far away across the great desert. Eliab had remained with them after Jared's death, for he had promised Jared on his deathbed that he would watch over Rachel now that she was alone.

When Nathan moved Mary back to her mother's home, Nathan wondered how long Eliab would stay. When Rachel had died, he wondered if Eliab felt he had repaid his debt to the family. He was sure Eliab would leave them now, and in his heart Nathan felt it would be soon. Eliab seemed to be waiting for something but kept his thoughts to himself.

Nathan had noted Mishma's behavior in the last few months. This was no atmosphere for a young boy. The boy's natural sympathy for Mary had turned to fear. He would not come near her and then seemed relieved when Nathan finally had to lock her in her room.

Nathan turned toward Keturah, whose eyes seemed guarded as she watched him approach.

"How is she?"

He shook his head slowly. "I had to bar the door

again. The evil one takes more and more of her. I don't know how much longer I can endure this."

"You have borne more than most men would have, Nathan."

He raised his eyebrows. The comment was unlike her. He thought for a moment. How long had she been with them? Too many years. She had not sought marriage again, devoting herself to her son and Mary. One evening Mary had shared with him the circumstances of Keturah's first marriage and how she had lived with an abusive husband. She told him Keturah had nearly lost her son to one of his rages when she was pregnant. It had almost been a blessing when he died suddenly in an accident.

Nathan thought on all these things and knew he must make a decision in some way. What was he to do?

"I must leave for Capernaum. I need to deliver the boat to Zebedee and his sons. When I return, I must decide what to do about Mary."

"Will Zerah go with you?"

"No, I promised the next trip to young Daniel. He's been a big help in the boatyard and has been begging to go along on one of my delivery trips."

She nodded, and Nathan noted that the same lines of fatigue he had seen on Rachel's face now touched Keturah's. He watched her knead the bread dough. She should have a life of her own, a husband and father for Mishma. Yet she stayed.

The soft folds of her shift moved with her and Nathan felt an emotion suddenly constrict his heart that he hadn't felt in a long time—the longing for a woman. Keturah was comely, a good mother and an able homemaker. On more than one occasion, he'd struggled with the temptation she presented living with them. When Rachel was there, it had been acceptable, but now Rachel was gone and he knew he must either send Keturah away or find a husband for her. He cringed inwardly, thinking of the words of their rabbi the previous Sabbath.

"It has come to my attention that after the death of your mother-in-law a young woman remains in your home."

"She cares for my wife, who is ill."

"It is not a good situation. We know of your wife's illness. It has continued for many years. This young woman must not remain unprotected in your home."

Nathan nodded. "I understand."

Now, as he thought back on the rabbi's words, he stopped at the gate and suddenly turned around. Keturah was standing in the courtyard watching him, and in that unguarded moment, her feelings were in her eyes. They stood staring at each other in silence, and Nathan felt an overwhelming urge to take her in his arms and comfort her, yet he knew if he did, he was lost.

He spoke first, but it was not what he wanted to say. "I pray things will go well with Mary while I'm gone. Huldah will help you and you have Eliab to watch over the household and protect you."

The moment passed. Keturah turned away abruptly and began to shape the dough into loaves. There was no resistance left in her.

He needed to be at the boat. He picked up the leather pouch of food Keturah had prepared for his journey, slung the strap over his shoulder, and strode briskly toward the docks, wrestling with his thoughts.

You love the boy, you could be a father.

With Keturah you could have more children.

Why should you stay with a woman who cannot be a wife?

Mary's words, flung at him in saner moments, haunted him, *Leave me, divorce me, we have no life together.*

Everyone would understand Nathan taking another wife under the circumstances, but then what could he do with Mary? He searched his heart. Did he still love her? It was true, they had no marriage. Mary couldn't bear to have him touch her. The forces that drove her caused her to cry out in fear lately whenever he came near. Bitterness raised its ugly head as Nathan contemplated his circumstances.

Several fishermen were washing their nets,

flinging them out again and again into the water to remove the sand and pebbles that clogged them. Some were mending their nets, torn by the violent waves from the sudden storms that plagued those who fished the unpredictable waters of the Sea of Galilee.

When he neared the boat, Daniel waved at him and Nathan brightened a little. At least this trip he would not have to put up with a sour mood from Zerah, who had not shown up at the boat-yard yesterday. No doubt recovering from one of his drinking sprees. Young Daniel would be better company.

The sea was relatively calm as they hoisted the sail. Nathan was proud of this boat. It showed their finest workmanship, and he knew Zebedee and his sons would be pleased. Their young apprentice at the boatyard begged to go along and Nathan relented and gave him permission. Now he scampered like a young monkey, doing Nathan's bidding as they readied the boat for its maiden trip to Capernaum. When he'd delivered the fishing boat, he would find passage on another boat heading for Magdala and return home.

A slight breeze blew and the sail filled, moving the craft across the water. Nathan turned his face into the wind and breathed in the salty air. He loved the sea and had sailed their new boats to ports on the Sea of Galilee as often as was possible. It lifted the burden he bore. Now, he listened to the cry of the ever present seagulls as they hovered over the boat, looking for scraps.

Daniel waved his hands at them good-naturedly. "You scavengers! We have no fish for you on this trip."

The birds seemed to sense this and eventually moved away over the water, looking for a more promising source of food.

The craft was made to cut through the water, and with fair weather they reached Capernaum in good time. Daniel leaped to the dock to tie the line and secure the boat. A lone figure stood waiting for them. Zebedee.

As Nathan stepped out of the boat and approached the older man, he was startled to see the sad look on the fisherman's face. Zebedee looked distracted.

"Would you care to inspect the boat, sir?"

"Yes, yes, of course." Zebedee walked closer and looked over the sleek craft from head to stern. "It is good."

Nathan frowned. "And how are those two strapping sons of yours?" He meant only to make conversation, but Zebedee's face was suddenly as dark as a storm cloud.

"Gone, both of them, their two cousins, Peter and Andrew also."

"Gone? Where?"

"They are off to follow an itinerant rabbi gathering followers. He came to our boats one day and merely said, 'Follow me,' and my sons left our boat and walked away with him." He shook his head slowly. "I don't understand. They just left. They have wives and children and now I must take care of their families."

Nathan stood dumbly, trying to imagine what Zebedee was telling him. A man counted on his sons to follow him into his trade, and now it was as if Zebedee had no sons at all.

"Who is this rabbi they are following? Is it the prophet you told me about earlier?"

Zebedee waved a hand in the air. "No, it is not the man called John. It is a new teacher by the name of Jesus. He goes around the countryside telling people the kingdom of God is at hand. They say he heals people. Preposterous stories! Who can believe these things? I say he's a sorcerer."

He had Nathan's full attention then. "Healing people? In what way?"

Zebedee shrugged. "I hear conflicting stories. Some say he has caused a blind man to see, healed lepers, driven out demons—"

"The man has authority over demons?"

"So it would seem, but unless I can see these things for myself, who can believe all he hears?"

Nathan thought of Mary. A glimmer of hope

tugged at his heart. He needed to find this rabbi and see what he could do. He had nothing to lose. Then he remembered he needed to complete this sale.

"Are you satisfied with the boat, sir?"

"It is well made. I am pleased." Then Zebedee remembered his hospitality. "Come, young man. Share a meal with my family. We will talk more."

Daniel was still standing by the boat. Zebedee nodded toward him. "Bring your young friend with you. My men will guard the boat."

Nathan and Daniel followed Zebedee down a series of narrow streets to his home. It was a simple one story with steps up the side leading to the rooftop where the family could sleep in the heat of the summer. The courtyard was surrounded by a wall with no gate. Two goats grazed on a pile of hay in one corner and a few sheep moved restlessly in their cramped pen in another corner. Three large clay jars containing water stood by the side of the house in the shade.

Two women came out of the house, one holding a baby on her hip. Zebedee glanced toward them. "Miriam, the wife of my son James, and my grandson, Eli. Also Dinah, the wife of my nephew Peter. A houseful as you can see." He shook his head sadly.

There was also sadness in the faces of the women as they gazed at Nathan a moment before respectfully lowering their eyes.

Another woman came out of the house and Zebedee introduced her as his wife, Salome. A thick carpet was unrolled on the ground and the men sat cross-legged as the women began to bring wine, bread, fruit, and date cakes, which they spread before their guests.

Daniel waited until Zebedee spoke the prayer of thanks before the meal, and then began to sample the variety of food, especially the platter of fish that had been fried to perfection in olive oil and leeks.

Zebedee settled himself and, as a good host, inquired about their journey and Nathan's family. Nathan spoke briefly about his mother-in-law and father-in-law's deaths.

Daniel watched covertly, no doubt wondering what Nathan would say about his wife.

"My wife suffers from an illness. It is worse since the death of her mother recently."

Zebedee's dark eyes studied Nathan's face, and Daniel had the feeling the older man saw a lot more than they realized. Zebedee stroked his beard and remained quiet, only nodding at Nathan's words.

Finally Zebedee spoke. "The fishing has been good and I am able to provide what is needed, but I must now work without the help of my sons. My brother is in the same circumstances. Both of his sons, Peter and Andrew, have gone after this rabbi."

Nathan shrugged. "Perhaps the interest in this new rabbi will wane and they will return."

Zebedee paused, a small bunch of grapes in his hand. "That is my hope. I pray each day to the Most High, blessed be his name, they may tire of wandering the countryside. May he hear my prayers."

"May he hear your prayers indeed."

When the meal was over, Nathan stood, and despite Zebedee's expected urging to stay longer and eat more, he thanked his host for his hospitality. He needed to go. Daniel had remained respectfully silent throughout the meal, listening eagerly to the older men's conversation, and now rose quickly and waited for Nathan. He was eager to find out more of this rabbi who healed people. Perhaps Nathan would take him to hear Jesus.

Daniel's eyes lit up when Nathan turned to their host and asked, "Can you tell me where I would find this Jesus?"

Zebedee frowned and eyed him suspiciously. "Do you wish to follow him also?"

"No, but I would see what it is about him that causes sons to leave their father's business."

"He is sometimes found out on the hills. Many people come to hear him speak and that is the only place where there is room for the multitudes. Ask anyone in the marketplace. They can tell you where he is."

Nathan walked toward the marketplace with Daniel hurrying beside him, eagerly anticipating the prospect of adventure.

❖ 21 ❖

Nathan transferred some of Zebedee's final payment to a small leather pouch in the front of his waistband. He tucked the larger bag of coins out of sight in his belt lest it be a temptation for thieves as he and Daniel strolled through the crowded marketplace. He paused, wistfully admiring a beautiful blue silk mantle. He considered buying it, but shocked himself when in his mind he saw how attractive it would be on—Keturah, not Mary. He hurried Daniel on to the next stall. Doves cooed in cages, their sounds almost mournful. Did they know they were destined for the Temple for a sacrifice? Nathan shook his head to clear away his foolish thoughts.

He purchased a cloak for Daniel, for the air was cooling and they would have to pass the night somewhere. He also purchased some dates and figs, which he shared with his young friend, who, like any twelve-year-old boy, seemed forever hungry.

The fruit merchant appraised him quietly. "You are a stranger here in Capernaum?"

"Not totally. I've just delivered a fishing boat to someone here."

The man smiled then, showing two missing teeth. "Ah, a builder of boats."

The man seemed amenable and Nathan decided to make an inquiry.

"I've heard news of a rabbi traveling around here preaching and healing people. Would you know of him?"

The man looked around and, with an air of conspiracy, sidled closer. "He is a sorcerer. No ordinary man could do the things he does."

Overwhelmed by the waft of garlic from the man's breath, Nathan casually stepped back, not wishing to offend his informant. "What if he is a man of God?"

The merchant shrugged. "See for yourself. He was here, but I hear he has left for Bethsaida."

"Many thanks for your kindness, my friend, I shall enjoy the fruit." With a tilt of his head, Nathan indicated to Daniel that they should move on.

Bethsaida. He would have to hire a boat. At least it was across the narrower part on the upper end of the Sea. The voyage would not take long. He contemplated what funds he could spare and decided he could chance the passage and still get back to Magdala in a short time. He sighed. Only the Most High, blessed be his name, knew what Zerah was up to in his absence. Sober, Zerah was a shrewd businessman, drunk, he was prone to rages, and Nathan prayed all was calm at the boatyard.

When they returned to the docks, they inquired about transportation to Bethsaida. A friendly fisherman, by the name of Puah, agreed to take Nathan and Daniel across to Bethsaida.

As they left the harbor of Capernaum, the conversation turned to the traveling rabbi. "His name is Jesus of Nazareth." Puah's face lit up. "He healed my daughter who had been sick with a fever. He had only to touch her and she was well." He shook his head slowly. "I saw him heal a lame man who threw away his cane and walked and leaped for joy."

"Do you think it was a trick?"

Puah's eyes bored into Nathan's. "When you see him, you will know who he is and what he is. No one speaks like this man."

Nathan was thoughtful. "Did you see any other healings when you were there?"

"Dozens. He healed everyone who was brought to him. He cast out demons and only had to touch the eyes of the blind and they could see. I would still be there, but I have to feed my family so I returned to my boat. You came at a good time. I've had a good catch, enough to take care of my family for this week. I would go with you to hear the teacher again, but I must return home to Capernaum."

Jesus casts out demons? A flutter of hope rose in Nathan's chest. Is it possible? Was this man the answer to his quest?

When they reached the harbor at Bethsaida, Nathan started to pay the fisherman, but surprisingly, Puah refused.

Putting a hand on Nathan's shoulder, he smiled. "What he has done for me I cannot repay. So, go, hear him for yourselves. You will never be the same."

Nathan stood watching the boat sail out of the harbor and thought of what Puah had told them. A man who had only to touch or speak and people were healed. Suddenly he felt he couldn't find Jesus fast enough.

The air was full of the smell of salted fish. Knowing they might be away in the hills a long time, he stopped at a fishmonger's stall. He needed to purchase food for the two of them. Who knows where they would find a place to eat later? He bought a couple of salted, dried fish, and in the street of the bread makers, he purchased several fragrant loaves to eat later. He knew Daniel would be hungry before long.

"You are seeking Jesus of Nazareth?" said a voice at his elbow.

He turned to see an older woman staring up at him. He nodded his head. How did she know?

"Come, follow me. I will show you where he is."

As they walked, Nathan considered that the woman had called Jesus a Nazarene. He knew the saying, "Can anything good come out of Nazareth?" It was a poor village with little reputation. How could such a man come from Nazareth?

After about half an hour, Nathan and Daniel were well out of the city and following the woman and other townspeople toward the hills. As they drew closer, Nathan heard a man's voice, speaking clearly. Amazed that the voice carried so well over the crowd, Nathan focused on a figure sitting on a large rock near the top of the hill. The man did not appear tall, he had a finely chiseled face, and his hair curled softly to his shoulders. There was little about him that was more than ordinary, except for a commanding voice that echoed through the crowd. Nathan put a hand on Daniel's shoulder to keep him close in the throng and began to listen.

As Jesus spoke, Nathan recognized that the rabbi was teaching from the Torah, the words of the Law. He simplified the words for his audience of unlearned townsfolk, but the way he taught captivated Nathan. Here was a man in simple garments, not in the fine clothing of a Jewish leader, speaking from great knowledge and with authority. Nathan urged Daniel forward and they made their way through the crowd to hear Jesus better. Who was this man?

The people hung on the Teacher's words and time seemed to be of little importance. When Jesus had finished teaching, the people were restless and hungry. Nathan heard one of the teacher's followers say, "Master, send the crowds away that they may go into the surrounding country and villages and buy themselves bread; for they have nothing to eat."

Jesus smiled at him and said, "You give them something to eat."

Nathan raised his eyebrows. How could his disciples feed this vast crowd? There must have been over 5,000 men, not counting women and children.

The disciple's eyes widened. "Master, two hundred denarii would not buy enough to feed them all."

Just then Daniel's stomach growled and Nathan looked down at the boy.

"Are you hungry?"

"Jesus must be hungry too, sir," Daniel whispered.

"I'm sure he is, Daniel. We need to find a place to eat our fish and bread, but let's wait a moment longer. I want to see what Jesus will do."

Daniel was looking straight at Jesus, who was looking right back at him, a smile playing around his lips. Before Nathan realized what

Daniel had in mind, the boy had stepped out of the crowd and was approaching the disciple Jesus had spoken to.

He held out the pouch with their dried fish and bread. "Jesus may have our lunch if he is hungry."

The smile on the Teacher's face broadened. "What have we here, Andrew?"

"A boy with some loaves and dried fish, Master."

Jesus beckoned to Daniel. "Come closer."

Daniel stepped up next to Jesus, who put an arm around the boy. "Your gift is most welcome, Daniel."

Daniel gasped. "You know my name?"

Jesus nodded. "You are just in time." He turned to his disciples. "Have the people sit down in companies of fifty." Then Jesus took the loaves and fishes and held them up as he looked up to heaven. He blessed the loaves and gave them to his disciples to pass out, then did the same with the fish. The disciples put some of the fish and bread in each of several baskets.

Nathan watched in amazement. While he applauded the boy's honest offer, there was no way it could feed this vast crowd. Before he could move to retrieve his young helper, a basket was passed to him containing fish and bread. People had been reaching in and taking food from the basket, yet it was still full when it reached Nathan. Startled, he took some bread and fish and passed it on. Everyone was reaching into the baskets and all were finding enough fish and bread for their needs. Nathan wanted to weep and laugh at the same time. The miracle was overwhelming. This teacher was no sorcerer. With sudden clarity, Nathan knew Jesus served the Most High God.

When he had eaten his share of the fish and bread with Daniel, he waited to see if Jesus would continue teaching. Instead Jesus began to walk through the crowd toward the water and a large fishing boat anchored nearby. He touched children on the head as he passed and people reached out to touch his garment, crying out blessings on him.

The disciples followed their master and Nathan suddenly recognized Zebedee's sons, James and John. They walked protectively around Jesus, but their faces reflected the awe Nathan himself felt. If he had not been here and observed for himself, he wouldn't have believed what he had seen. Jesus had fed thousands with a boy's small offering.

The people, their stomachs filled, began to drift in groups back toward the town. Some grumbled about the lateness of the day as they passed Nathan, so soon forgetting what they had seen and heard.

Nathan and Daniel also sought out the local khan, an inn where lodging was provided for strangers at no cost. At least they would have some straw to bed down on.

As they settled for the night in the cubicle

assigned to them, Daniel was asleep at once. Nathan listened to the boy's steady breathing and thought again of the events of the day. Sleep was impossible, for in his head he still heard the words that had been impressed on his mind as Jesus passed by. They were as clear as if Jesus had spoken aloud.

Bring her to me.

❊ 22 ❊

Mary tossed and turned through the night, calling out for Nathan and her mother, but there was no answer. Then she remembered. Her mother was dead. She would never feel the gentle arms around her and her mother's voice soothing her. Tears rolled down her cheeks when she remembered she had not even been allowed to follow her mother's body to the burial site. She had listened to the weeping and wailing of the neighbor women from her room and cried with them.

The voices plagued her again and again as she begged HaShem to stop their torment. In a lucid moment she remembered Keturah and Huldah trying to dress her and how she had fought them. She didn't want to hurt anyone, but she had no control over some of her actions. Now Nathan had locked her in the room. The forces that ruled her life were strong, and she had beaten herself against the door over and over, but it had remained closed. Her hands were bruised and bloody from pounding on the unyielding barrier.

Eliab had entered cautiously with food for her, but even he had difficulty restraining her. He flung her away when she tried to claw him, and she'd crawled under the table and watched him with wary eyes as he tried to gently speak to her. Finally, he left the bread and fruit and closed the door behind him. She heard the bolt slide into place and whimpered in despair.

Everything she could have used to injure herself had been removed. Even her bed was only a pallet. She had tried to kill herself by placing her own hands on her throat, but it didn't work. How long was she destined to live in the prison of her mind?

She chewed slowly on a piece of bread, remembering the times she had helped her mother bake bread in the mornings. Heavy wooden bars had been installed on her window after the kidnapping years before, to protect her, but now they only reminded her that she was a prisoner in her own room. She stood at the window looking out at the Sea of Galilee in the distance. She imagined the seagulls crying and the fishing boats along the shore, half of which had been built by her father. Would she ever go down to the sea again?

Then her thoughts turned to Nathan. Beloved Nathan. What kind of wife was she to him now? He refused to divorce her, but every time he tried to come close to her, a voice that didn't even sound like hers cried out, "Leave me alone! Go away!"

She had seen the sadness on his face, yet his kindness to her had not wavered. Why did he stay? Why did he not leave her? At least, here in her room, she couldn't hear the snickers and whispers of the neighbors and the words "Mad Mary."

Nathan had gone somewhere. Eliab told her in a calmer moment when she cried for him. Where had he gone? Had he left her as she had begged him to do so many times?

"He is delivering a boat, mistress. It can take many days."

Then Eliab had slipped out again.

Hours passed, and as the unease came over her again, she approached the door.

"Eliab, are you there? Let me out, dear Eliab. Please let me out."

There was no answer, but she knew he was there. He was there—every night and most of the day. He was guarding her. Why did he need to guard her? She was mistress of the house. A sly smile formed on her lips. *No, Keturah is mistress now. She bakes the bread and feeds the household.* Why was it Keturah and not herself? *Because you are mad,* her mind told her and she heard the faint laughter. *Keturah will take care of Nathan.* Mary frowned and shook her fist at the door. *No, I'm his wife, not her.* Keturah had stolen him from her with her soft words. She had a child. Nathan loved children. Now he would have a son to raise. Her lips trembled and the tears began to flow again. No children. She was a barren wife because of her madness. No children for Nathan.

She sank down on her bed, whimpering and letting self-pity run rampant in her mind. What was she good for? Nothing. Nothing at all.

She lay down and pulled the simple rug over her. Mad Mary. Mad Mary. That's who she was. She lay staring at the ceiling until at last she fell into an exhausted slumber.

❋ 23 ❋

After asking in several places, Nathan was finally directed to a small merchant ship bound for Magdala and paid passage for Daniel and himself. They stood on the deck, watching as bundles of goat and camel hair were carried on board, along with spices and a load of silks. A large cage was lowered onto the deck and the golden eyes of a young lion looked into Nathan's. The confines of the cage angered the beast, and it growled and clawed at the sides, chewing on the heavy wood. If it was going to Magdala, Nathan knew it was destined for the Hippodrome, and he shuddered. He had heard Eliab's bone-chilling stories of the fights between man and animals. The man seldom won.

He turned his thoughts toward home and Mary. He had to find a way to bring her to Jesus. It was the only hope he'd felt in a long time. He knew that if she had one of her spells, the sailors would not let her on board a ship. Their superstitions against having a woman on board was enough of an obstacle, let alone a woman obviously mad. He leaned his forearms on the railing of the ship and considered his options. Not only did he have to learn where exactly Jesus was preaching, but he would have to transport Mary to that area. If a boat was out of the question, he would have to travel by donkey or walk. He sighed heavily. It was too far and too long a trip. His shoulders slumped. The prospect seemed impossible. Then there was the problem of Keturah. He had to find a husband for her. She couldn't remain in his home, her reputation was already at risk.

Daniel joined him at the rail. "The captain says the weather will hold for our voyage. That is good news, is it not?"

Nathan turned to smile down at the boy. "That is good news, indeed. We shall have some stories to tell when we arrive home, won't we?"

The boy was somber. "Yes, if they will believe us. Do you think the Teacher can heal your wife?"

Nathan raised his eyebrows. "So you were thinking of Mary? I have thought of that too, but getting her to the Teacher may be an impossible task."

"Then we can pray for the Teacher to come to her, can't we?"

Nathan looked into Daniel's eyes that were full of trust and confidence. It was the one thing he had not thought of.

When the ship docked in Magdala, Nathan hurried Daniel off and sent him on to the boat-yard with the money from Zebedee carefully concealed in his rolled-up cloak. Nathan knew he could count on Daniel to deliver it safely. His own footsteps turned toward home, for he was anxious to see what state Mary was in and what his possibilities were. He wanted to share with Keturah what he had seen and heard in Bethsaida.

When he reached the courtyard, he was surprised to see Keturah in tears, her belongings placed by the gate.

"Oh, Nathan. The rabbi was here. He says I cannot stay or I will be branded a fallen woman. He says it is not safe for my son either. I don't know what to do. I don't have any place to go."

Nathan closed the gate, and looking around quickly for any prying eyes, he gently took Keturah in his arms. "Do not weep. I will find a place for you and Mishma." Then, realizing he was on dangerous ground, he suddenly released Keturah and stepped back.

"Forgive me. I should not have done that, Keturah. You have been good to Mary, and I don't want to compromise your reputation any more than it has been. How is Mary?"

She gave a slight shrug. "The same. She remains in the room and I can only go to her with Eliab present. She has the strength of five women. We have to get out the door quickly and bolt it so she cannot escape. She got past me one day and Eliab chased her nearly into the village. This morning she was under the table in her room, growling at me."

His shoulders slumped. "I had hoped I might find her on a good day." He brightened. "I have good news, Keturah, and harder news."

Her eyes were wide as she studied his face. "You have made a decision then?"

"There is a rabbi, traveling the country around Galilee who is healing people, Keturah. I saw him lay hands on the sick and they recovered. Every one of them. The most amazing miracle was when Daniel gave him our lunch of two fish and five loaves of bread, and it multiplied in the baskets until over five thousand people, including women and children, were fed."

She frowned and stepped back, eyeing him skeptically. "How could he feed all those people with just that small amount of food? That is hard to believe."

"I thought the same thing. If I had not been there and seen with my own eyes, I would never have believed someone telling it to me. Keturah, he cast demons out of people and they were healed. I saw it myself and so did Daniel."

"You are thinking of Mary." It was not a question, and the sadness in her voice betrayed her emotions. "Nathan, how can this one man do what the local rabbi and even the high priest in Jerusalem could not do?"

"I saw it happen."

Keturah glanced toward the house. "Eliab is outside her door. He sleeps there every night." She shook her head. "A thankless vigil, but he loves her as a father loves a wayward child."

Nathan knew why. It was Eliab's promise to Mary's father.

Keturah spoke again. "I know that you feel you have hope, Nathan, but how will you get her to this man? If you let her out of her room, she is like a wild woman and will run off."

He sighed heavily. "That is my biggest problem. I will have to send a messenger to find out exactly where the Teacher is, then get Mary to him."

"You ask the impossible."

"Perhaps, but I have to try, if not for Mary's sake, then for mine."

Nathan had been so engrossed in his conversation with Keturah that for a moment he did not see Mishma sitting quietly in the corner of the courtyard. He was watching them with eyes that were wary and too wise for a young boy.

He called the boy over and put an arm around his shoulder. "Has it been a hard day for you, Mishma?"

He hesitated.

"It's all right, Mishma. You can tell me."

"I am afraid. They taunt me at school."

"Because of Mary?"

He hung his head. "Yes. They say we live with a . . ." He stopped abruptly and peered fearfully up at Nathan. "I'm sorry . . ."

"It's all right, Mishma, I understand. Mary won't hurt you, she is just sick, that's all. I'm going to find a way to make her well."

"She scratched me."

"When?"

"The last time she was free."

Nathan looked down at Mishma's face and knew he was telling the truth. So it had come to that. The boy had been sympathetic to Mary, but now he was afraid of her, and suffering the consequences at school. Nathan had forgotten how cruel children could be to one another.

Just then, there was a voice at the gate. It was Huldah. He welcomed her and brought her into the courtyard.

"Huldah, I have a situation . . ."

"I know about what Keturah must do, Nathan. It is something you should have thought of sooner. Samuel and I have talked it over. She may come to us. We have a spare room she can share with Mishma." She turned to Keturah. "Come. Bring your things. You and your son are welcome in our home."

Keturah embraced the older woman and let her tears flow freely. "Oh, Huldah, thank you for your kindness."

Before the women left with Mishma, Nathan

took Huldah aside and told her about what he'd seen and what Jesus could do.

She listened, her eyes wide. "I believe you would not lie, Nathan, but this is very hard to believe. I pray you will find a way. None of us can handle her and she is almost too much now for Eliab. He is not as young as he used to be and the forces that rule her are strong."

"I know, Huldah, but I'm going to do everything I can."

Huldah shook her head sadly, and with a last glance back at the house where they could hear Mary crying out, the two women left with Mishma.

When they'd gone, Nathan walked reluctantly toward the house. He must talk to Eliab and see what they could do. It would depend on how Mary was.

He paused, thinking. If he sent out a scout to see where Jesus was teaching, he would have some direction. He pounded his fist into his palm. Yes, that is what he must do. Daniel's words came back to him. *"Maybe we should pray Jesus comes to Magdala."* That indeed would solve his problem.

As he climbed the steps to Mary's door, he saw Eliab sitting next to it, carving. The man lifted his dark eyes to Nathan's and shook his head. Inside the room, things were being flung around and sounds of weeping alternated with harsh shrieks.

Nathan listened a moment and then, gathering his courage, sat down on the floor beside Eliab and began to tell him about Bethsaida and the Teacher.

❖ 24 ❖

Nathan ran his hands along the rail of the new boat, feeling its smoothness. This one was going to a young fisherman in Tiberias; it had been paid for by the father to set his son up in business. The father raised sheep and goats, but the boy loved the sea. As Nathan studied the structure of the boat, he remembered his own joy as he sailed out on the blue waters, even just to deliver a boat. He had once been an apprentice like Daniel, but now, thanks to Jared, he owned half of the business.

Deep in thought, Nathan was unaware of Amos until the young man was standing next to him, speaking his name. Amos had become a friend when they worked together, and even though Nathan was now half-owner and his employer, it had not affected their friendship. Amos was one who had sought news of the Teacher.

"You are miles away in your thoughts, my friend."

Nathan turned and smiled. "That is true. What news do you have for me?" He was aware stories were running rampant through Magdala of the amazing rabbi who could merely touch sick people and they were healed. Never before had there been a leader so powerful that demon spirits fled before him. Neighbor whispered to neighbor of the lame healed and the blind eyes opened. Nathan had watched and listened, considering what would be his best opportunity to bring Mary to Jesus. Word came that Jesus was in Gennesaret, and Nathan wanted to see where the Teacher would go from there.

Amos shrugged. "He travels through much territory. I know this. He angers the scribes and Pharisees. They do not understand him. He breaks tradition. They follow him and condemn his actions, in spite of the miracles he does. The Teacher called them hypocrites, for they honor God with their lips but their hearts are far from him."

"He has courage, I'll say that."

"Courage or he's foolhardy. He is up against powerful leaders."

"More powerful than the Most High?"

Amos was thoughtful. "True. If he is indeed the Messiah, they would be protesting against God."

Nathan pulled on his beard and looked out again toward the sea. "Do you know where the Teacher is headed from Gennesaret?"

"My sources say he is moving in the direction of Tyre and Sidon."

Nathan's heart sank. That was far from Magdala.

Seeing the sadness on Nathan's face, Amos clapped him on the shoulder. "His home is in Capernaum. Surely he will return there soon. Take heart, my friend. There will be the right time."

"That is the hope I cling to, every day."

The two men were silent, each with their own thoughts, and finally Nathan shook himself mentally. "We have work to do. The new load of pitch will be delivered this afternoon. Tell the men to prepare the buckets."

Nathan watched Amos stride away. It was good to have a friend to count on who knew what he was seeking to do. He turned toward the stone building that served as the business center for the yard. Zerah had entered the boatyard a short time ago and gone in to talk to Beriah. Whatever Zerah was up to was usually not good.

As Nathan approached the building, he heard laughter. Was he hearing things? Zerah, laughing with his father? Puzzled, he entered and found his father smiling up at Zerah from the low table where the scrolls were laid out for accounting.

"Nathan, my son. Come and join us."

He approached, frowning, his mind full of questions.

Zerah came forward. "We were discussing an

encounter I had with a Roman soldier while you were gone."

"You are lucky you escaped. They do not handle encounters with our people well."

"Ah, this one was drunk." Zered smiled broadly. "Fortunately, he was more drunk than I, but it caused me to think about some things. I have been too harsh with you. For a successful business, we must work together."

Nathan stared at his partner, eyebrows raised.

"I am a changed man, Nathan. HaShem spared my life and there was no reason for him to do so. I was unworthy of his mercy."

Did he see tears in the eyes of this man who had been so harsh and unfeeling? Zerah's countenance was indeed changed, softened. In his heart Nathan realized the man was telling the truth.

"I am glad to hear that. I have need of your advice and there is work enough to benefit us both."

Wine was poured all around and they drank to Zerah and the future.

Daniel burst into the yard running toward them and, spying Nathan, made straight for him. "Sir, I have news."

The men crowded around him.

Nathan gave the boy a chance to catch his breath. "What is it, Daniel?"

"The Teacher. Remember when we saw him feed the crowd in Bethsaida?"

"Yes, over five thousand by my estimate."

"He did it again. Some say there were more than four thousand this time, on the mountain near Capernaum."

"Capernaum? He is heading this way?"

Daniel beamed. "HaShem has heard our prayers, sir. The Teacher crossed the Sea near here and has landed in our region."

Here. Jesus was coming here. Nathan's heart raced with excitement. "Then he will come to the city." He pressed a coin into Daniel's hand. "Go and let me know exactly where the Teacher is. Go quickly."

Daniel grinned, nodded, and clutching the coin, raced off again.

Zerah had watched this all with his eyes wide and, when the boy was gone, turned to Nathan. "What is this the boy is talking about? The Teacher coming here? Do you mean the Jesus I've been hearing about?"

"Yes. He lays hands on the sick and they recover. He has even cast demons out of those afflicted—"

"And you are thinking of Mary?"

Nathan spread his hands. "What other hope do I have for her?"

"Then I will help you. She is my niece and I wish to see her well also. If Jesus comes to Magdala, I will do whatever I can to bring him to her."

"Thank you, Zerah, your kind words mean a great deal to me at this time."

Nathan returned home in high spirits and told Eliab of Daniel's news. A slow smile spread on the dark, wrinkled face of their servant. "It is time then. I have felt it. I must be on my way to my home, but not yet. I will wait."

"I understand, Eliab." He stood for a moment, noticing there was silence from Mary's room. "How is Mary?"

"She sleeps now, but do not let the silence fool you. If you enter the room, she will awake and try to attack you. The evil one gives her great strength."

"But not for long, Eliab, not for long."

Nathan went to see what Huldah had left for their evening meal. He hated eating alone, and since no one else was around, he convinced Eliab to join him. The servant was reluctant, even after so many years, but gingerly eased himself down at the table. When he saw how it lifted Nathan's spirits, he relaxed and dipped his bread in the stew.

As Nathan ate, his mind turned and the two men discussed all the possibilities.

"There will be a way, young master. Your God will show you the way."

Nathan looked at him and said earnestly, "If you saw the miracles he did, and listened to him speak, he would be your God too, Eliab."

Eliab's face was passive, but the dark eyes looking back at him held a fire. "The young mistress will be healed and then I will return home."

Nathan laughed softly. "I could use your confidence, my friend." Whatever happened, they would get Mary to Jesus if they had to carry her kicking and screaming. He sighed. That might just be what they had to do.

As if reading his thoughts, Eliab nodded. The two men finished their meal. There was nothing to do now but wait.

❧ 25 ❧

Nathan was aware of a low buzz of excitement stirring through the neighborhoods of Magdala. Word came to him that people were flocking out to the hills where this rabbi named Jesus was teaching. Pushing, shoving, hurrying to be the ones closest to see, they came for the excitement —to see the miracles Jesus performed. Like a sea of hungry children, they murmured among themselves and stretched their necks to watch what the Teacher would do next. Those who were closest passed the word to those behind as the sick were brought and healed. Samuel and

Huldah went to hear Jesus and came back changed. They believed he was from God.

That evening, Zerah came to the house and he, Nathan, and Eliab discussed how they might get Mary through the crowds.

Mary's uncle raised his eyebrows when Eliab slowly came to stand near them. Then with a shrug, he went on dipping his bread in the warm goat meat stew. He chewed thoughtfully as he listened to Nathan's ideas. Eliab hung back, puzzled, his dark eyes upon the two men. Nathan motioned for him to join them.

"Eliab has been part of the family for many years. He is not a slave." Nathan knew the old Zerah would have angrily objected. The new Zerah merely nodded and went on eating. Nathan raised his eyebrows at Eliab. In one fluid movement, Eliab sat down beside Nathan and reached for a chunk of warm bread, and for the first time in a long time, Nathan saw Eliab smile.

Nathan, almost too excited to eat, had an idea. He set his cup of wine down on the low table. "What if we put her in a cart?"

Zerah shook his head. "A thought, my friend, but not practical. She could easily climb out and be lost in the crowd. What if we tied a rope around her waist?"

Nathan snorted. "And lead her like a goat?"

Eliab listened to the various suggestions and finally spoke up. "If two were at her side, holding her arms, and I was behind her, could we not guide her to the Teacher?"

"Like a human wall around her?" Nathan nodded. "That might work, Eliab."

Eliab gathered some grapes, cheese, and bread dipped in the stew from the table and put them on a platter. "She is hungry," he said simply, and turned toward the house.

Nathan watched him go. "He has a way with her. She lets him in and has not attacked him." He hung his head. "Such is not the same with me. Why?"

Zerah shook his head slowly. "It is the ones closest to us that the enemy would devastate. She loves you, but the enemy will not let you near her, and that is torture to her soul and to yours."

He was right, and Nathan knew it, yet now there was hope. His heart burned with the expectancy that something was going to happen that could change their lives. He didn't know when or how, but he clung to that hope with all his being.

"Stay the night, Zerah. The Teacher is close. Tomorrow is our best opportunity while the Teacher is as close as he will get to us."

Zerah nodded. "I will stay. Let us both think on what we can do. HaShem will show us the way."

Nathan settled his guest and then blew out the lamp in the courtyard. The small lamp in the main room of the house burned, giving off a dim glow.

He checked the oil, noting there was enough. As he wearily lowered himself down on his bed, his mind turned. Slowly he moved onto his knees and, in the darkness, poured out his heart to the only One who could help him.

Mary listened to the footsteps on the stone stairs. It was Eliab. She had been sitting on the floor but crawled to her bed and now slowly got up. She had eaten little and her stomach let her know its craving for food. She longed for light, but lived in the darkness. They could not trust the forces that drove her. A lamp and fire would provide ways for her to harm herself.

She watched the door, cowering back. The bolt slid and it moved open. She waited. Eliab stepped carefully into the room, a platter of food in his hand.

"I have brought you your dinner, mistress. Come, partake and be strengthened."

She eyed the door.

If you move quickly, you can escape!

You do not need food!

Just run!

He cannot catch you!

The voices cried at once in her head, urging her, petulant, demanding. Her eyes found Eliab's and he watched her calmly.

"It is not time to go, mistress. But soon. You will be free soon."

Free? She tilted her head and stared at him. "What is free, Eliab?" Large tears began to roll down her cheeks. "This room is my prison. My body is my prison. How can you say I will be free?"

"There is One nearby who can help you. You must conquer those who try to guide you, and let us bring you to him. Tomorrow."

"One who can help me? No one can help me. No one." She wrapped her arms around her body, swaying back and forth.

"His name is Jesus. He is a healer. He heals the sick and has made lame legs walk. He has driven out the forces of the evil one from those afflicted—"

Her eyes widened. "He has healed those like me?"

"Yes, mistress, but you must help us. You must not run away. You must let us bring you to him."

Raucous laughter erupted in her head.

Do not listen to him.

He tells you lies.

No one can EVER free you from us.

She tried to ignore the voices. She was hungry and the food looked inviting. She grabbed the chunk of bread and began to devour it greedily, letting the sauce run unchecked down her chin. She kept her eyes on Eliab as if he would steal a morsel from her.

The sadness in his eyes moved her as nothing

else would. She paused with the bread in her hand. "I would see this Teacher."

He smiled broadly. "Tomorrow, mistress. Be ready."

She eyed the doorway again and he followed her gaze. Shaking his head, he slipped through the door, moving even more quickly than she did. His swiftness in gauging her actions always surprised her.

After a moment she heard the bolt slide into place and she slumped against the door, desolation once again covering her with its shadow. She crawled slowly over to the platter on the floor and reached for the small bunch of grapes. Holding them in her hand, uneaten, she stared at the darkness outside her window a long time.

As dawn slowly colored the sky with its palette of pink and gold, Nathan rose and, stretching his arms, moved to the doorway to stare at the panorama before him. He was surprised he had slept so well. Usually the night hours found him prowling about the house or courtyard wrestling with his thoughts. A sense of expectancy filled him. What would the day hold? Success or failure? He only knew that if he didn't try, life would go on as it had, and the thought of that made his heart heavy. If Mary wasn't healed, would he find a place for her and take a second wife? He'd been without the comfort of a wife too long. He bowed his head and beseeched HaShem for a miracle.

Zerah joined him a few moments later, just as Huldah, who had been cooking for Nathan's household, came with fresh bread and some fruit for their breakfast. Since being taken in by Huldah and Samuel, Keturah had stayed away. Considering the risk, Nathan decided not to tell Huldah what they had in mind for Mary that day.

Eliab came back to join the men and Huldah nodded to him. Nathan knew she had a soft spot for the huge man who had been so faithful to the family.

When Huldah returned to her home, Nathan and Eliab went up the stone steps to Mary's room. Eliab lifted the bolt on the door and quietly opened it. Nathan caught his breath. The sight of his wife always jolted him. She was sprawled on her bed, asleep, her hair unkempt, her garments dirty and torn. No one had been able to help her bathe or get near enough to comb her hair in weeks. Today, though, instead of the feelings he'd considered earlier, his heart melted again with pity for her. The miracle he had prayed for wasn't a change in Mary; it was a change in his heart, a renewal of tenderness for the woman he had loved so long.

Mary had paced her room by the hour, fighting the mind-bending headache that had come upon her during the early hours of the morning. Voices screamed in her head until she fell in a sobbing heap on the floor. Finally, crawling to her pallet, she fell into an exhausted sleep.

At the sound of the bar being lifted, her eyes flew open. She heard whispered voices. Was it Nathan? Or Eliab? When the door opened, she shrank back. She pretended to sleep. Maybe she could catch them unawares and escape. Then sensing something in the silence as they stood there, her eyes opened. It was Eliab and Nathan. They had something in their minds. She could see it in their faces. What were they going to do? Was Nathan taking her somewhere? Yes, the day had come. *He is getting rid of you, a useless wife. He is putting you away.*

Then the voices were silent. She watched Nathan's face, frightened. "Why have you come?"

To her surprise, the look she received from her husband was one of tenderness. "We want you to meet someone, Mary. We want you to come with us."

They were taking her to meet someone. A new caretaker? Certainly he was getting rid of her at last?

Resigned, she looked down at the floor and barely nodded her head.

As the two men came on either side of her, Mary was aware of the odor that came from her clothes and person, but it didn't matter. Nothing mattered anymore. She looked from one to the other fearfully. Where were they taking her?

The two men had a firm grip on her arms as they led her out of the room and down the steps to the courtyard. Zerah watched them and then came forward.

"My dear niece, it is good to see you again." He smiled at her, but Mary could only stare at him listlessly.

Zerah took the arm Eliab held and Eliab stepped back to walk closely behind them. As they made their way through the streets, Nathan glanced warily at her from time to time, and his anxiety only reinforced the idea in her mind that he was taking her somewhere to get rid of her.

Self-pity whispered in her mind. *You are not worthy to be his wife anymore. He will find someone young and beautiful to take your place.*

As they passed people in their neighborhood, many stopped and stared at her and whispered to each other.

"It's Mad Mary. What are they doing with her?"

"Watch the children, that crazy woman is about."

"Is that Jared's daughter, Mary, the same woman we have known? She looks like a witch."

The hurtful words echoed in her mind, cutting into her heart. No one cared. She was the local madwoman. Wherever Nathan was taking her, it didn't matter anymore. With head bowed, she kept walking with her husband and Zerah holding tight to her arms.

At the edge of town, the voices began screaming in her head and she could stand it no longer. A large crowd of people were gathered ahead of them. She could flee from Nathan and his plans for her and lose herself in the crowd.

Get away!

Get away!

RUN!

With almost superhuman strength, Mary broke away from Nathan and her uncle and ran for her life, blindly plunging into the crowd of people who parted hastily to get away from her. She knew the three men were right behind her, but she would not let them catch her. She laughed, wild with freedom, and darted through the crowd, until suddenly she was stopped by a man standing in her path.

RUN!

Get away!

But this time the voices were not strong and forceful, they were fearful. She tried to move, but her feet were like stone. She stared up into a rugged yet tender face, beautiful in its compassion. Sunlight seemed to be in the eyes that held her captive, and she was wrapped in a love so profound she swayed toward him.

"Mary."

She struggled to speak. "Y-you know my n-name?"

"I have always known you."

Then he spoke to the forces that whimpered and struggled within her. "How many are you?"

Through her mouth a terrified voice cried, "We are seven. Do not torture us, we know who you are, you are the Son of—"

"Be silent." Then in a voice that echoed with authority, "Leave her!"

Tossing her onto the ground like a sack of flour, with a low wail, the forces that had troubled her for so long left her body. She lay still a moment, then, gentle hands lifted her to her feet and she heard a strong, compassionate voice. "You are free, daughter of Abraham. They shall trouble you no more."

Relief and joy poured through her being. Her head cleared, and for the first time in years, she felt herself again. The voices that had assailed her every moment of the day were silent. A mantle of peace settled over her as she looked slowly around and up at the blue sky. She felt the sun in her face and let the warmth flow over her body. Then she looked at this man who had freed her.

"Who are you, Lord?"

"I am Jesus."

She knelt at his feet. "My Lord and my Master. This time I know I am healed. Whoever you are, I will follow you, wherever you go, forever."

He gently lifted her again and spoke softly,

"You shall indeed follow me, Mary of Magdala, but it is not time. Return with your husband to your home, and tell what great things God has done for you."

Tears streamed down Nathan's face as he came and stood at her side. "How can I express my gratitude, Lord, for breaking the bondage that has held Mary for so long? We will follow you together."

Jesus did not answer; he only smiled, but there was a touch of sadness in his smile.

"Return home, Nathan, son of Beriah, and enjoy your wife. Rejoice in the days you have together."

Zerah had watched Mary's deliverance with amazement and now came and fell at the feet of Jesus.

"I am a sinful man, Lord, but I believe in you. I have done a terrible thing that has caused suffering to ones I love. Forgive me, Lord."

Jesus put a hand on his shoulder. "Your prayers have been heard by my Father. You are forgiven. Now you know what you must do."

Zerah gathered himself and slowly turned to Mary, his face twisted with anguish. "It was I, Mary, who hired the kidnappers. I thought only of money that I needed. They were told not to hurt you. I didn't know that they would . . . hurt your father. You have suffered because of me." His voice broke. "Can you find it in your heart to forgive me?"

A sudden rush of emotions flooded Mary. Her uncle? Responsible for her father's stabbing—for her ordeal with those two terrible men? Anger began to rise within her. How could she forgive such an act that had ruined years of her life? She covered her face with her hands. She could not forgive. Then, though no one actually touched her, she felt her hands gently being pulled from her face. She looked up at Jesus and suddenly realized that she herself had been set free and given new life. How could she turn away and deny forgiveness to one who had suffered as much in his own way with guilt and remorse?

One word came to her mind. *Forgive.*

The anger slowly dissipated and she took a deep breath and turned to her uncle. Putting a hand on his cheek, she looked at him with new eyes of compassion. "As I have found healing today, Uncle, so may you also. I do forgive you with all my heart."

Zerah wept in relief and embraced her.

Eliab stepped forward then and knelt before Jesus. "I have waited, Teacher, for what I knew not. Now I know why I stayed. I too believe you are from God. The one true God."

"Well done, faithful Eliab. Return to your home and your people. You have much to share with them."

Eliab rose. He could not speak, for his emotions overwhelmed him. He turned to Mary and Nathan.

Mary looked at the ebony face, now wrinkled with age, of the man who had watched over her family for so long. "Go in peace, dear Eliab. May the Most High, blessed be his name, watch over and protect you."

Nathan clasped him on the shoulder, but no words came, nor were they needed. Eliab nodded his head slightly and turned. He walked through the crowd and was soon swallowed up in the masses.

Mary felt laughter bubbling up inside her. Not the raucous laughter of a deranged woman, but one very much full of life. The past years seemed but a moment, blurred and distant. She laughed, a wonderful, freeing laugh, a laugh of joy and wonderment. Then she turned to her husband. She had years to make up for.

She whispered in his ear. "I believe I would like a bath."

26

Mary kneaded the bread, enjoying a familiar task denied her for so long. She was content to be in charge of her household again, with no one looking over her shoulder.

As a bird sang its joyful solo in the sycamore tree, she felt her heart would burst with happiness. This last year had been like the early days of her marriage as she and Nathan found one another again. She put her hand on her flat stomach, barren still, but she felt hope once again. Surely now the Most High would give them a child.

She smiled to herself, thinking of Nathan almost singing as he left for work in the morning. She had lain in his arms last night as they talked of his plans for the future.

"We have been building fishing boats and an occasional larger boat. I think we have the means to build a merchant ship, Mary. We have good workers, men who are skilled at their craft. I've talked with Zerah and he agrees." Nathan gave a small laugh. "Zerah is becoming a most cooperative partner these days. You have seen the change in him. There are even rumors that he has spoken of marrying again."

"That is good news, Nathan. I hope he will find someone to share his life."

When Keturah had left Mary and Nathan's home, Mary learned that Samuel and Huldah had wasted no time searching for a husband for her. A matchmaker was consulted, and with Samuel acting as her father, a match was found.

"A brick maker," Huldah told Mary. "He can provide for her—a widower with no children. What could be better? He is older—a few years." She shrugged. "So Keturah is not young herself. He will make a fine father to Mishma."

Keturah and Benjamin had found they liked each other and a wedding took place.

Mary's reverie was interrupted by a knock at the gate. Huldah entered the patio, her face rosy with excitement. Mary could tell she was bursting with news and waited for the older woman to collect herself.

"It is a boy! They have named him Seth after Benjamin's father."

Keturah was with child soon after her marriage, and Mary felt the old pain of her barrenness, yet was glad for her. With her own marriage restored, Mary held no grievance against Keturah. She was secure in Nathan's love, and she also realized how much Keturah had helped her, putting her own desire to be married again aside to tend to Mary's needs.

Mary smiled at her neighbor. "That is wonderful news. I'm glad Keturah has a home of her own again. It has been a long time."

The two women were silent a long moment and Mary knew Huldah was thinking, as she was, of the years of anguish Mary had gone through, and Keturah's years of care. Now that she was healed, Mary realized what a temptation Keturah had been for Nathan. She realized all too clearly the terrible state she had been in for so long. How had he loved her through all she had put him through?

Huldah lifted an eyebrow and gave Mary a knowing smile. "It is good with you and Nathan?"

Mary felt her face warming. "It is good."

"And . . . ?"

She shook her head. "No. The time of women came again."

Huldah sighed. "You have waited so long. It will be soon now. I'm sure of it."

Mary laughed then. "I'm glad you are so sure."

"HaShem has heard your prayer, Mary. He knows the longing of your heart and he will answer."

With a wave of the hand, Huldah was off again, no doubt to apprise the rest of the neighborhood of the new baby.

Mary looked up at the blue sky and wondered where Jesus was at this time. She and Nathan had gone back to the hillside the day after her healing. Friends and neighbors had joined them, so excited and awed at Mary's miracle that they wanted to see this amazing Rabbi. Many became believers, not only because of Mary's healing, but because they heard him for themselves.

The Pharisees and Sadducees, instead of silently observing Jesus, began to taunt him and question his right to do the things he did.

"Show us a sign from heaven, and we will believe in you," one of them called out.

Jesus observed them steadily for a moment, then sighed deeply. "Why does this generation seek a sign? Listen to me. When it is evening you say, 'It will be fair weather, for the sky is red'; and in the morning, 'it will be foul weather today, for the sky is red and threatening.' Hypocrites! You know how to discern the face of the sky, but you cannot discern the signs of the times. A wicked and adulterous generation seeks after a sign, and no sign shall be given to it except the sign of the prophet Jonah. For as Jonah was three days and three nights in the belly of the great fish, so will the Son of Man be three days and three nights in the heart of the earth."

The leaders and the people began to murmur among themselves.

"What does he mean?"

"How does he compare himself with the prophet Jonah?"

Jesus taught for almost three hours and the people listened with rapt attention. No one spoke as this man. He healed those who were brought to him, and the crowd murmured and exclaimed with each miracle.

Finally, Jesus rose from the knoll he'd been sitting on and his disciples formed a barrier around him. He passed through the crowd and they realized they would see no more miracles today. They began to disperse. Mary knew he was departing from the area. As he passed by the place where Mary, Nathan, and their neighbors were standing, his eyes found Mary's and he smiled at her.

Her heartbeat quickened and she smiled back. She was still trying to comprehend that she had been set free from the dark forces that had imprisoned her mind for so long. She watched the small group of disciples and noted that some women accompanied him. She wondered what it was like for them to go with him from place to place, hearing him teach and seeing the miracles.

Her reverie was broken by Nathan's gentle touch on her arm. "Let us go, beloved, the hour grows late."

When they returned home, Nathan was still pondering the words of the Teacher. "What did he mean by the sign of Jonah?"

She set the pot of warm lentil stew on the low table. "Was not that prophet three days in the belly of a great fish?"

Nathan nodded, his brow furrowed in thought.

"Three days. He said the Son of Man would be in the earth three days. There is meaning in the three days, but for the life of me, I cannot comprehend it."

She put a hand on his shoulder and he covered it with his own. "He speaks in parables, stories the people can understand, but sometimes I wonder at his words."

"True, his words make the Scriptures come alive. He teaches with wisdom that is beyond that of the rabbi who taught us in school. He was always quoting another distinguished rabbi, but Jesus speaks with authority." He looked up at her and his eyes searched her face. "You are the treasure of my life. You are so beautiful."

She laughed softly, shy at the depth of feeling behind his words and yet still half incredulous that after all these years he could still look at her and make her feel like a young girl again.

The next morning Nathan ate some fruit and drank a cup of milk and prepared to leave. The look in his eyes caused the warmth to rise in her face.

"I would linger," he said softly, "but a man must work. The merchant we are building this new boat for is coming to inspect our progress."

"This boat is different somehow?"

"Larger than our usual fishing boats. He carries pottery and livestock to different ports. He wants his own boat rather than paying to use a larger merchant vessel."

"Will he take delivery himself?"

"No, we will sail the boat to Bethsaida when it is finished. He'll meet us there." He drew a slow line along her chin with his finger and, with a warm smile, left the courtyard.

Two weeks later, as she packed food in his goatskin bag for his trip to Bethsaida, she looked up at the sky and thought of the words of Jesus when he talked about discerning the weather. The sky had a sullen look to it and she felt a shiver of apprehension. It was the time of sudden storms that swept down on the Sea of Galilee from the mountains.

"Could you not wait, Nathan? I do not like the look of the sky."

He glanced up. "The boat is big and sturdy and I have two good men who know the sea to go with me. We will be all right."

She paused, her voice small. "I do not wish to be parted from you, even for a week. Even a year seems such a short time together since Jesus freed me."

Nathan put his arms around her. "I will be careful, beloved. The thought of you waiting for me will hasten my return."

"Is young Daniel going with you?"

"No. His brother's Bar Mitzvah is not something his parents will allow him to miss." Nathan laughed. "He has let us know in no uncertain terms of his great disappointment. Amos and Levi have agreed to go with me."

He kissed her then, a promise of their time together when he returned.

❋ 27 ❋

Five days after Nathan left, Mary was awakened early by the sound of rain. Her first thought was that she was glad she'd brought her small cooking stove and kitchen items into the main room of the house the night before. Suddenly another thought pierced her consciousness. Nathan. Was he out on the sea? He would be returning home by now. She listened to the wind and knew there was a storm.

She fell to her knees and cried out to HaShem, "Oh Lord, protect him and bring him safely home to me." She stayed on her knees for a long time, praying for her beloved husband and the men in the boat with him. Finally, peace flowed over her being, yet as her head was still bowed, she saw the face of Jesus as he spoke to the crowd of people. There was majesty in his presence. How he put the Pharisees and Sadducees in their place.

They watched him with disdain and asked him ques-tions, yet seemed astounded at his answers. He spoke as one taught by the scribes, not a simple carpenter from Nazareth. Surely he was the one her people had waited for throughout the centuries.

She reasoned to herself that there must be some way she and Nathan could send money to Jesus and his followers. Surely they needed funds for food and lodging. She would speak to Nathan when he returned. It was the least they could do to show their gratitude for what he had done for her.

There was a knock at the door. Huldah and Merab came to stay with her.

"There will be news soon, Mary." Huldah sounded like she spoke with more confidence than she felt.

The next morning Mary stood at the window of her room upstairs and shivered as she felt the cold, moist air come through the latticework. As a child she had moved her bed as far from the window as she could and then snuggled down under a heavy lamb's wool rug. Safe and content with her parents nearby, she'd not thought of the storms and the fishing boats that were lost. It was beyond her immediate world and meant little to her.

Now, as she'd gazed out at the dark clouds and the restless sea, and watched the wind churning the waves, she knew Nathan was out in that storm.

She struggled against the fear that threatened to rise up within her.

Word spread quickly and Mary's friends rallied around her, keeping her company while she waited. Huldah brought mending to do and Merab twirled her spindle, pulling the lamb's wool into a fine thread. Mary worked on her loom, weaving a new tunic for Nathan. This one would be one piece and she worked steadily, sending the shuttle back and forth. Keeping her hands busy helped keep her mind from dwelling on the storm.

Samuel came at evening and ate with them. He had been checking the docks for word of any of the fishing boats, but no one had heard anything as yet.

When Mishma returned from Hebrew school, and the rain stopped for a little while, Keturah hurried over with the new baby and remained awhile. Mary held little Seth and her heart constricted as he curled his small hand around her finger. As he looked up at her, with eyes that seemed so wise in such a tiny face, he captured her heart. She was reminded of the first time she held Mishma, who was growing tall. He would soon be ready for his Bar Mitzvah, the ceremony that made him a man in the eyes of the Law.

As the evening mealtime approached, Keturah took the baby from Mary. Calling to Mishma, who had been looking at one of the scrolls, she returned home. Merab had a sick neighbor to attend to, and she and Keturah assured Mary they would return in the morning. Samuel went to feed their animals, but Huldah stayed so Mary would not be alone.

The women kept their vigil until the seventh day, when Samuel pounded on the locked gate. "Mary, open the gate. There is news."

She threw a warm mantle over her head and pulled it around her as she hurried across the courtyard to let him in.

"A merchant ship has brought Nathan and Amos to our port."

She searched his face and her heart beat faster as she sensed there was more to his news. "What of Nathan?"

Samuel shook his head. "They are bringing him home. He is alive, but seriously wounded."

Mary gasped as four men came to the gate, carrying someone on a litter. It was Nathan. His face was pale and his eyes closed. The side of his head was matted with blood and a large lump had formed at his temple.

She had the men gently lift Nathan and place him upon his bed. He let out a small groan, but his eyes remained closed.

Someone had already sent for Merab and she came quickly with her goatskin bag of herbs and powders. She looked down at the unconscious man and shook her head. When Mary finished cleaning the dried blood from the wound, Merab made a poultice and applied it to the side of Nathan's head to stop the bleeding. Mary helped her wind a clean cloth around his head to hold the poultice in place.

One of the men went to bring Nathan's father from the boatyard.

Merab watched Nathan carefully, and as he began to stir, he suddenly rolled to one side. Anticipating his next act, she grabbed the basin of water Mary had used to clean his wound with. She held it for Nathan, who vomited into the basin and then lay back, his breathing heavy and labored.

"Will he be all right?" Mary searched Merab's face for any sign of hope.

"Only time will tell. We do not know if there is damage we cannot see. If he lives through the night, we may hope, but his breathing is not good, nor is the sickness."

Her heart was like a lump of lead in her chest. Mary found herself reliving the moments at the bedsides of her father and then her mother as they died. She must not lose Nathan.

"What more can I do?" she cried.

Merab touched her shoulder. "Pray. Pray that HaShem will spare him."

Mary turned to Amos. Though weary from his ordeal, he had come with the men who carried

Nathan, and stood watching, his face the picture of anguish.

"Amos, what happened?"

"The sea was calm when we bartered for the fishing boat to take us back to Magdala. Nathan thought we could take a chance and make it home. We had only been at sea for a short time when the storm clouds rolled out over the water and the waves began to whip up from the wind. I wanted to turn back, but Nathan felt we were only going a short distance and he was anxious to get home."

Mary's eyes filled with tears as he paused. She knew Nathan was trying to get back to her as he promised.

Amos went on. "The boat was not as sturdy as the one we delivered to the merchant, but we worked hard to take the sail down in the wind and bailed with a clay pot the fisherman had on board. It wasn't enough. One large wave, almost the height of the top of the mast, slammed into the boat. The mast snapped like a mere twig. Nathan tried to get out of the way, but there was nowhere to go. In an instant it struck him and he fell overboard into the sea. I dove in after him, knowing he was wounded, and just then another wave broke the boat up completely and swept the fisherman and Levi into the sea. I never saw them again. Nathan had somehow grasped a plank from the boat and we both clung to it, I kept hold of him as best I could. As suddenly as the storm came up, it passed on and the sea calmed. A merchant ship had made it through the storm. They spotted us and somehow managed to pluck us from the sea." He paused, shaking his head. "The rest you know."

She listened to his words, picturing the storm in her mind and the men's struggle to save the boat. She nodded slowly. "Thank you, Amos."

Just then Beriah came, his face a picture of silent agony as he saw his son. He put a hand on Nathan's shoulder and spoke quietly to him, but Nathan remained silent and unmoving.

The hours dragged by, and the family kept watch. Beriah's wife, Beulah, brought food, as did other women in the neighborhood. The women stayed with Mary and Beriah. Her uncle Zerah stood with the other men in the courtyard, talking quietly among themselves.

About the ninth hour, Nathan suddenly opened his eyes. His voice was hesitant. "Am I dreaming —is it you, Mary?"

Wild with joy, she put his hand to her cheek. "I am here, beloved. You are home."

He gave her a weak smile and hope made her heart flutter.

"Rest, my husband, you will be well soon."

He began to mutter, his words coming in short spurts. "The storm . . . so strong . . . knew I should have waited . . . wanted to return to you. Boat too small . . . something fell . . ."

Beriah's eyes were moist as he smiled down at his son. "Don't try to talk, my son, you must rest so your head can heal."

Nathan blinked his eyes several times as if trying to clear his vision and peered up at their anxious faces. "I feel strange." His voice was hoarse.

He grimaced and she knew he was in pain. "Head hurts . . ." His breathing became more ragged.

Suddenly his eyes widened. "Do you see them?"

Those in the room followed his gaze toward the ceiling. Mary shook her head. "I don't see anything, Nathan."

"They are there . . ."

She frowned. Was he having delusions? "Who?"

His voice was almost a whisper. "The angels."

"No!" A cry of agony left her as she clung to his hand.

"They—are—beckoning—to me."

"No!" She cried again.

"My son, save your strength. You are dreaming."

Nathan reached out with his free hand and clasped his father's.

"Watch over Mary for me, Father. Promise me."

"I promise, my son. I will look after her." Beriah promised, his voice cracking as tears slipped down his wrinkled cheeks.

Nathan looked up at her. "I love you, Mary. Have—always—loved you." His arm went limp, pulling the hand she held downward. Slowly she put his arm by his side, the shock keeping her immobile for a moment. Then a heart-wrenching cry of pain and loss rose up and spilled out of her, and the other women took up the lamentation as Beriah tore his clothes and stumbled out into the courtyard.

Mary could not just sit and weep. The Law required that a body be laid to rest the same day, a commandment from the Lord. In a daze of shock and grief, she helped the women bathe his body and prepare him for his burial.

The procession wound its way through the streets, gathering mourners who wept and cried out, flinging dust into the air as they commiserated with the family in their time of mourning.

Mary wanted to die and be buried with him. How could she go on now? They had weathered so many years of struggle and heartache, only to have just this one year to enjoy one another again. She cried out to HaShem, asking "Why" over and over, but the heavens were silent. She stumbled on, bewildered.

When the family returned to the house, they sat in mourning for the seven days of shivah. Beriah was inconsolable. Beulah sat with him, giving him strength by her quiet presence. Huldah,

Merab, and Keturah sat with Mary, lending their comfort as only women can do for one another.

Near the end of the first month of mourning, Mary sat in the courtyard, letting the warm sunshine pour over her. Huldah and Merab came when they could and Keturah brought little Seth. Caring for the baby seemed to help Mary in her grief and from time to time even brought a smile to her face.

The courtyard was quiet. Even the bird that sang in the sycamore tree had stilled his voice. She had slept little for days, unable to speak for the well of grief that settled over her heart. How could God take Nathan away from her so soon? She could not understand.

Little by little, thoughts of Jesus began to infiltrate her mind. She recalled the day she had found him on the hillside, in the middle of her headlong, terrified flight. She once again saw his face with his eyes of compassion and felt again the sense of love that he had poured into her. Was he not the Messiah? She believed that with all her heart, as did many of her neighbors. No one could do the things he did and be a mere prophet. She relived the moment when he had lifted her from the ground. She told him she would follow him anywhere, but he had gently refused.

It seemed so long ago, that day that had brought her back from the living dead. Such joy she felt. Now, the weight of her widowhood pressed upon her. What was she to do now? Her parents were gone, Eliab had returned to his own country, Keturah was married and busy with her own family. She was alone. She had no children to tend. What could she do now? Samuel suggested a kinsman redeemer, a relative of Nathan's who would be willing to marry her. Yet remembering Nathan and the love they had shared, she could not think of another man taking his place.

On and on questions raced through her mind. She was a woman, and the men in the boatyard would be uneasy if she came alone.

Then, as she sat staring at the ground, she thought of the small group that followed Jesus. Women were in this group. Were they wives of the disciples? Surely women were needed to prepare meals for the men. They looked like good and decent women.

As she mused, a thought began to form in her mind. Her eyes widened and she sat back. It was as if a voice in her head was speaking to her. It was not the same as the voices that had plagued her. She knew this gentle voice.

Daughter of Abraham, be strong and do not falter. Come. The heaviness that had weighed on her heart began to lift. Suddenly she knew what she must do.

❉ 28 ❉

Zerah listened quietly. "You are sure this is what you have been told to do?"

"It was clear, Uncle. I heard his voice, calling me. I must go."

He stroked his beard and gazed out at the courtyard. "I would dissuade you, Mary, but under the circumstances, you must obey God, not man. He is the Messiah, and if you can be of help to his ministry, how can I tell you not to go?"

"Oh, Uncle Zerah, I knew you would understand. There is nothing here at home for me now. I want to serve him."

Zerah put a finger under her chin. "You will serve him for both of us and others who are not free to go."

Beriah took a little more convincing. She was under his protection as her father-in-law, and he had promised Nathan to take care of her. He had to give his permission.

"This is madness, daughter. My son has been dead only a few weeks and you are ready to leave our city to follow this Jesus on the road?"

"He has called to me and he is the one who healed me after all those years of madness. There are other women who support his ministry. I would not be alone."

Beriah pulled at his beard. "How will you live?"

Zerah had been standing in the background, listening, and now stepped forward. "I shall send funds each month with Daniel or another trusted messenger. She can use them as she sees fit."

Beriah shook his head in consternation. "And what of your home? Will you let it fall to ruin?"

"I have thought of that also, Father Beriah. Keturah's husband has a very small home. They need room for their growing family. They could live there and act as caretakers until I return."

"If you return," Beriah muttered.

Zerah spoke again. "If he is truly the Messiah, as Mary and I and others believe him to be, and he is calling her, would you set yourself against God?"

Beriah looked from Mary's face, her eagerness almost palpable, to Zerah's, whose eyebrows were raised in question.

Her father-in-law sighed heavily. He flung one hand in the air. "It seems you have thought of everything. My son is dead; there are no grand-children to sit on my knees. I am getting older, just a man who will one day be gathered to his fathers. I am the last of my clan, and there will be no heirs. What does it matter now?" He sat down suddenly and great tears rolled down his cheeks.

Mary put her arms around his shoulders. "You have been kind to me when I could not return the kindness. Who knows, Father Beriah, what the Most High, blessed be his name, has in mind for all of us? Can we read his mind? Does he not work in ways beyond our understanding?"

His eyes met hers and he slowly nodded. "So you will send word from time to time?"

Her heart sang. He was relenting. "Yes, Father Beriah, I will send word."

Zerah's practical mind became evident. "Let us consider how she will travel. She must have an escort. A woman alone would be vulnerable. Also, we will transport some food and other goods with her that will be helpful."

The two men put their heads together and Mary sat down and listened respectfully to Zerah's suggestions.

The men at the boatyard carefully crafted a small cart for Mary's journey. It was sturdy, yet not so cumbersome that the donkey would balk at pulling it when it was fully loaded. It was the spring of the year and the best time to travel. Zerah had learned that Jesus and his disciples had returned to Capernaum, and Mary would catch up with him there.

Keturah was moved to tears when Mary told her she and her new husband could stay in the home without paying any fee, as long as they took good care of it. "The house has known much sadness. It will be good to have the sound of children in it once more."

"We will care for your home, Mary, and pray for you each day as you travel with the Teacher."

Mary packed the cart with a grinding stone, a small clay stove for cooking and warmth, her lamb's wool rug to sleep under on cold nights, two changes of clothes, and an extra pair of sandals. In a small woven basket she packed the spices she used for cooking, some cheese, and date cakes. She added a cooking pot for stews. She opened the basket that held what was left of Nathan's clothes. What should she do with them? She lifted the linen tunic she had woven in one piece and smiled to herself. She turned and packed it among her clothing. Perhaps there was someone, about Nathan's size, who might need it.

Zerah stood by while she checked her provisions. As her closest male relative, he would travel with her and see her safely to her destination. Amos had offered, but it was not deemed proper. He was an unmarried man and she was a widow.

When all seemed in order, she turned to her uncle. "I am ready."

"And I."

Neighbors came to see them off, and Huldah wept, as did Keturah. "You must send us word," they told her.

"I will send word back with Daniel or Amos, whoever my uncle sends each month."

With her uncle leading the donkey and Mary walking by the donkey's side, they passed through the marketplace with the stalls of the fishmongers, dye makers, cages of doves, merchants of silks, and she listened to the sounds of the sellers extoling their wares. For a brief moment, Mary hesitated. Was she doing the right thing? *Come and follow me.* The words echoed in her head, reassuring her and calling her.

As they climbed through the hills, Mary looked out at the vast city of Magdala, her home for so many years. She was heading into the unknown with only the words of Jesus ringing in her head.

They spent the first night with another group of travelers returning from Jerusalem. Mary prepared food for the two of them and they rolled up in their cloaks and warm rugs for the night.

The next day as they approached Capernaum, Mary and Zerah saw the crowds gathering on the hillsides and knew Jesus must be somewhere nearby. They stabled the animal and cart and paid the innkeeper to give the donkey some straw. They passed through the crowd and Mary searched for Jesus. At last, in a group on the top of the hill, she saw him. Her heart expanded within her with joy. She was here. She would be listening to his words, walking with him. She hesitated. What should she do next?

As if he heard her thoughts, Jesus suddenly turned and looked straight at her. As he approached her, his welcoming smile was all she needed.

"Mary, come and meet my disciples and friends."

Then Mary noticed a small group of women standing to one side. He introduced her to them, indicating each one with his hand.

"This is Mary, wife of Cleopas; Susanna; Joanna, wife of Chuza; and Salome, mother of my friends James and John. Dear women, this is another Mary, she comes to us from Magdala."

The women embraced her and welcomed her. Susanna saw Mary's uncle standing to one side. "Is this your husband?"

"No, he is my uncle, the brother of my father. He came along to see me safely to you, but must return to Magdala."

Zerah spoke with Jesus quietly and then, embracing Mary, took his leave.

"I will miss you, Uncle."

"May HaShem watch over you, Mary."

She patted her girdle where the money pouch was hidden. He had given it to her in a quiet moment on the road when no one was around. "This is for your journey and any other needs you may have. Do not show it. When you are alone, take only what you need for the moment and keep it in another small pouch. Thieves are everywhere and watching. Be wise in your use of it."

She had hidden these words of warning in her heart, recalling them as they embraced. Her heart overflowed with gratitude. "I will be careful. Thank you for supporting me in my decision." She paused and then looked up at him. "I pray you will find a wife who will fill your heart, Uncle. Loneliness is not a good companion."

He raised his eyebrows at her boldness, but smiled. "I might just do that."

Now he was gone, lost in the crowd who was gathering. He planned to hire a boat to return to Magdala.

Mary turned to the women who clustered around her. "I have a donkey and a cart at the innkeeper's. I've brought cooking pots and provisions to share."

Susanna looked relieved. She had glanced around to see what Mary had brought with her and her face had been apprehensive. Now she beamed. "A good meal will be most welcome, though we never know how many we are to feed. Usually it is the closest disciples and those of us women who prepare the food."

Jesus taught from the top of the hillside and, toward the end of the day, dismissed the crowds. A handful of people remained—the disciples and the women.

Salome, the mother of Zebedee's sons, beckoned to Mary. "Jesus has the use of a house in Capernaum. We will go there." She called to her sons nearby. "John, James, come with us. Mary has brought a donkey and a cart with provisions. You can help her bring it to the house."

As they walked toward the town, some of the priests stopped Peter and one said loudly for all to hear, "Does your Teacher not pay the temple tax?"

Peter answered quickly, "Of course he pays the tax."

The priest nodded with a disdainful look and went on his way.

When the group reached the house, Mary overheard Peter asking Jesus about the tax.

"What do you think, Peter? From whom do the kings of the earth take customs or taxes, from their sons or from strangers?"

Peter answered, "From strangers."

"Then the sons are free, nevertheless, lest we offend them, go to the sea, cast in a hook, and take the fish that comes up first. When you have opened its mouth, you will find a piece of money; take that and give it to them for me and you."

Mary listened to this exchange in amazement. It was a strange way to provide the money for the tax. Was there nothing this "Son of Man," as he called himself, could not do?

The donkey, tired from the journey and now well-fed, seemed relieved to have the harness removed and be free of the cart he'd been pulling. They tied him in a corner of the courtyard and pulled the cart near the house.

Peter had brought back fish from the docks and the women set about frying it. Mary stirred a lentil stew in her cooking pot, and Suzanna broke up some flat bread for their meal.

The men gathered at a low table near the house, and the women ate in a group a short distance away. Mary, looking around at the faces of the women, felt welcome and accepted.

She was taking a bite of the bread she'd dipped in the stew when she felt herself being watched. When the feeling persisted, she turned slightly and met the eyes of one of the disciples.

Suzanna noticed her glance. "That is Judas. He is the treasurer of the group. When anyone gives us money, he keeps it in his bag and takes care of purchasing food and, in bad weather, lodging."

Mary thought of the pouch her uncle had given her. Was she to turn it over to this man? She was in new circumstances. When she had an opportunity, she would speak with Judas. She was eager not only to help but also to share her funds when they were needed.

As the women sat in a small group on the side, Mary's curiosity rose and she turned to Joanna, the wife of Herod's steward. "Was Jesus ever married?"

Joanna raised her eyebrows and smiled. "No, he has never married. The Most High has called him to a purpose greater than that of family. He came to tell us what the kingdom of God is like and how that, if we follow him, we will know God. While he has no wife, he is a friend to women and feels we should be accorded respect. He gives us self-worth. He has no children of his own, but loves children and never seems to miss an opportunity to hold a child on his knees and bless them."

Mary nodded, then looked across the group. "How did you come to follow him?"

Susanna glanced over at Jesus a moment. "I know his father and mother. I grew up knowing his brothers and sisters. Jesus was always kind, a gentle soul. I always felt he was destined for more than our small town of Nazareth. He was friendly, but somewhat aloof from the other men. He seemed always to be waiting for something and looking off into the distance. Sometimes I would see his mother, Mary, watching him and the look on her face puzzled me. It was as if sadness and joy wrestled within her. When he announced his ministry and began to travel, I heard amazing stories of miracles he performed. When he was rejected twice by the elders of our town, some of us decided to seek him out and see if the rumors were true. We were on the hillsides when he broke some bread and blessed a few small fish and . . ."

She paused, overwhelmed by what she remembered. "He fed thousands, there on the hillside. The baskets never seemed to empty, no matter how much people took out of them. I knew then that he was who he claimed to be, the Light of the World, God's Son."

Mary leaned forward eagerly. "My husband was there. He saw Jesus heal everyone who was brought to him. That's when he believed also."

The women smiled and murmured among themselves.

Susanna spoke again. "His own family does not believe in him. They came to get him once here in Capernaum when he was teaching. They wanted him to return home, but he looked around at all of us gathered there and said that whoever does the will of God were his mother and brothers and sisters."

"Does Mary, his mother, ever come with you?"

Salome shook her head. "Rarely, unless he is near to Nazareth. She is elderly now, almost fifty years old. It is hard for her to travel, and she also has the rest of her family to look after."

"Does his father live?"

"No," Susanna answered, "he has been gone many years now."

Mary looked over to where Jesus had been sitting and realized he was no longer there.

At the puzzled look on her face, Susanna put a hand on Mary's arm. "It is his way. When evening comes, he goes away to a place by himself to pray to his Father. He is often alone. Sometimes it seems he is with us, yet not with us." Her words seemed almost wistful.

The fire burned down and the disciples sought places in the courtyard to sleep. The other women made a place for Mary in the main room of the house with them. Wrapping her rug around her, she felt the weariness of her journey and closed her eyes.

The next morning as the group was eating some bread and cheese, Mary approached Judas.

"You are the treasurer?"

He raised his eyebrows. He had a handsome face, but something about it seemed closed. The dark eyes studied her. "Yes. Do you have something to contribute to our needs?"

"Well, I, that is, my uncle gave me some funds for my use, and of course to help Jesus."

"You are new with us. I keep the funds that are donated and distribute them as needed, for food or lodging." He waited expectantly for her to reply.

She wanted to do what was right, but thinking of how her uncle entrusted her with the funds, it was hard to turn them over to someone else. She hesitated.

"You can turn the coins over to me," he answered confidently and waited again.

"I have the coins hidden, but will bring them to you."

Judas nodded and turned away.

✣ 29 ✣

Mary got her pouch of coins. Her uncle had cautioned her to keep it safe. Surely it would be safe with Judas. They all seemed to trust him, including Jesus, so it was the right thing to do and her uncle was no longer here. She handed the pouch to Judas. He lifted it up and down in his hand briefly and gave her a pleased smile before tucking it in his waistband and striding quickly away.

The supplies were left at the house in Capernaum and the group followed Jesus out to the hills where he would teach most of the day. Since Peter, James, and John were subdued as they walked, Mary turned to Joanna walking near her.

"Is there something wrong? Peter, James, and John are very quiet."

"They have been acting strangely ever since Jesus called them to go up on the mountain with him several weeks ago. He didn't take the other disciples. We believe something happened. When they returned, they could hardly speak. They kept watching Jesus with this wonderment

257

on their faces. The only thing they would say is that they know he is the Messiah."

Mary smiled. "I too am sure of that."

As they walked, the women were aware of a murmured argument going on between the men. It would not have been the women's place to inquire, but soon it was apparent they were quarrelling about who was the greatest in the kingdom of heaven. Mary was surprised, but remained silent.

People from Capernaum began to come from the surrounding streets and join them along the way. Jesus listened to his disciples' comments, then paused. He picked up a small child whose mother had brought him close.

"Assuredly I say to you, unless you are converted and become as little children, you will by no means enter the kingdom of heaven. Therefore, whoever *humbles* himself, as this little child, is the greatest in the kingdom of heaven. Whoever receives one little child like this in my name receives me, but whoever causes one of these little ones who believe in me to sin, it would be better for him if a millstone were hung around his neck and he were drowned in the depth of the sea."

Mary listened to the words and marveled at his teaching. She, like the other women traveling with Jesus, made herself inconspicuous in the crowd. She listened to the story of a lost sheep, and how the shepherd went out of his way to leave the ninety-nine to search for the one that was lost.

I was lost, she thought to herself, *a madwoman, feared by the children and neighbors, of no use to my dear husband.* She remembered the day she was healed and the joy of feeling life again. She had cast off her filthy clothes when they got home and later burned them. After a bath, she felt human again. She had been enfolded in the arms of her beloved and had known once more the joy of being one. At the thought of Nathan, she forced back the tears forming behind her eyes. It was not time to look back. All the love she had felt for her husband she now poured into the joy of serving her Savior and Lord. She would follow him, no matter what it cost her.

When Jesus finished talking to the crowd, he began to move on. His disciples and followers moved with him. They found a shady place in a grove of trees and settled on the grass to rest and share the bread, fruit, and cheese the women had packed in cloth bundles. One of the women brought a jug of water and passed it among the group.

As they rested and enjoyed the peaceful afternoon, Mary sat near Jesus, just happy to be where she was. Then Peter rose and approached Jesus. He frowned as though troubled. Mary wondered if he was struggling with something Jesus had said when he talked to the crowd. He sank down near Jesus.

"Lord, how often shall my brother sin against me, and I forgive him? Up to seven times?"

Mary listened carefully. Peter was quoting the letter of the Law, which Mary, from her studies with Nathan, knew well, but kept to herself. The words of the rabbi in Magdala briefly came to mind. "It is better that the words of the Law should be burned than that they should be given to a woman." She would keep her knowledge to herself and be silent unless HaShem showed her it was to be shared. She leaned forward to hear the answer Jesus would give.

"I do not say to you, up to seven times, but up to seventy times seven. Therefore the kingdom of heaven is like a certain king who wanted to settle accounts with his servants. And when he had begun to settle accounts, one was brought to him who owed him ten thousand talents. But as he was not able to pay, his master commanded that he be sold with his wife and children and all that he had, and that payment be made. The servant therefore fell down before him, saying, 'Master, have patience with me and I will pay you all.' Then the master of that servant was moved with compassion, released him and forgave him the debt. But that servant went out and found one of his fellow servants who owed him a hundred denarii; and he laid hands on him and took him by the throat, saying 'Pay me what you owe!' So his fellow servant fell down at his feet and begged him, saying, 'Have patience with me, and I will pay you all.' The servant would not, but went and threw him into prison till he should pay the debt . . ."

Jesus went on to tell how the king heard of his servant's deed and called the servant to him. " 'You wicked servant! I forgave you all that debt because you begged me. Should you not have had compassion on your fellow servant, just as I had pity on you?' His master was angry, and delivered him to the torturers until he should pay all that was due to him. So my heavenly Father also will do to you if each of you, from his heart does not forgive his brother his trespasses."

Peter sat back and appeared to be thinking about the story. In the silence, Mary remembered her uncle's confession of his part in her kidnapping and how she was at first angry with him, realizing the pain and agony he had cost her. Yet in the wonder of being forgiven and healed, she'd found the strength to forgive her uncle for what he'd done. His remorse was real and she'd forgiven with all her heart. Yes, she understood what Jesus was teaching them.

Over the next few days there were many parables. Mary realized Jesus was trying to help them understand the concept of following not the letter of the Law, but the reasoning behind the

Law. He had glanced at her with a twinkle in his eye and smiled. It was as if he were looking deep into her soul. He was aware of how much of the Law she knew. Her understanding grew as she listened to him teach on patience and loyalty. It was not following the Law that brought them eternal life but purifying your heart and receiving the good news Jesus brought concerning the kingdom of heaven.

When the group left Capernaum for Galilee, Mary learned that Jesus would soon be in his hometown of Nazareth. With eagerness, she looked forward to meeting his mother.

It was late afternoon when they approached the small village of Nazareth. Word of his coming had spread quickly. They camped on the outskirts under some trees, and the women began to prepare the evening meal.

Mary was surprised that the crowd meeting Jesus was so small. Everywhere else he went, people flocked to him. As she watched the people approach, there was one group of men in the front with stern looks on their faces. She felt she knew who they must be. The other women had told her Jesus's family did not approve of his ministry, and he was able to do few miracles in his hometown because he was such a familiar figure that they scoffed at the idea he could be the Messiah. He'd grown up with them from boyhood, worked in his father's carpentry shop, built their tables and chairs. Susanna said it saddened him, but their minds seemed to be set. They had almost stoned him when he claimed to be the Messiah, but now the people of the town, including his own family, just regarded him as slightly demented.

As the family of Jesus approached, Mary knew immediately which woman was his mother. She stood out to Mary because she had eyes only for her firstborn son.

Jesus embraced his mother and greeted his brothers by name—James, Joses, Simon, and Judas. With an air of reservation, each of the brothers embraced Jesus in turn.

Mary watched the mother of Jesus speak quietly with him and then they both turned as Jesus nodded in her direction. Jesus's mother walked slowly toward her and smiled.

"My son tells me you have recently come from Magdala to support his ministry. You are alone?"

"Yes." Mary sighed. "My husband is dead."

The older woman studied her face a moment, and Mary saw pain and joy mingled in her eyes.

"Come apart with me, Mary of Magdala. The Most High brings me out to the hills today, not only to see my oldest son, but to seek you. There is much in store for us in the months to come. Let us walk a ways together."

❈ 30 ❈

As the sun climbed higher in the clear sky, the two women sought the shade of a large tree and settled themselves in its shade.

Mary had been told the mother of Jesus was almost fifty, yet her skin had few wrinkles. Her eyes held wisdom and something more. Mary sensed a timelessness about her, and great strength, but also great sorrow. She felt honored that the mother of her Lord had sought her out.

"Tell me about yourself, Mary. How did you come to follow my son?"

Mary mulled her question over a moment, then began with what had happened to her when she was eleven and the suffering she'd endured through the years. Over an hour passed while she shared her story up through the death of Nathan. The older woman listened without comment, nodding from time to time, but Mary sensed her empathy.

"I am sorry about your husband. I lost mine just after the last of Jesus's brothers, Simon, was born. Joseph was older than I by twelve years and his lungs were not good. I miss him, but Jesus was such a comfort to me. He was head of the house until the day he told me he was leaving. He said it was time. His brothers and sisters were angry. As the oldest, they expected him to be the family patriarch."

His mother looked down at the grass and sighed. "I knew the day was coming, but I didn't know what it meant. It was when he was twelve I was reminded of his mission."

Mary tilted her head. "When he was twelve?"

The elder Mary smiled. "We had been to Jerusalem for the Passover and were returning to Nazareth with family and friends. We thought he was with us—it was a large company—but we didn't miss him until we had gone a day's journey and had not seen him. When we inquired among our relatives and acquaintances, we realized he had stayed behind in Jerusalem. We returned at once but had no idea where to look for him. I was sure something had happened to him and was beside myself. Joseph kept telling me that HaShem would look after him, but I was weeping. By the time we found him, three days had gone by and we were frantic. Sure he'd been kidnapped or come to harm."

Mary leaned forward. "Where was he?"

"In the Temple, in the midst of the learned scholars and scribes, listening to them and asking them questions."

"He was asking questions of the Jewish leaders?"

"Yes. They were consulting their scrolls and he

seemed so at ease there, not intimidated in the least. Of course I was torn between anger that he had not consulted us, and pleasure at the astonishment of the elders and scribes."

Mother Mary shook her head. "When Joseph asked him why he had done this to us and told him how anxiously we had sought him, he calmly smiled at us and said, 'Why did you seek me? Did you not know that I must be about my father's business?' "

"So he knew even then."

"Yes, and I had forgotten why he was given to me. Life had gone on in such a normal way for so many years—and now I remembered the words of the Most High to me, 'You shall give birth to a son and shall call his name Jesus, for he will save his people from their sins.' "

"My lady, many years ago, my father sought to have me taught by the local rabbi in our town, but he refused because I was a girl. My husband, Nathan, then just my friend, was hired to teach me. I studied much about the Messiah to come and the prophecies." Mary stopped, unsure whether to ask, but something leaped within her and her excitement made her bold. "Tell me, where was Jesus born?"

The elder Mary smiled again. "Due to a decree from Caesar Augustus, each man was to return to his own city with his family. Though I was nearly at my time of delivery when the edict came, we were required to travel to Judea, to the city of David, for Joseph was of the house and lineage of David. There I gave birth to my firstborn son."

Joy filled Mary's heart, for she knew what the mother of Jesus was saying. "Bethlehem, the city of David. Jesus was born in Bethlehem."

The elder Mary nodded. "Yes."

Mary caught her breath and the words came, "The prophet Micah! 'But you, Bethlehem Ephrathah, though you are little among the thousands of Judah, yet out of you shall come for me the One to be Ruler in Israel . . .'"

"You do know the Scriptures, as my son told me."

"So at twelve, he knew even then . . ."

"He knew who his Father was."

"He came with you then?"

"Oh yes, he was obedient to us and returned to Nazareth. Yet from that day on, it was as if he was so much more mature, his knowledge far beyond the knowledge of the other boys of the town. He spent many hours walking the hills and talking to his Father. Something he still does."

Mary put a hand on the older woman's arm. "Oh, dear lady. Every Jewish mother dreams of such a thing—to be chosen as the mother of the Messiah. They pray for sons, with the hope they will be the one to bring him into the world. How blessed you are."

"And you are blessed, dear Mary of Magdala, to

have a father anxious to teach his daughters the Scriptures." She looked off in the distance. "Perhaps there will come a day when all women will be taught as the men are."

Mary was glad to hear another woman voice the same thoughts she had. Then another thought crossed her mind. "I've been told that his brothers and sisters do not believe in him."

"No, they knew him only as their older brother. He worked in the carpentry shop with Joseph until Joseph died, then became the head of the family. Everyone knew him as the son of Joseph. The years went by and it was easy to forget all the things that happened before."

She smiled at Mary. "At thirty, there was much gossip and speculation as to why I had not found a wife for him. Many a young woman in the village dropped hints."

"He would have made a good husband."

His mother shook her head. "But that was not what the Most High sent him here to do. Always, in the back of my mind was the feeling that one day something was going to happen. His Father would call him in some way. I'm not sure where his path is leading, I only know I was told that a sword would pierce my own soul." His mother shuddered. "Something is coming, Mary, that is going to bring great sorrow. I feel it. I just do not know what it is."

Mary sat quietly, thinking of what she'd been

told. It was almost too much to comprehend, yet she had seen Jesus heal every disease and deliver not only herself but others from demonic powers. Many evenings by the fire, she'd heard the disciples discussing miracle after miracle. She was awed when she heard of the time the disciples and Jesus were all in Peter's boat, out on the lake, when one of the fierce storms arose that swept the lake from time to time. Mary had thought of Nathan and the night he and his friend had been swept into the sea. She'd leaned forward eagerly to hear what happened . . . Jesus had merely spoken to the wind and waves and suddenly all was calm. Only the Son of God could do such things, she reasoned, and hearing the story of Jesus's birth, it began to all fall into place.

"I do not know what part you are to play in the coming events, Mary. I was only told to find the Magdalene."

"Perhaps, my lady, it was meant to strengthen my faith for the days to come."

"That could be his reason. We cannot question his plans for us."

The older woman rose slowly. "I am glad to meet you, Mary of Magdala. I'm sure we will see each other again in the days to come. I would ask you to watch over my son, but his Father above does that, and guides him on a path we can only follow as spectators."

Mary had risen also and now embraced her. "I

am indeed blessed by your words. I shall look forward to seeing you again."

One of Jesus's brothers approached them. "Are you ready to return?"

"Yes, my son, I am ready." She turned to Mary with a smile. "We have had a nice talk."

The young man gave Mary a searching look, but with only a brief nod of acknowledgment, escorted his mother back toward Nazareth.

Mary watched them go. What a wonderful woman the mother of Jesus was.

She hurried back to the camp to help the other women prepare their meal. It had been nearly a month since she'd joined the group. If her uncle kept his word, a messenger should be coming with the funds Zerah said he would send her. She wondered how the messenger would find them. She just had to trust Zerah to do what he'd promised. The group was running low on supplies. The donkey could graze on grass by the side of the road, but he needed some other feed. She looked toward the group of disciples. If her uncle sent the pouch, she was honor bound to turn it over to Judas.

As she walked, she thought again of the storm on the Sea of Galilee that had injured Nathan. A thought brushed her mind. If only Jesus had been in that boat with Nathan, he could have stilled the storm.

❋ 31 ❋

From Galilee, the disciples traveled back to Jerusalem for the Feast of Tabernacles. Jesus had stayed behind with his family but sent the disciples on ahead. When Mary and the group reached Jerusalem, Judas made arrangements for them to stay in the local khan. The inn was free to travelers and there were too many of them to stay at a single house.

Susanna, Joanna, Salome, and the other women set up camp in the open courtyard. Mary unhitched the donkey from the cart and made him comfortable in a stall with some hay. While the men prepared for the ceremonies of the holy day, there was much discussion about what Jesus would do and when he was coming. Restless, the disciples and the women milled about as they waited for word of him. What would he do next?

In the morning, Mary and the other women entered the Temple's Court of Women for the ceremonies. Four great lights had been erected to light the Temple. The Court of Women was lit up through the day and night of the seven days of the festival, reminding Israel of how the Lord's

271

presence was a column of cloud by day and a column of fire by night to be a light in the camp after they fled Egypt.

Mary looked around, awed at the great number of priests, tribal leaders, and renowned men of Israel crowding into the Temple. All had come in obedience to the command that every man of Israel was required, if able, to journey to Jerusalem for these holy days. The courtyard was filled. Mary, Susanna, and the other women sought out places on the side behind some of the pillars where they could be inconspicuous yet keep a watchful eye out for their Lord.

As they moved through the crowd, Mary overheard people murmuring, wondering where the Teacher was. *They are like eager children, anticipating entertainment,* she mused. They wanted to see the miracles he performed. She knew the common people also enjoyed his inter-action with the haughty priests and scribes, putting them to shame with his answers to their probing questions.

Suddenly there was a stirring of the crowd, and to Mary's delight, a familiar figure strode into the courtyard. Jesus had quietly slipped into the city. He settled on the steps and began to teach the people. Once again he began to upbraid the Pharisees and scribes for their hard-heartedness about the Law. Yet, as the elders remained silent, the people began to murmur.

"Isn't this the one the leaders seek to kill? Here he is, teaching openly, and they do nothing. Do they believe that he is the Christ?"

Others cried harshly, "We know where this man comes from; but when the Christ appears, no one will know where he comes from."

Dissention began to sweep through the crowd as supporters of Jesus began to argue with those who opposed him. Mary hung back in the shadows, fearing the crowd could become dangerous and take Jesus by force. What would happen to his followers? She brushed the fearful thoughts aside and focused on listening to Jesus.

When he had been teaching awhile, he leaned forward with one hand on his thigh and waved the other hand for emphasis as he said firmly, "You feel you know me and where I am from; but I have not come of myself. He who sent me is true, whom you do not know. But I know him, for I am from him, and he sent me."

The crowd murmured among themselves again, and once again Mary waited to see what would happen. Then Jesus rose and walked directly into the crowd, saying, "I shall be with you a little while longer, and then I go to him who sent me. You will seek me and not find me, and where I am you cannot come."

He then continued through the crowd and passed out of Mary's sight. When she and the other women were able to make their way through the throng to the street, Thomas, who'd remained behind briefly to meet them, said he was going to Bethany. Mary and the others were to return to the khan and wait for further word.

The Temple sacrifices continued and the other disciples brought word each evening to the khan as to what had happened that day. Over the course of the week, seventy bulls, fourteen rams, ninety-six lambs, and seven male goats were offered.

Mary looked forward to one special ceremony on the final day of the feast. The culmination of all that occurred in the Temple during the week, the Water Ceremony.

Her father had carefully explained the ceremony to her many years ago. A single priest was sent from the Temple to the Pool of Siloam, which meant *sent.* The priest was referred to as *he who is sent,* a reference to the one sent from heaven, represented by the Temple mount, down to Siloam, the lowest part of the earth, represented by Jerusalem. When the priest, who carried a golden pitcher, came to the pool, he would draw water. The waters were called the *waters of salvation* or the *waters of Yeshua.* Mary had learned in her studies of the Law, the words of the prophet Isaiah: "Behold, God is my salvation, I will trust and not be afraid; for the LORD God is my strength and song, and he has become my salvation. Therefore you will joyously draw water from the springs of salvation."

Now Mary was to see the words of the Scripture come to life before her eyes. She waited joyously for the priest to return with the golden pitcher, a flute player leading him. The flute player, her father had explained, was called the *pierced one* because of the holes in the tube of the flute.

Suddenly the priest entered the Temple court and silver trumpets sounded to draw everyone's attention. The priest with the golden pitcher was joined by a priest carrying a silver pitcher of wine. Mary craned her head to see as the two priests walked up the ramp to the altar, and each separately poured the contents of their pitchers down two funnel-shaped goblets that would drain the fluids down the side of the altar. One funnel for water and one for wine. Mary and the other women smiled and nodded to each other, for it was an exciting sight to see.

No sooner had the final ceremony been completed, when Jesus suddenly stood up among the people and cried, "If anyone thirsts, let him come to me and drink. He who believes in me, as the Scripture has said, out of his heart, will flow rivers of living water."

Mary listened and was puzzled. How could rivers of water flow from her heart? She sighed. He would tell them in private the meaning of his words. He spoke in parables, telling stories the people could relate to, driving home his point. She knew that only those whose hearts had received his message could understand truly what he taught them, and she wanted to learn all she could. Jesus had said that they would know the truth and the truth would set them free. Mary felt she understood. Since following Jesus, even though the hardships of being always on the move had been difficult, she felt more free than she had in her entire life. She had walked many miles, holding on to the bridle of the donkey as the small cart rolled along. She had found places in streams to wash, eaten food people had shared with them or whatever they were able to purchase from markets. Some nights had chilled her to the bone as she wrapped herself in her rug and slept on the ground, yet Jesus and the others endured the same hardships. It seemed a small price to pay to be able to walk with the one she called her Lord.

She had been witness to so many miracles. She remembered the day they had been walking through a town and a man who had been blind from birth called out to Jesus. When his disciples brought the man to Jesus, he was asked what he wanted.

"I want to see!"

Peter, ever bold with his questions, asked loudly enough to be heard by the rest of them. "Rabbi, who sinned, this man or his parents, that he was born blind?"

Jesus put a hand on Peter's shoulder and turned to his disciples and the others following. "Neither this man nor his parents sinned, but that the works of God should be revealed in him. I must work the works of him who sent me while it is day; the night is coming when no one can work. As long as I am in the world, I am the light of the world."

When he had said this, he spat on the ground and made a small ball of clay with the saliva; then he anointed the man's eyes with the clay and told him to go and wash in the Pool of Siloam. The man was led away by friends to the pool and in a short time came back almost running to Jesus.

"I can see! Rabbi, I can see!"

The townspeople began to murmur among themselves. "Isn't this the beggar who used to sit there in that place, begging every day?"

Some agreed he was, others cried, "No, he just looks like him."

The man who had been blind looked around at his neighbors. "I am the man who was blind."

Jesus passed on with his disciples and they later heard there was a huge argument among the Pharisees when the man was brought before them. When he tried to tell them how a man healed his eyes, they ridiculed him. Even with his parents testifying that he was blind from birth, the leaders wouldn't believe that a mere man had healed blind eyes. Finally, the man had been cast out of the synagogue. When the formerly blind man found Jesus, he fell down and worshiped him.

Rejoicing once again at the marvelous works of God, the disciples had followed Jesus out of the town to find a place to rest for the night.

Her reverie was interrupted by the people streaming out of the Temple area, talking among themselves as they headed in the various directions of their towns and homes. Mary and the others watched for Jesus and, when they saw him leaving the courtyard, joined him outside the Temple. This time he told them they would go to the Mount of Olives for the night.

Mary needed to retrieve the donkey and cart from the khan, and Jesus asked Matthew to accompany her for protection. As they left the khan and walked toward the outskirts of the city, Matthew, who had been mostly silent, asked how she had come to join the disciples.

"Where is your husband, your family?"

She told him her story as briefly as she could, and he listened thoughtfully.

"You have known much sorrow also. I lost my wife many years ago and sought to fulfill my life by gathering all the wealth I could. I was a tax collector for the Romans."

Mary paused. "A tax collector?" She knew how

they were hated by the Jews for serving the oppressors of their people. "How then did you come to follow the Lord?"

Matthew looked off into the distance and for a moment Mary thought he was not going to answer her question. Then he gave a slight shake of his head. "I was at my booth by one of the gates of the city when Jesus came by. I had heard rumors about him, and when he walked through the gate, he stopped at my table and looked at me."

Matthew paused again. "It was as if he saw my entire life, laid bare in a moment of time. Then I knew he knew about my wife and everything that had happened to me. I had never felt such compassion from a human being. His eyes looked deep into mine and he only spoke two words. 'Follow me.' In an instant I knew there was nothing else I'd rather do, and I got up and left the tax table. I invited him to eat with me in my house and invited my friends to join us." He chuckled to himself. "Two of my friends were Pharisees. They were indignant that Jesus would eat with the likes of my guests and said so."

He pulled a little harder on the harness of the donkey, which had been slowing down.

"What did Jesus say to them?"

"He said, 'Those who are well have no need of a physician, but those who are sick. Go and learn what this means, *I desire mercy and not sacrifice* for I did not come to call the righteous but sinners to repentance.' "

Matthew suddenly became silent and frowned. He glanced sideways at her. Mary knew he'd been carrying on a rather deep conversation with a woman in public and was embarrassed. She honored his silence and they walked quietly on to join the group waiting at the Mount of Olives.

James was restless during the evening meal, and finally looked up at Jesus and asked, "Master, what did you mean when you spoke of rivers of living water?"

"I spoke of the Spirit, but it is not yet time for you to know of these things. There is coming a time soon when it will be revealed to you."

James appeared to want to continue, but held his peace. The disciples had learned over the months of following their Lord when it was time to be silent.

Jesus spoke to the people about many things, and Mary listened carefully, pondering his words and seeking understanding of what he was teaching them.

Just before they again left the Temple, Jesus spoke words that stayed in Mary's heart. He said, "When you lift up the Son of Man, then you will know that I am *he,* and that I can do nothing of myself, but as my Father taught me, I speak these things. And he who sent me is with me. The Father has not left me alone for I always do those things that please him."

What did Jesus mean by being lifted up?

Something was in the air. Mary watched Jesus gather the larger group of his disciples and talk quietly with them. He chose seventy men and began to instruct them. Then the disciples clapped each other on the shoulder and came to where they had laid their belongings.

Salome watched her sons James and John, but they merely stood as the other men sorted through their things.

"What is the Lord doing with those others?" she asked.

John looked up, his face jubilant. "Jesus is sending them out in pairs to minister for him. They will go through the towns he plans to visit and prepare our way. They have been given authority to heal the sick, cast out demons, and share the good news of the kingdom of God."

His mother sighed and glanced at James, who was also watching. "And you are going with them?"

James shrugged. "I wanted to go, but Jesus told us we would remain. We have already ministered to the sick in his name."

Mary moved closer as Jesus faced the seventy he had chosen.

"The harvest is truly great, but the laborers are few; therefore, pray the Lord of the harvest to send out laborers into his harvest. Go your way; I send you as lambs among wolves. Carry neither money bag, knapsack nor sandals, and greet no one along the road. Whatever house you enter, first say, 'Peace to this house,' and your peace will rest on it; if not, it will return to you. Remain in the same house, eating and drinking such things as they give, for the laborer is worthy of his wages. Do not go from house to house. Whatever city you enter, and they receive you, eat such things as are set before you. Heal the sick and say to them, 'The kingdom of God has come near you.' But, whatsoever city you enter, and they do not receive you, go out into the streets and say, 'This very dust of your city which clings to us we wipe off against you. Nevertheless, know this; that the kingdom of God has come near you.' I say to you all, that it will be more tolerable in that day for Sodom than for that city."

He looked off in the distance and cried, "Woe to you, Chorazin! Woe to you, Bethsaida! For if the mighty works which were done in you had been done in Tyre and Sidon, they would have repented long ago, sitting in sackcloth and ashes."

He continued his instructions, and as Mary listened, she caught her breath, aware of the enormous responsibility and challenge these men were being given. They were to do the same miracles they had seen Jesus do.

At last, the seventy said goodbye to those who remained behind. One or two of the men whose wives had followed for a time stood aside with them, talking quietly, and Mary sensed they were reassuring them of their return.

Those who had not been chosen appeared wistful as they watched their comrades stride off eagerly down the road. Many of those watching appeared disappointed and some turned back from following Jesus, returning to their homes in other towns.

Jesus spoke with those remaining and called the Twelve and the women to him. It was agreed to meet in Jericho in two weeks. Peter and his wife returned to their home for a time, as did Andrew and Philip, and others went to stay with friends. Only Matthew and Thomas would go to Bethany.

Judas disappeared, as he did many times, not telling anyone where he was going. He troubled Mary, for she often saw him observing Jesus from under those heavy brows with a scowl on his handsome face. Whenever Judas was absent, there was a lighter atmosphere among the group.

Joanna went to her home in Jerusalem, and James and John returned with their mother to Galilee to fish with their father, Zebedee. It was a good time to fish and they would bring fresh supplies back with them.

Mary turned to Susanna. "What shall we do? It will be many days before the seventy return, and some of the followers have gone back to their homes."

"Will you also return home, Mary?"

"There is no one but my uncle there. I would stay with the Lord, but I don't know if we have been included in the invitation to the home of the Lord's friends in Bethany."

Susanna hung her head. "I have no place to go either." She brightened. "Perhaps we could return to the kahn?"

"But how long will we need to stay there? I have only a little money." Mary shook her head. "That innkeeper will not take too well to two single women. We might be in danger there." She put her hand on her belt. Bound in her garments was a small leather pouch. At the risk of alienating her friends, Mary had decided to keep some of the recent funds from her uncle. She didn't understand why, but felt impelled not to turn over the entire amount to Judas. She justified this, since he was not always available. There had been times when they needed supplies and Judas was nowhere to be found. As she pondered their dilemma, someone called to them. Jesus had turned and looked back.

With a smile, he lifted his arm and gestured. "Come."

Mary's heart leaped. Thomas came quickly and

pulled on the harness of the donkey as the two women hurried down the road to join Jesus. She only hoped she and Susanna would be as welcome with his friends as the other disciples.

❈ 32 ❈

Mary was a little apprehensive, for she and the other women had never gone to the home of Martha, Mary, and Lazarus. Jesus had only taken his closest disciples, the twelve he had chosen. Yet the women were warmly welcomed by the family in Bethany.

Jesus and his followers stayed two weeks, giving Mary and Susanna much-needed time to wash and repair clothing. They baked bread and added to the provisions of the cart. Martha was friendly but reserved. She ran a well-kept home and kept the women busy with many tasks. Her sister, Mary, was easier to talk to and was interested in hearing of their travels and the words Jesus spoke. Martha, with tight lips, would go about her duties, but her sister wanted to sit with the other disciples and listen to Jesus.

One evening Martha's sister played the lute for them and sang one of the songs from the Psalms that was often sung on the Sabbath.

It is good to give thanks to the LORD,
And to sing praises to your name, O Most
  High;
To declare your loving kindness in the
  morning
And your faithfulness every night.
On an instrument of ten strings, on the lute,
And on the harp,
With harmonious sound,
For you, LORD, have made me glad
  through your work;
I will triumph in the works of your hands.

As the sweet clear notes rang out in the evening air, Mary looked over at Jesus. He was watching Martha's sister and nodding to the music. His face seemed peaceful as he leaned back against the wall, listening and smiling.

Some of the men helped Lazarus with his brick making and repairs to the house. It was a time of rest and refreshment for all of them.

In the early evenings, Jesus would make himself comfortable in the shade of the courtyard and continue his teaching. Then he would quietly leave the house to walk the hills in solitude. Many times he stood for long moments looking toward Jerusalem, and Mary wondered what he was thinking.

Mary and Susanna cleaned the small cart and Mary was able to rearrange her things. One morning Mary opened a bundle that had been hidden under other household goods and cooking items and recognized the robe she had woven for Nathan. She wasn't sure why she had packed it and then forgotten about it. Now, as she examined the garment, woven in one piece without a seam, she knew who she would give it to. The next morning, when Jesus returned from a sojourn in the hills, she approached him. She noted how threadbare his robe had become.

"My Lord, there is something I would give you." She held out the robe.

He took the folded garment and unfolded it. She waited, holding her breath. Would it fit him?

His smile was as if the sun had risen in his face. "You made this." It was not a question but a statement.

"Yes, Lord. I made it for my husband, but he never wore it, he . . ."

"I know, Mary, and I will be honored to wear it. Thank you."

As she looked into his eyes, her heart filled with love for him—not the love she felt for Nathan, but love born of worship and devotion. At last she had been able to do something for her Lord.

He turned toward the house and came out a few moments later, wearing the new robe. The white linen caught the sunlight and he seemed to emanate a radiance all his own.

They left Bethany and moved on through other towns in Judea, always drawing crowds. Mary noted that along with the people, the inevitable priests, Sadducees, and Pharisees were present. They seemed relentless in their efforts to trap him into saying something incriminating.

Jesus listened patiently to their questions but always seemed to see through their schemes and, to the delight of the crowd, confounded the Jewish leaders with his answers. Finally, after being embarrassed again and again, the leaders refrained from asking questions. Yet they remained, observing, their faces grim and silent.

When the time came to reunite with the seventy who had been sent out, the group looked forward with great anticipation to hear the results of their journeys. The disciples who had returned to their homes for a time greeted the others, and once again a sense of camaraderie permeated the air.

As the seventy straggled in, many looking tired and dusty, but exultant, they were eager to share what they had seen and heard.

"A child who was blind could see, Lord."

"A man's crippled leg straightened before our eyes!"

"I was able to cast a demon out of a young man and restore him to his mother."

"Lord," exclaimed one, "even the demons are subject to us in your name."

Jesus smiled at their eager faces. "I saw Satan fall like lightning from heaven."

At their obvious puzzlement, he continued. "Behold, I give you the authority to trample on serpents and scorpions, and over all the power of the enemy, and nothing shall by any means hurt you. Nevertheless, do not rejoice in this, that the spirits are subject to you, but rather rejoice because your names are written in heaven."

The stories continued—blind men healed; lepers cured; those who were sick, raised up from their beds of pain. As each team told of the places they'd gone and the events that occurred, Mary and the others listened in wonder. They were mere men, these seventy, yet Jesus had the power to entrust them with the gifts of miracles that he himself performed. She sat quietly, hugging her knees and listening until she felt her heart could not contain the glory of it all.

Mary followed the group as they returned to Jerusalem for the Feast of Dedication in the winter of the third year of Jesus's ministry and then moved on to the region of Perea across the Jordan. The wives and many of the large following of disciples returned to their homes and responsi-bilities. Only the twelve whom Jesus had chosen to be his close companions remained, along with Mary, Susanna, and Joanna.

In one town, the Pharisees were able to stir up the citizens and Jesus came close to being stoned.

Yet, to Mary's amazement, he would pass through the midst of them unharmed. When the disciples would comment on this, feeling they'd had a close call, he would merely smile and say, "My time is not yet come."

He continued through the cities and villages teaching, and Mary realized they were heading again toward Jerusalem. One day some of the Pharisees came to listen and told him, "Get out and depart from this place. Don't you know Herod is trying to kill you?"

Jesus sighed heavily. "Go tell that fox, 'Behold, I cast out demons and perform cures today, and tomorrow and the third day I shall be perfected.' Nevertheless, I must journey today, tomorrow, and the day following; for it cannot be that a prophet should perish outside of Jerusalem."

Shaking their heads, the leaders departed. Jesus looked after them and spoke almost to himself, "O Jerusalem, Jerusalem, you kill the prophets and stone those who are sent to you. How I would have gathered your children together, as a hen gathers her brood under her wings, but you were not willing! See, your house is left to you desolate; and I say to you, you shall not see me until the time comes when you say *Blessed is he who comes in the name of the Lord!'* "

Later, in the darkness, when most were asleep, Mary and the other women whispered together, and Mary was troubled. "He speaks so much lately of death." In her mind she remembered the scrolls she studied and the Messiah who would come and rescue them from their oppressors. If he was coming as their King and Messiah, why would he speak of his dying? It was as if he was facing something terrible. She had no scrolls to study here and could only search her memory for what she'd read many years ago.

Joanna whispered, "I know, Mary. Perhaps we should avoid Jerusalem. There are many there who would do him harm."

Mary shook her head in the darkness. "He will not turn. He teaches the people each day, but in the evening, his face is always toward that city. I do not think he will be deterred from whatever purpose he has in mind."

As she settled down, wrapping herself in her rug for warmth, Mary pondered the Lord's words and the talk with the Lord's mother that day outside Nazareth. She too had sensed that he was heading for something they could not name.

Mary gazed out over the campsite at the bundled forms of the sleeping disciples and became aware of a lone figure silhouetted in the moonlight. The Lord stood quietly, the soft breeze moving the robe he wore. He had his back to her, but she knew which direction he faced. She shivered as a coldness brushed across her heart.

❧ 33 ❧

Several days later Jesus and his disciples were passing through Jericho, and one of the most notorious of the tax collectors by the name of Zacchaeus actually climbed a tree in his fine robes to be able to see Jesus. He was short and evidently couldn't see over the crowd. To Mary and the other disciples' astonishment, Jesus stopped under the tree and invited himself and all of them to the tax collector's house for a meal.

Zacchaeus lived well and his dining hall was large. Mary wondered if somehow Jesus knew he had room for them. The little man seemed so excited and invited other tax collectors and some of the Pharisees to come also.

Mary and the other women sat down on cushions in the back of the room. They were uneasy and felt hardly welcome. To their surprise, they were served at the order of Zacchaeus by his equally surprised servants.

Jesus seemed quite at home and began to share how valuable each of them was to the Father. Mary drew her cloak around her and settled back to listen. She marveled at how Jesus used the things of everyday life to make his point.

"What man having a hundred sheep, if he loses one of them, does not leave the ninety-nine in the wilderness, and go after the one which was lost until he finds it? And when he has found it, he lays it on his shoulders, rejoicing. He calls his friends and neighbors to rejoice with him, for he had found the sheep which was lost."

He told of a woman, losing a coin and sweeping the house until it was found. She too called her friends and neighbors to rejoice with her. It seemed to Mary that the Lord strove to help the people understand how much the Father loved them all.

Finally he told the story of a prodigal son, who had convinced his father to give him his inheritance and had gone to a far country where he spent all he had on all the wrong things. The young man ended up starving and was hired by a man to feed his pigs. The young man remembered all he had at his father's house, and dirty and hungry, he stumbled back to his own country. Knowing he'd spent his inheritance, he'd ask his father if he could become one of the servants. At least he would have a place to sleep and food to eat. When he at last came to the road leading to his father's house, the father, who had grieved for his son and watched every day for his return, saw him coming.

The father ran down the road and, before the son could speak, embraced him with tears of joy.

The son made his humble request to become a servant, but the father said to his servants, "Bring the best robe, kill the fatted calf, and put my ring upon his hand. My son was dead to me and now he is alive. Let us eat, drink and be merry."

Then Jesus looked pointedly at his listeners. "Now the older son was in the field and when he neared the house and heard the merriment, he asked what was happening. When a servant told him it was for his younger brother who had returned from the far country, he was very angry. He said to his father, 'I have served you all these years and you have never killed the fatted calf nor let me make merry with my friends.' And the father said to him, 'Son, you are always with me, and all I have is yours. It is right to make merry, for your brother was dead and is alive. He was lost, and is found.' "

Mary listened eagerly, for with parable after parable Jesus taught them about the kingdom of heaven. *We are like lost sheep,* she reflected, *and the lost coin, and the young man who returned from the world to be welcomed in the father's house.* As they believed in the kingdom, they too would be welcomed home to heaven in the Father's house.

The two Pharisees looked around at the motley group gathered around them, and their eyes flashed with indignation. Mary knew Zacchaeus, though Jewish, was a sinner in their eyes, for he worked for the oppressive Roman government, collecting taxes from his own people and lining his own pockets as most tax collectors were known for doing.

She glanced over at Matthew, a former tax collector. He was listening and watching Zacchaeus intently.

Suddenly Zacchaeus stood and cried out, "Look, Lord, I give half of my goods to the poor, and if I have taken anything from anyone by false accusation, I restore fourfold."

Jesus beamed at him. "Today salvation has come to this house, because he is also a son of Abraham. For the Son of Man has come to seek and to save that which was lost."

The two Pharisees nearly sputtered into their beards and rose hastily to leave the house.

When Jesus and his followers also rose to leave, Zacchaeus saw them to the door. Jesus clasped him on the shoulder and spoke a few words quietly. Zacchaeus merely nodded his head, his face alight with happiness.

Mary's feet were tired. It seemed as if they had been walking for hours and she brightened as they neared a town. She had been thinking of her uncle, amazed that he could find the group so easily, for each month, either Daniel or Amos appeared with a small pouch of money as her uncle had promised.

Sometimes Daniel or Amos would stay with the group a day or two and share news of Magdala. Amos was hoping to start a family soon, having been married a few months. So far, his wife had not become pregnant. Keturah's little boy was growing and starting to walk. Daniel had his eye on a girl in Magdala and was anxious for his father to present him to her family. Mary always felt a little sad when they left, but she had only to hear Jesus speak and her heart would lift again. She was where she belonged, following her Lord.

The company would rest when they reached the town and she and the other women looked forward to possibly staying at an inn. Just then, a messenger hurried up to Jesus. It was obvious he had been traveling hard.

"Master, I have been sent to you from Bethany. Your friend Lazarus, whom you love, is very ill and his sisters have sent me to find you. Come at once, Master. He needs you."

Jesus put a hand on his shoulder and bowed his head a moment. Then he turned to the women. "Give him some refreshment and let him rest before he returns."

When the messenger had gone on his way, Jesus looked at his disciples who were waiting word to pack up and start for Bethany.

"This sickness is not unto death, but for the glory of God, that the Son of God may be glorified through it."

There was nothing to do but wait for his command. Two days passed and the disciples became restless.

After the evening meal, Mary turned to Susanna and murmured, "If Lazarus is sick, should we not go to him? The Lord needs only to lay hands on him for his recovery."

The next morning Jesus rose and told them, "Let us go to Judea again."

Mary sighed. At last.

Thomas looked at the other men and back at Jesus. "Lord, the Jews have lately sought to stone you, should we go there again?"

Jesus picked up his traveling bag. "My friend, are there not twelve hours in the day? If anyone walks in the day, he does not stumble, because he sees the light of this world. But, if one walks in the night, he stumbles, because the light is not with him."

At their puzzled looks, he sighed deeply. "Our friend Lazarus sleeps, but I go that I may wake him up."

A sense of relief flowed through the group. Lazarus would recover.

Peter shouldered his mat. "Then if he sleeps, he will get well."

Then Jesus told them plainly, "Lazarus is dead. And I am glad for your sakes that I was not there, that you may believe. Nevertheless, let us go to him."

The disciples looked at each other in surprise. Why had they tarried? They set out, with much murmuring among themselves, but like the calm before the storm, they sensed this journey was different. They feared the Jewish leaders and knew there was danger in going near Jerusalem.

Thomas turned to the others and said, "Let us go also, that we may die with our Lord."

Though they were not strangers to miracles, having traveled so long with Jesus, they were uneasy facing the unknown.

Jesus set a pace that was almost hard to keep up with. Mary noted that even the donkey protested being hurried. They camped only to rest for the night, then were on the road again at first light.

When they neared Bethany, a villager told Jesus that Lazarus had been laid in the tomb four days before. The disciples began to murmur among themselves again.

"Why then did we wait two days?"

Peter voiced what Mary was thinking. "Could we have gotten to Lazarus in time if we had left sooner?"

Just then a distraught figure came running up the road toward them, her face streaked with tears. It was Martha.

She could hardly speak for the tears, but cried,

"Master, if you had been here, our brother would not have died."

Jesus spoke to her for a few moments and then Martha ran back to the house to get her sister, Mary.

Mary also ran up to Jesus with the same words, "If you had been here, our brother would not have died."

The face of the Lord appeared troubled and he put his hand over his eyes. Mary had never seen him weep before in all the time she had traveled with him. *He must have truly loved his friend Lazarus deeply.*

Jesus turned to those following him. "Come." With purpose they all hurried to the tomb where Lazarus had been laid. Mary thought he wanted them to share his grief.

What followed, she could never have imagined.

❋ 34 ❋

They approached the crude cave that had been carved into the rock. A large stone had been rolled in front of the opening to seal the cave. Mary, the disciples, and people from the village stood around the site. Some of the Jewish leaders pushed their way to the front of the crowd and stood with disdainful looks on their faces. People murmured among themselves and some even asked out loud, "What is the man going to do?"

The two sisters were weeping quietly with their arms around each other.

The Lord stared at the tomb for a long moment and then in a firm voice, cried, "Take away the stone!"

Mary and Susanna looked at each other, their eyes wide. Take away the stone?

Mary heard Martha voice what they were all thinking. "But Lord, he has been dead four days, there will be a stench."

Jesus turned to her. "Did I not say to you that if you would believe, you would see the glory of God?"

Martha looked at her sister and then at the crowd, but finally ordered the stone to be moved

300

away. Some men from the crowd came forward and put their shoulders to the stone, finally moving it aside.

Martha put her arms around her sister, and Susanna gripped Mary's hand as they watched, their eyes wide with both hope and anxiety.

Then Jesus lifted up his eyes toward heaven and in a firm voice said, "Father, I thank you that you have heard me. And I know that you always hear me, but because of the people who are standing by I said this, that they might believe that you sent me."

Mary had never heard Jesus pray out loud to the Father before, and she gripped Susanna's hand tighter as they waited to see what would happen. Would God send lightning, or answer in an audible voice?

In the silence that followed, people began to be restless. "Who is he talking to?" Others near Mary murmured, "What does this fellow think he is going to do?"

Then Jesus cried out, "Lazarus, come forth!"

The crowd held its collective breath, watching the opening of the cave.

Mary stared, her eyes wide with amazement. A figure shuffled to the entrance of the cave, still bound in the graveclothes. She strained to see better. Was it Lazarus?

Oh praise to the Most High God, it was, for his sisters rushed forward, frantically tearing the graveclothes away from him and removing the cloth that covered his face.

Mary felt tears of joy pour down her face and there were tears on the faces of others around her. An astounding miracle. A man who had been dead four days, alive again, embracing his sisters and weeping with them.

She felt her heart would burst with excitement and amazement. Never had one of the priests ever raised a man from the dead. She looked at the astounded leaders, who watched with open mouths. The priests and scribes quickly collected themselves and, pushing angrily back through the exuberant crowd, hurried back to Jerusalem.

Mary turned to look at the Lord, who was watching them with an unreadable expression on his face, and wondered, Were they in even more danger than they were before they came here?

Sitting under the shade of an olive tree at the Mount of Olives days later, Mary and Susanna still spoke with a sense of wonderment. If they had not been there and seen the miracle with their own eyes, would they have believed?

Susanna sighed. "Oh Mary, I felt so sad for Martha and Mary. They loved their brother Lazarus. Even the Lord himself wept. How could we imagine what the Lord was going to do?"

"I know. When Lazarus stumbled out of the tomb and his sisters unwrapped the graveclothes, it was as though he had never died. My heart nearly stopped beating. Then, only a short time later, he was hosting all of us in their home. It's a good thing we offered to help with the food and serving, for all Martha and Mary wanted to do was sit near Lazarus and bask in the fact that he was alive again. Did you see the scribes and Pharisees who had come out? They ran like rabbits for the city. All of Jerusalem must surely know of this great miracle by now."

Susanna shook her head slowly. "He calms storms, heals the sick, casts out demons, gives sight to the blind—how can the people who see these things not know who he is?"

Mary turned to look toward the group of men reclining on the grass near Jesus. "His time is coming, Susanna, when he will take his place and lift our people from their oppression."

"Surely he is the Messiah we have prayed for. Do you think he will do this soon?"

"He has some great purpose in Jerusalem," Mary answered. "He looks toward the city no matter where we go. Now I know that he is going there and something is going to happen."

Susanna gave a light laugh. "He will drive out the Romans as he drove the money changers out of the Temple."

The disciples rose and John came to where the women were sitting. "Come, let us prepare to travel. We move on to the city of Ephraim. The

Lord says that we will remain there awhile."

Mary stood and brushed herself off. "I thought we were going into Jerusalem."

John shrugged. "Passover is coming and I believe we will go there for that, but . . . I fear for him. There are rumors that the leaders are angry over the miracle of Lazarus."

Mary stared at him. "Why would they be angry about such a thing?"

He looked off toward the city. "I have relatives in certain places. It is not good. The Sanhedrin wants to arrest him."

Mary could not suppress a gasp. "Arrest him? Why?"

"The people follow him and he shows those high-and-mighty ones up for the self-righteous fools they are."

When he had turned away, Mary and Susanna looked at each other, and Mary saw in her friend's eyes what was reflected in her own. Fear.

The women harnessed the donkey and made sure that all the cooking pots and other belongings were carefully packed in the cart. The disciples graciously took turns leading the animal, for he was less stubborn with a firm male hand on his bridle.

They stayed in Ephraim nearly a week, until time came for the Passover. Then they traveled through the back country, skirting Jerusalem, and came again to Bethany, six days before Passover.

Joanna and Salome joined them again, and the four women and twelve disciples came with Jesus to the home of Martha and Mary.

The women helped Martha and Mary prepare a supper. Lazarus sat at the low table with Jesus, love and devotion aflame in his eyes. The sisters were overjoyed to have Jesus with them again and couldn't do enough for his comfort. The disciples, always treasuring a good meal, basked in Martha's cooking. Their eyes lit up when she brought out a lentil stew with chunks of lamb, bowls of ripe figs, and loaves of warm baked bread. There were fresh fava beans marinated in olive oil and garlic, spiced pomegranate wine, and goat's milk cheese.

To the puzzlement of his guests, Jesus spoke more and more of his death. He spoke of the Temple being torn down stone by stone.

Finally, James asked, "If all these things are to happen, what sign should we look for to know when that time is drawing near?"

Jesus sighed. "Take heed that you are not deceived. Many will come in my name, saying 'I am he, and the time has drawn near,' but do not go after them. When you hear of wars and commotions, do not be terrified; for these things must come to pass first. But the end will surely come."

He paused, making a sweeping gesture with his hand. "Nation will rise against nation, and kingdom against kingdom . . ."

Mary wondered to herself if he meant that the kingdom Jesus spoke about would rise against the Roman rulers.

He went on, "There will be great earthquakes in various places, and famines and pestilence, and there will be fearful sights and great signs from heaven. But before all these things, they will lay hands on you and persecute you, delivering you up to the synagogues and prisons. You will be brought before kings and rulers for my name's sake."

The disciples and the women looked at each other, their faces full of apprehension. Mary turned to Salome and they both shook their heads. What was going to happen to them?

Jesus continued. "But it will turn out for you as an occasion for testimony. Therefore, do not be concerned about what you will say, for I will give you wisdom, which all your adversaries will not be able to contradict or resist."

Mary sighed inwardly. That sounded better.

"You will be betrayed even by parents and brothers, relatives and friends; and they will put some of you to death. And you will be hated by all for my name's sake. But not a hair of your head shall be lost. By your patience, possess your souls."

He pointed a finger at them. "But when you see Jerusalem surrounded by armies, then know that its desolation is near. Let those who are in Judea flee to the mountains, let those who are in the midst of her depart, and let not those who are in the country enter her." He went on to describe signs in the sun and moon, and in the stars; distress with nations and the roaring of the sea and the waves. To Mary, it sounded like the end of the world.

Finally he ended, "Watch therefore, and pray always that you may be counted worthy to escape all these things that will come to pass and to stand before the Son of Man."

Mary's heart pounded, and in glancing at the others, she sensed they felt as she did. Strange and terrible times were coming, but they would not know when.

As the group whispered among themselves as to what the Lord meant, there was a sudden silence. A wonderful perfume was permeating the room. Mary, Martha's sister, had quietly taken a vial of costly spikenard, broken it, and was pouring it on the Lord's feet, then wiping them with her hair.

Judas snorted and said, loudly for all to hear, "Why wasn't this fragrant oil sold in the market-place? It could have brought almost three hundred denarii. The money could have been given to the poor."

Mary pursed her lips. She had seen Judas taking money from the bag when he thought no one was looking. With all the trees around, he hadn't seen her. The man was not to be trusted, but she didn't feel it was her place to expose him. The Lord knew all things—Judas would be found out soon enough. She was thankful she had decided not to turn over all the money her uncle sent each month. Judas watched her and she wondered if he knew, yet he never spoke to her about it.

"Let her alone," Jesus answered, putting a gentle hand on the sister's shoulder. "She has kept this for my burial. The poor you have with you always, but me you do not have always."

Mary listened to his words and what he taught them in these recent days, drinking in the truths he shared, and becoming more and more uneasy about entering Jerusalem.

To Mary's joy and delight, the mother of Jesus joined them, coming down with her family for Passover in the Holy City. The brothers of Jesus remained in Jerusalem, but the elder Mary traveled with Joanna to join them at the Mount of Olives. She embraced her eldest son and they held each other a long time.

Mary watched the two in earnest conversation. Jesus seemed to be telling his mother things she didn't want to hear, for she covered her face with her hands. She finally put a gentle hand on his face and then turned away and came toward Mary.

The two women embraced.

"Dear lady, it is good to see you again."

"And you, Mary. The long months on the road have seasoned you."

Mary knew her skin had felt the effects of the weather, but she felt stronger than she had been when she joined the disciples. "We have experienced much."

The older woman nodded. "My son tells me he is going to Jerusalem for the Passover. I tried to persuade him that it was dangerous for him in the city right now. He told me he must be about his Father's business." She looked off into the distance. "They are the same words he said to me many years ago, which I shared with you." His mother turned toward Jerusalem. "He is entering the city tomorrow."

Mary nodded. "The other disciples told me he is going to enter with the crowds openly. I pray there will be no trouble with the leaders."

"My sons will not hear of me spending the night here in the open and have made arrangements for our family in the city. I will be watching his entrance from a house built into the city wall."

"It will be a joyful day, my lady. Perhaps it is now that he will show his power and step up to lead our people."

Jesus's mother looked at Mary sadly. "I feel such a heaviness in my spirit. We will wait to see . . . tomorrow." She embraced Mary. "Be careful, Mary of Magdala. Pray with all your might. He needs your prayers."

"I do pray, my lady, every day. He is weary and some great sorrow weighs on his countenance."

As she watched the mother of Jesus walk away with her family, Mary was puzzled, but before she had time to think more on it, Joanna was calling her and it was time to prepare the evening meal.

※ 35 ※

In the morning the sunrise was beautiful to behold. Mary never got tired of seeing the soft golden and orange palate of the awakening day. Surely a morning that began with such beauty would become a good day.

The women prepared a simple breakfast of fruit and cheese, and as they were finishing, Jesus gathered them together.

"The hour has come that the Son of Man should be glorified. I say to you, unless a grain of wheat falls to the ground and dies, it remains alone; but if it dies, it produces much grain. He who loves his life will lose it, and he who hates his life in this world will keep it for eternal life. If anyone serves me, let him follow me; and where I am, there my servant will be also. If anyone serves me, my Father will honor him."

Jesus paused to look toward the magnificent city gleaming in the morning sunshine. "My soul is troubled, and I cannot say, Father, save me from this hour. For this purpose I came to this hour."

He looked up toward heaven. "Father, glorify your name."

Suddenly there was a voice that came clearly on the still air. "I have both glorified it and will glorify it again."

The disciples looked at each other in wonderment. Mary clasped her hands to her heart. Did she truly hear this?

As they questioned each other, Jesus said plainly, "This voice did not come because of me but for your sake. Now is the judgment of this world. Now the ruler of this world will be cast out. And if I am lifted up from the earth, I will draw all peoples to myself."

Mary did not realize the significance of what he said then until days later. He was saying he was going to rise up and lead the people against the Romans. It was an exciting day for all of them. To think they had been privileged to hear the very voice of God from the heavens. She was sure it was, because HaShem wanted them to know beyond a shadow of a doubt who Jesus was. He was truly their Messiah.

Excitement was building. Mary's heart was pounding and she felt she could almost burst with joy. Matthew, standing nearby, stepped up and took hold of the donkey's bridle as the animal became skittish. He led the animal firmly as Mary and the other women happily followed Jesus and the crowd that was forming along the sides of the road.

Just as Mary approached Jesus, he turned to Peter and John who were close by, and said quietly, "Go and prepare the Passover supper for us that we may eat."

Peter nodded. "Yes, Lord, but where shall we prepare it?"

"When you have entered the city, a man will meet you carrying a pitcher of water. Follow him to the house where you will prepare."

As the two disciples hurried off, Mary stood looking after them. What unusual instructions. No man carried a water pitcher. That was women's work. She shook her head. She had heard and seen stranger things in her walk with the Lord.

Jesus was waiting for something, and as everyone watched, a colt was led up to Jesus and after someone had spread their cloak on the animal's back, Jesus seated himself and began to ride toward the long ramp that led into the city.

Mary glanced around happily and suddenly noticed that Judas was conspicuously missing, again. *He seems to disappear at the wrong times,* she thought. *He should be here to share this moment with the Lord.* She turned to Susanna who walked beside her.

"I don't see Judas with the others."

Susanna scanned the crowd ahead of them. "Perhaps the Lord sent him on another errand for our Passover meal."

"Perhaps, but he has a strange way of disappearing. One moment he's there and the next he's gone. You are probably right. He does have the moneybag to pay for what we need."

Andrew and James cut palm branches and, with a flourish, handed them to Mary and the other women in their group. Villagers were also cutting palm branches to hand out to people around them.

The cries of "Hosanna, blessed is he who comes in the name of the Lord" and "Hosanna to the Son of David" rang in their ears. The tumult was deafening as, along with cries of praise, the people waved their palm branches. Some of the pilgrims took off their cloaks and laid them in the road ahead of Jesus.

Mary could hear the tambourines and flutes along with the sounds of the Levites who sang and played musical instruments at the entrance to the Temple. It blended in a cacophony of sound with the voices of the crowd that had swelled into thousands of people.

Now that she'd been healed, Mary looked up at the majestic walls of the city as though it were the first time. As they approached, she could see the top of the Temple, its white walls gleaming in the morning sunshine. Her father had told her once that you could not look at the Temple in the daytime as it would blind you. She now knew what he meant.

The crowds entered the city through the southern or Hulda gates, flowing like a great river of humanity into the streets toward the Temple mount. Mary looked up at the stone walls built with heavy stones, some weighing many tons. Yet they were carefully placed one on top of another with no space in between. She had been to the Temple before, but today it seemed even bigger than she remembered, almost as a conquering king brooding over his tiny subjects.

When the triumphant procession reached the city, people waved from rooftops as Jesus approached the Temple. As she walked, Mary scanned the nearby houses for the mother of Jesus, but every window was full of people leaning out and adding their cries to the throng.

She waited as did the others, holding her breath. What was he going to do now? The people were ready to crown him their king. All he had to do was acknowledge them and they would sweep him into the Temple and proclaim him King of the Jews.

He dismounted from the donkey and stood for a long moment looking at the huge edifice and then strode into the Temple. Matthew appeared at Mary's side. He seemed nervous as he glanced at the large number of Roman soldiers quietly moving into place near the Temple.

"Come, I am to show you women the upper room where we will celebrate Passover. You can prepare the meal there."

Mary looked at him in astonishment. "But this is his moment. Are we to miss what we have all waited for?"

"We do not know what is to happen. He will not be crowned king. He has told us that much in many ways. It is better that you are out of the crowds." He tilted his head at Susanna and Joanna. "Come."

Mary was confused. Why were they being led away at this time? She had been wondering what to do next, but it was with reluctance she and the women followed Matthew. If the Lord had asked him to take them to the upper room, she would be obedient. She sighed. Others would have to tell her what happened at the Temple.

Joanna embraced Mary and Susanna. "I'm returning to my home to celebrate the Passover with my family. Several have come from other towns and they are waiting for me."

When she hurried away through the crowd, Mary and Susanna followed Matthew through the narrow streets to the far side of the city. They stopped in the marketplace and Mary used most of her remaining coins to purchase the supplies they needed: bitter herbs, fruit, apples, nuts, wine, horseradish, and lamb shanks. She knew she already had the spices.

They wound through the narrow streets and came to the building Matthew indicated. Mary was surprised to see her donkey and cart. Someone had brought it here for them. She shook her head. This was a strange day and not at all what she had imagined.

After climbing up some steps, they entered a large room where a table had been laid with platters and wooden cups. They brought the supplies up to the back of the large room and began to prepare for the meal.

Matthew helped bring up the food and then turned to them. "I am returning to the Temple. Jesus will be there awhile. I think you will have plenty of time."

They thanked him for his help and set to work. Mary put kindling in the small clay stove and soon the lamb shanks were simmering. Susanna cut up the apples and mixed them with almonds, cinnamon, and sweet and dry wines to make *charoset*, the sauce that represented the mortar used to build the Temple. Mary had purchased the *matzah* bread in the marketplace as they had no time to bake it. They had also purchased roasted eggs, a symbol of life. Mary chopped up the horseradish for the bitter herbs that represented the bitterness of slavery, and the parsley that represented hope and redemption. She filled a bowl with salted water for dipping the parsley, representing the tears shed by her people.

As Susanna poured the wine in each of the cups, a voice was heard at the entrance of the room. The mother of Jesus entered with her son Joses and a younger woman. "This is my youngest daughter, Rebecca. We wanted to celebrate this night with you, and my son so kindly escorted us here."

The look on the face of Joses didn't support his mother's words, but she ignored him.

Mary moved forward to greet Rebecca, and embrace the Lord's mother. "Dear lady, it is so good to have you with us. Did you both see the procession this morning?"

The older woman sighed. "Yes, it was wonderful to see—the people and the children, the palm branches. He entered like a king."

"He is a king, dear lady. He has the support of the people now. You saw that yourself. Soon he will take his place as our leader."

"Mary, he is a king, but not as you have imagined. The kingdom he speaks of, as you have heard many times, is not of this world."

Mary stood as though struck dumb. What had she missed in the Scriptures? She'd been wrong, but she didn't know why.

Before Mary could respond, Jesus's mother

turned and nodded her approval at the set table. "I wonder how many there will be?"

Mary gathered her turbulent thoughts and turned to the task at hand. "I believe it will just be the Lord and the Twelve." She turned to the others. "The four of us and . . ."

She glanced at Joses, but he was already shaking his head. With a frown at his mother, he left them.

"Salome, the wife of Zebedee, is with her family, as is Joanna," Mary added.

The elder Mary looked after her son. "His brothers think their older brother is demented. They wanted to take him home to Nazareth, but it was impossible. Even with the miracles, he is still just their older brother."

Rebecca had seemed to Mary a timid soul, but she spoke up. "He has always been kind to me. He was different from the other young men in the village. I believe in him." She turned to Mary and Susanna. "What can we do to help?"

❖ 36 ❖

When the Passover meal was ready, the women sat down to wait for the men to arrive. It was nearly sundown when they heard footsteps and voices on the steps and Jesus entered the room. He embraced his mother and smiled at the other women.

"You have done well. All is ready for this night."

To Mary's surprise, Judas was with them. He looked around at the food and quickly attended to the ceremonial washing of his hands in the basin the women had provided. His face was sullen as he glanced at Mary. He knew she'd purchased the supplies. She gave him a hard look as he almost slunk into his place at the low table and pursed her lips. If he'd been around when he should have been, he could have purchased the supplies himself. He should be glad she had a little money left.

Just as the four women were ready to begin serving, Jesus rose from his place and removed his robe. He took a towel, and picking up the bowl of sacred water used for the ceremonial washing of their hands, he began washing the disciples' feet. They were too astonished to comment, struck silent until Jesus came to Peter.

Peter pulled his feet back and exclaimed, "Lord, are you washing my feet?"

"Peter, what I am doing now you do not understand, but you shall know after this."

"You shall never wash my feet!"

"If I do not wash you, you have no part with me."

Peter's eyes grew wide. "Lord, not my feet only, but also my hands and my head!"

Jesus eyed Peter intently. "He who is bathed needs only to wash his feet, but is completely clean; and you are clean but not all of you."

Mary watched this strange act of their Lord, and when Jesus came to Judas, he paused a moment looking up into the disciple's face. Judas opened his mouth as if to say something and quickly closed it again. He merely watched Jesus wash his feet and dry them. When Jesus moved on to the next disciple, Mary was surprised to see the disciple's face contorted, almost as if he were in pain.

When Jesus had put on his robe again, he looked around at his twelve disciples.

"Do you know what I have done to you? You call me Teacher and Lord, and you say well, for so I am. If then, your Lord and Teacher has washed your feet, you also ought to wash one another's feet. For I have given you an example that you should do as I have done to you."

The women sat in the back of the room, still astonished at this act of servitude. It was a task done by the lowest slave in a household for their master's guests. Jesus never failed to surprise them.

Then, as the women got up to serve, Jesus spoke to all of them. It seemed to Mary that there was an urgency about his words. As if it was vital that they understand what he was telling them.

The women listened to the traditional prayers as they refilled platters and wine goblets as needed.

Jesus said the *Kaddesh*, and the men went through the steps of the meal. The story of the exodus from Egypt was told by Matthew, the oldest of the disciples. There were no children to ask the traditional questions, and that part was omitted.

As they were eating, Jesus put down his food. "Assuredly, I say to you, one of you will betray me."

The women, who had retired to the far corner of the room to partake of their meal, looked at each other, as did the Twelve, who began murmuring among themselves and asking, "Lord, is it I?"

Jesus glanced at the bowl of lamb shank stew in front of him. "He who dipped his hand with me in the dish will betray me." Then he looked at each of them. "The Son of Man indeed goes just as it is written of him, but woe to that man by whom the Son of Man is betrayed! It would have been good for that man if he had not been born."

Peter motioned to John, who was next to Jesus, to ask of whom the Lord spoke. John then asked, "Lord, who is it?"

Jesus answered, "It is the one to whom I shall give a piece of the matzah when I have dipped it."

Then Jesus gave the bread to Judas. The other disciples were looking at each other, still not understanding. When Judas leaned forward and asked, seemingly innocently, "Lord, is it I?" Jesus answered quietly, "You have said it."

Mary frowned. What did the Lord mean, one would betray him? Then she glanced at the Lord's mother. From the look on the older woman's face, she knew his mother had also heard the words.

Judas rose suddenly, and without looking at anyone, gathered his cloak and strode out of the room.

Mary wondered what errand Jesus had sent him on.

Jesus took some of the matzah bread and blessed it. When he had broken it, he passed it around to his disciples. "Take, eat; this is my body that will be broken for you."

Then he took the final cup of wine for the meal and held it up. He gave thanks for it and then said, "Drink from it, all of you. For this is my blood of the new covenant, which is shed for many for the remission of sins. Do these things in remembrance of me. But I say to you, I will not drink of this fruit of the vine from now on until that day when I drink it new with you in my Father's kingdom."

Slowly the disciples passed the cup, one to another. The women watched. Since it was not an intimate gathering with their own families, they would not participate.

Jesus leaned on the table and spoke to them again. "All of you will be made to stumble because of me this night, for it is written: 'I will strike the Shepherd, and the sheep of the flock will be scattered.'

"But after I have been raised, I will go before you into Galilee."

Peter, who had been surprisingly silent through this, suddenly blurted out, "Even if all are made to stumble because of you, I will never be made to stumble."

Jesus turned to him, sadness evident on his face, and said gently, "Assuredly I say to you, that this night, before the rooster crows with the dawn, you will deny me three times."

Peter balled one fist. "Even if I have to die with you, I will not deny you!"

Jesus spoke of many strange things to them, that where he was going they could not come, and he gave them a new commandment, that they love one another as he had loved them. Then he told them that from now on, his disciples would be known by their love for each other.

The women listened, with Mary almost holding her breath as he spoke of his Father's kingdom, and of the Helper, the Holy Spirit, which the Father would send in his name, who would teach them all things. He spoke of leaving his peace with them—not the peace the world gave, but a different kind of peace.

"Let not your heart be troubled, you believe in God, believe also in me. In my Father's house are many mansions; if it were not so, I would have told you. I go to prepare a place for you. And if I go and prepare a place for you, I will come again and receive you to myself; that where I am, there you may be also. And where I go you know, and the way you know."

Thomas, the one the others had nicknamed the Doubter, spoke up. "Lord, we do not know where you are going and how can we know the way?"

As Jesus spoke the next words, Mary sensed power emanating from him.

"I am the way, the truth, and the life. No one comes to the Father except through me."

He spoke of many things and the hours seemed as moments, so rapt was their attention to their Lord.

Finally, he lifted his eyes toward heaven and

began to pray for all of them, words of eternal life and hope. Words to comfort them, beseeching the Father for those the Father had given him as Jesus walked the earth. It was a prayer to sanctify them—Peter, James, John, Matthew, Thomas, Andrew, Philip, Bartholomew, James the son of Alpheus, Thaddaeus, and Simon the Canaanite. Eleven only, with Judas still absent.

As Mary listened to his prayer, she felt joy rise up within her as she realized it was for her also. She pondered the meaning of his words when he said he had kept them all, except for the son of perdition, that the Scripture might be fulfilled.

Jesus then prayed, not only for his disciples, but for those who would believe in him by the word of his disciples. "And the glory which you gave me I have given them that they may be one just as we are one."

When he finished his prayer, there was a profound silence and Mary knew something had changed in her. She felt emboldened to go and tell the world who her Lord was. She almost laughed out loud at the joy that bubbled up inside. Jesus turned and looked straight at her, and in his smile she felt the love he had for her and for the others who had been with him so long.

She returned his look with devotion and in her heart whispered, "My Lord, and my God."

Jesus led them in a familiar hymn of Passover,

Eliyahu HaNavi (the song of Elijah the prophet). The words seemed to burn within her:

> Speedily and in our days, come to us,
> with the Messiah, son of David,
> with the Messiah, son of David.

At last, Jesus rose from the table and, beckoning Mary, said quietly, "When you have completed your tasks here, take my mother and sister to the place where they are lodging. Someone will come to accompany you."

Mary nodded. "Yes, Lord. But where will you and the others go?"

"We will cross the Kidron Valley to the Garden of Gethsemane, and spend the night there."

Mary was puzzled. "Can we not attend you there, Lord? Why must we be sent away?"

"You will understand soon enough, Mary of Magdala. Your devotion touches my heart, but your moment is not yet. Do as I ask, for my sake."

She bowed her head. "Yes, Lord, we will go with your mother."

"Thank you, Mary."

She watched the men go down the steps and suddenly felt a great loss.

❦ 37 ❦

Rebecca began to gather the platters while her mother and Susanna cleaned the olive wood wine goblets. The dishes would be left for the householder who had given them the upper room to use. Mary began to pack up the food that was not perishable to place in the cart. The rest would have to be thrown away, for it would not keep in the heat.

Susanna paused, holding a clay jar of the charoset. "Where are we to meet the Lord and the other disciples tomorrow? Will he be at the Temple?"

Mary shrugged. "He knows where we are staying. I'm sure he will send word with one of the men."

When the three women had completed what they had to do, they carried the small clay stove and the other things down to the cart. Mary's son Joses was waiting, having hitched the donkey to the cart. Joses held up his lamp and the women followed him through the darkened city. They huddled together, glancing from side to side as they walked. Clouds passed across the moon and gave Mary an eerie feeling. A dog growled in the shadows and she jumped in fright.

When they came to the house of Joanna where the women were staying, Mary learned that Chuza, Joanna's husband, was away at the palace.

The women embraced each other and were welcomed into the house.

Joanna took the elder Mary's arm. "My lady, and Rebecca, it is good you have returned safely." She turned to Joses. "Put the donkey in the stall in the corner of the courtyard."

The women each carried in the food left over from Passover to share with the household. When all was put away, Joanna led Mary and Susanna to a small room with two narrow beds where they would spend the night.

"How did the Passover supper go? Who was there?" Joanna looked eagerly at Mary.

"Just the Twelve—and Jesus of course. Judas was with them, but the Lord sent him out to do something."

"I'm sure you are both tired from the long evening. I hope you will be comfortable here. It was the room of my sons before they were grown. Our lady and Rebecca are sharing a room nearby. I will see you in the morning."

The hour was late and Mary was weary, but she looked forward to the morning when she and Susanna could once again join the Lord.

She slept fitfully. Not since before her healing had she had such a bad night. She was awake just as dawn was breaking over the city. Vowing to be as quiet as possible, she rose so as not to wake Susanna, who was still sleeping soundly. She dressed quickly and was about to leave the room when there was a pounding on the gate of the house.

She hurried down the corridor to the main room just as Joanna went with Joses to open the gate. It was Bartholomew. Tears ran down his cheeks as he almost fell into the courtyard, breathing heavily.

"They have arrested him!"

Joanna frowned. "Who have they arrested, and who are they?"

The disciple took a deep breath. "The Sanhedrin. The leaders have arrested Jesus. They came to the garden where we were sleeping. A crowd with swords, clubs, you'd think they were after a terrible criminal. They bound Jesus and took him away to the house of Caiaphas."

Mary stood in shock. Her gentle Lord, arrested and dragged away like a criminal?

Susanna appeared, as did the Lord's mother and Rebecca, wondering what all the excitement was about.

Mary went to his mother. "Dear lady, they have taken him."

The Lord's mother put a hand to her heart. "What happened?"

Bartholomew spat angrily, "They came with

clubs and swords to arrest him, led by Judas!"

Mary gasped. "Judas? He was the betrayer?"

Bartholomew nodded. "He came up to the Lord and kissed him. Evidently that was the signal, for they rushed forward and grabbed him. Peter had a sword and cut off the ear of one of the men." He shook his head in unbelief. "The Lord, even at that moment of arrest, reached out and healed the man's ear." He flung his hands up. "Could they not see who he was?"

The Lord's mother bowed her head and clasped her hands. "So the time has come."

Joses looked at her strangely. "Mother, I know you seek to protect him, you always have, but he has been flinging his teaching in their faces too long. Now he will have to suffer retribution. They will probably flog him and let him go."

Bartholomew nodded. "That is true. They cannot put him to death, it is against the Roman law they themselves imposed on us."

The distraught disciple sat down on a low stool and a small cup of wine was handed to him.

Joanna clasped her hands. "What else can you tell us?"

"John is related to the high priest. He was allowed into the hall, but Peter could only follow and remain outside for news. One of them will let us know what has happened as soon as they can."

The Lord's mother sat down on a bench. "We

can only wait and pray. He is in the hands of his Father."

Joses started to answer her, but pursed his lips and remained silent.

She has had grief enough, Mary thought, *she needs comfort now, not opinions.*

It was midmorning before there was another quick knock at the door. It was John. The agony of the night's events had aged him overnight. There were lines of grief on his face and dark circles under his eyes.

"The high priest has sentenced him to death. They are taking him to Pilate to carry out their terrible plan."

The elder Mary gasped. "They have sentenced my son to death? For what crime? He healed people, raised the dead, taught them from the Scriptures. What crime could they possibly sentence him for?"

John turned to her and went and knelt at her feet. "My lady, it is for the crime of blasphemy, for saying he was equal with God and claiming to be the Son of God."

She stood then, regal and tall, looking around at all of them. "For so he is!" Then she turned to her son. "Your father, Joseph, knew this."

Facing the group again, there was a look of wonder on her face. "Our people have looked for the Messiah, the promised Savior, for centuries. I have known who he was from his birth and carried that secret in my heart all these years."

Joses came closer. "What are you talking about? Why did you not share this with us?"

"Who would believe me? He was a normal child, growing up in a small village. How would anyone understand what your father and I experienced?"

"What did you experience? Are you sure you are not protecting him? You have always favored him above the rest of us."

She put up a hand. "You were not there in the stable in Bethlehem where he was born, when the shepherds came, and later when kings from the Far East came to the small house we were living in, following a star. Those great men presented him with gifts of gold, frankincense, and myrrh. You were not there when we fled to Egypt to escape the wrath of Herod who sought your brother to kill him. The men from the East told him a king had been born according to the Scriptures."

Joses put a hand to his beard and frowned. "Then Jesus was not born in Nazareth?"

She looked down at her hands. "No. I didn't know what the Father's plan was. For thirty years he was only my eldest son, yet in my heart I knew that his time would come one day. I just didn't know it would come to this." She put her face in her hands and began to weep.

Mary moved to put a comforting arm around her shoulders. The Lord's mother wiped her eyes on her shawl and again faced her son.

"He is not the son of your father but the son of the Father of us all."

Joses shook his head. "I don't know what to believe."

Rebecca interrupted them, crying out, "What can we do? We must save him!"

Her mother shook her head. "It is in the hands of the Most High, blessed be his name. I have felt great sorrow these past few weeks. He was moving toward something and determined to go to Jerusalem."

Mary looked around at their faces. "Then this is what he has been telling us all these months, that he would be taken? We did not really listen to what we were hearing. We did not want to believe."

John beckoned with his arm. "We'd better hurry. Let us go to the court of Pilate to see what he will do."

Mary thought a moment and then blurted, "Where is Peter? I thought he was with you."

John shook his head. "I have not seen him since we entered the house of Caiaphas. He was warming his hands at a fire in the courtyard. When we came out, he was gone."

Bartholomew rose from the stool. "I'll try to find him and the other disciples. They need to know what has happened. We scattered and I don't know where any of them are." He put a hand on John's shoulder briefly and left.

The small group hurried through the streets and was almost unable to enter the court for the crowd of people shaking their fists and crying out, "Crucify him!"

John held the Lord's mother up, for she was almost overcome with emotion.

The four women stood in the shadows with him. When the soldiers brought Jesus out to the crowd, the small loyal group collectively gasped. He was a horrible sight to see. They had flogged him and put his robe back on. Blood seeped through the fabric as he stood swaying before Pilate. A crown of spiked thorns had been pressed onto his head and small rivulets of blood ran down his face.

The Jewish leaders were moving among the crowd, stirring them into a frenzy.

Mary couldn't believe her ears. The same people who had followed the Lord and had him heal their sick were now crying out for his death. Tears ran unchecked down her cheeks as she realized what was happening.

The elder Mary turned to her son Joses, but he had disappeared in the crowd.

To her horror and those with her, Pilate, following his custom of releasing a prisoner to mollify the people each year, sentenced Jesus to be crucified and released Barabbas, a known murderer and zealot. It could not be. Jesus was innocent of any crime!

People brushed past her as the soldiers brought out a large wooden cross and forced Jesus to bear it as they led him out into the street.

John took the arm of the Lord's mother. "Come, I know a shortcut, we can get closer to him."

The women hurried behind them as they went through back streets, coming out a short distance ahead of the procession.

People were crying out, some denouncing Jesus as a fraud, but others weeping and begging for his release.

Ahead of Jesus came two men, condemned criminals, carrying crosses. Their backs also showed the effects of the Roman whips as they were driven toward Golgotha. Then his mother gave a horrified sob as Jesus came into view.

Mary gasped, feeling almost physically ill. The Lord's body and face were hardly recognizable as they watched him stagger under the weight of the cross. Blood dripped from his body onto the stones of the street.

Rebecca wrapped her arms around herself and rocked back and forth with grief. "What have they done to him? Oh what have they done?" she cried over and over.

Suddenly, the procession stopped for a moment for something up ahead they couldn't see. Jesus, almost on his knees under the weight of the cross, looked up directly into the face of his mother.

"My son, my son," she whispered through her tears, and slipped out of the crowd to kneel at his side. "My dear son." She wiped his face with a corner of her shawl.

Just then a Roman soldier rudely pushed her away. "Leave the prisoner alone. Get back." He raised his whip.

She looked him in the eye. He was young, younger than Jesus. "I am his mother," she said quietly.

The soldier glanced at his fellow soldiers in front who were not looking his way. A brief look of compassion crossed his face, but he shook his head. "I'm sorry for you, woman, and for your son, but you must step away."

"Please, help him," she begged the soldier as she stepped back.

John took her arm and pulled her back into the crowd. To their immense relief, the soldier grabbed a large, heavyset man out of the crowd and ordered him to help carry the cross. The eyes of the young soldier sought his prisoner's mother in the crowd, and for a brief second, they acknowledged one another, then he moved on, snapping his whip in the air, but not at Jesus.

Mary and the others followed the procession to the hill called Golgotha and the women wept openly. Mary felt each blow of the hammer as the nails were driven into the gentle hands that had touched and healed so many. Her stomach churned at the pounding of the large nail into his feet and hearing him cry out in agony. She struggled to keep her composure to strengthen his mother, whose body also jolted with each strike of the hammer.

At last the huge cross was lifted and a soldier tacked on a sign above him, supposedly telling his crime.

Mary, thanks to Nathan, could read both Hebrew and Greek. Her eyes widened. "It says, 'Jesus of Nazareth, the King of the Jews.' "

Salome cried out, "Pilate must have ordered that to be placed on his sign. Is there a crime listed?"

Mary stared and shook her head, feeling the anger rise up. "He committed no crime. Pilate only gave in to the people because he feared their displeasure. You heard them threaten to complain to Rome. He posted that sign deliberately to taunt the priests."

John murmured. "They were jealous of him and the way he exposed them. Now they have their revenge."

Some of the priests and scribes almost strutted in front of the cross. "He saved others, let him save himself, and we will believe in him."

Behind the cross, the soldiers were throwing

dice, and to Mary's horror, she realized the prize was the robe she had woven and given to Jesus. She felt the heat rise to her face at the thought of it being in the hands of a Roman soldier.

"It is in one piece," one of the soldiers said. "We'll cast lots for it."

Jesus, in agony, looked at his mother and then toward John. "Woman, behold your son." Then he looked at John and indicated his mother. "Behold, your mother."

John nodded his understanding. She stoically endured her son's agony but could hardly stand. Almost in a daze, she allowed John to move her back from the scene. He glanced back at Mary and the other women, a question in his eyes.

"We will stay also," Mary told him, and turned back to the cross. They were not leaving him now, in his darkest hour.

❖ 38 ❖

Mary and the small group of women huddled together, watching as the hours went by. John kept a strong arm around the Lord's mother and Rebecca leaned against her mother during the long vigil. From time to time Mary looked back at the crowd, now strangely subdued. Where were the other disciples? The men who had walked with the Lord these past three years? Where was Peter? He had promised to give his life for the Lord. How quickly they had deserted him when he needed them the most.

She looked back at the cross. The Lord knew they were there, his eyes had flicked in their direction once or twice in his agony. They would be there—until the end.

The men on either side of Jesus at first taunted him, and she wanted to shout at them to be quiet.

Finally, one of the thieves looked over at Jesus and spoke through cracked lips. "We deserve our punishment, but you do not. Lord, remember me when you come into your kingdom."

"Today, my son, you will be with me in Paradise."

There was silence for a long while and someone held a sponge up to him with sour wine on it. He tasted the sponge, and then cried out, "It is finished." He looked up again. "Into your hands, Father, I commit my spirit."

As his body slumped on the cross, Mary moaned and put her fist to her mouth. His ordeal was over. He had died at last.

Many of the crowd who had at first come to see the spectacle had dispersed. She looked defiantly at their faces, but no one looked back at her. They slunk away from their places as if suddenly ashamed at what they'd done.

Mary stood with the others and they exchanged glances. What were they to do now?

The centurion who had overseen the crucifixion was waiting for his task to be over. A soldier hurried up to him and spoke a few words. The centurion nodded. He turned to the soldiers standing nearby.

"The Jews want the legs broken to hasten their death so they won't remain on the crosses—some high holy day is approaching."

The soldiers took one of the hammers and broke the legs of the two thieves, who barely had the strength to cry out. Death came quickly as they slumped on their crosses. When they came to Jesus, Mary wanted to beg them to leave him alone. He had suffered enough at their hands. She put a fist to her mouth, and she and Susanna clutched each other. Strangely, when the soldiers saw Jesus was already dead, they didn't touch him.

One turned to the centurion. "This one is dead already," but he drew his sword and pierced the Lord's side just to be sure.

He had no sooner done that when there was a rumbling in the sky and great dark storm clouds gathered out of nowhere. The earth began to shake, sending rocks tumbling down the hill. A sudden wind blew down on those who frantically ran from Golgotha. Mary and Susanna clung to each other in fear and trembling.

The centurion looked about at the people running back to Jerusalem to escape the storm and then back at the cross. The words he spoke engraved themselves on Mary's heart.

"Surely this man was the Son of God."

When the wind died down as suddenly as it began and all was quiet, two figures made their way up the hill. To Mary's surprise, they were priests. One looked familiar to her. She had seen him before.

They approached the centurion and the soldiers who were in the midst of taking the bodies down. One soldier laid the body of the Lord on the ground. Mary, the Lord's mother, John, and Susanna rushed to him, and his mother cradled the head of her son in her lap, sobbing quietly and stroking his face.

Mary turned to hear what the priest was saying to the centurion.

"I am Joseph of Arimathea. I have been given permission to take the body of Jesus. The Sabbath draws near and the body must be taken care of. I have a tomb nearby where he may be placed." He handed the centurion a small scroll.

The centurion glanced at the seal on the scroll and nodded curtly, as the soldiers unceremoniously flung the bodies of the two thieves on a cart and left. The second priest stepped forward and put a hand on the shoulder of the elder Mary. She lifted agonized eyes to his face and saw not scorn but compassion. John helped her up and the women stepped back as the two priests, after carefully wrapping the Lord's body, carried it toward the tomb.

Mary turned to Susanna. "I don't know Joseph of Arimathea, other than that he is a member of the Sanhedrin, but the other man is Nicodemus. He came to the Garden of Gethsemane one night to speak with the Lord."

Susanna nodded. "He is a leading priest, and I have heard that he is a believer. Let's follow them and find out where they are taking the Lord's body."

When they turned from the cross, they saw another small group of women who had followed Jesus—Salome was among them. They did not speak, but the women acknowledged each other.

Zebedee's wife joined them, but the women with her made their way back to the city.

John would have gone on with the Lord's mother, but she stopped him. "You may leave us for now, John. I will see you back at the house of Joanna. We wish to see where the priests are putting my son's body. After the Sabbath we can go and prepare him for burial."

John nodded. "I need to be less visible. Who knows what the wrath of the Sanhedrin will bring. I'm going to inquire in Jerusalem of some of the believers. They will know where the rest of us are."

"I will be at the home of Joanna for the Sabbath and you can join me there. I hope you find Bartholomew and Peter."

The four women followed the two priests to the tomb. Nicodemus took a package from a bag he carried over his shoulder, and the men went into the open cave.

The women noted the place of the tomb.

The Lord's mother spoke softly. "We will return after the Sabbath and prepare my son's body for a proper burial. Come, let us return to Joanna's, the sun is low and the Sabbath is near."

They had just reached the home of Joanna when the shofar sounded the beginning of the Sabbath.

Joses was sitting in the courtyard, his face drawn and gray. As his mother approached, he looked up at her with eyes that seemed like sockets in his head. "Forgive me, Mother, I could not stay. I did not agree with him, but he was my brother. Forgive me."

Mary put a gentle hand on her son's cheek. "You always had a weak stomach, Joses, even as a little boy. There is nothing to forgive. I knew."

He covered the hand with his own and leaned against her. "I'm so sorry. I'm so sorry," he moaned over and over.

She drew him to his feet. "The Sabbath must be attended to, Joses. Since Joanna's husband is not here, you must do his part." She looked into his eyes, willing her strength to him.

Then he stood and gathered himself, and led them into the house to do what they needed to do.

It was a somber group that went through the ceremonial motions of the Sabbath that night. They did as commanded, but there was no joy in this Sabbath. The songs echoed through the city, but it seemed to Mary to be subdued and more the sound of mourning than praise.

❄ 39 ❄

When the shofar sounded, marking the end of the Sabbath, Mary, Rebecca, and Susanna hurried to the marketplace to purchase burial spices. It took the last of the money Mary had kept back from Judas, but she had enough to buy what they needed. They hurried back to the house where they found Jesus's mother and Joanna tearing linen into strips to wrap the Lord's body. Tired and weary from grief, they all rested for the night.

The next morning Mary was up before the sun rose. She met the Lord's mother and Rebecca in the main room of the house.

Joanna had set out some bread and strained goat's milk, and they ate quickly, not knowing how long they would be at the tomb. They gathered all the things they had prepared the night before. The four women left the household and, huddling together in the cold and darkness of the early morning, hurried to the tomb where they had seen Joseph of Arimathea and Nicodemus take the body.

His mother murmured, "I'm worried about the stone. Who can we get to roll it away for us? I'm afraid it is too heavy to move."

Rebecca whispered, "Remember, there were soldiers coming toward the tomb as we left—a guard of some kind. Maybe the leaders wanted to check and be sure he was buried. I'm sure we can find someone."

Mary looked at her with alarm. "If Pilate has sent soldiers, they may not let us near the tomb at all."

"They would not let me properly bury my son?"

The women stopped walking. Mary looked around at them. "I think we should pray for HaShem to lead us."

They bowed their heads and fervently prayed to be able to do what they had come for.

When they reached the tomb, they stopped and stared. There were no soldiers, and the large stone had been rolled away. Fearfully they approached the entrance to the tomb. There was a strange light inside. Staying close together, they ducked through the narrow opening. Mary gasped, as did the others. The light was emanating from a being nearly nine cubits high. He was clothed in a shimmering white robe.

"Do not be alarmed. You seek Jesus of Nazareth, who was crucified. He has risen! He is not here. See the place where they laid him." He swept one hand toward the slab where the linen burial cloths lay, along with the head cloth. "Remember what he told you when he was still in Galilee, saying, 'The Son of Man must be delivered into the hands of sinful men, and be crucified, and the third day rise again.' "

The Lord's mother clasped her hands and her face glowed with joy. "It is true then!"

The being smiled at her. "Yes, most blessed one. As you were told many years ago, he has fulfilled his purpose."

"Are you the one who came to me?"

"Yes, most blessed one."

Mary listened with awe to this conversation. She tried to speak, but no words came out of her mouth. What could this being be but an angel sent from the Most High God? She fell to her knees, as did Susanna and Rebecca.

The voice of the angel filled the tomb. "Go, tell his disciples—and Peter—that you will see him as he said to you."

There was a great flash of light and the angel was gone.

The four women hastily fled the tomb and stood in the middle of the garden in uncertainty.

Joanna ventured, "How are we to tell the disciples if we don't know where they are?"

Mary took a deep breath, pulling herself together. The Lord's mother was weary, as they all were, for lack of sleep and overcome by the emotion of what they had just experienced. Mary put an arm around the older woman's shoulders.

"Dear lady, why don't you and Rebecca go back

to the house with Joanna and tell them what we saw and heard. Perhaps John or Peter will bring word there. Susanna and I will go to the upper room and see if they are there."

The women parted and Mary and Susanna hurried as fast as they dared in the early morning light to the house where they'd celebrated the Passover. Mary prayed fervently that she could find it again.

To her relief, she spotted the house. When she and Susanna came pounding up the stairs and entered the upper room, some of the men jumped up suddenly and stared at them. The eleven disciples were indeed there, along with some of the women. Their faces were stark with fear.

Peter stepped forward. "We thought you were the Temple police! How did you find us?"

Mary gathered her breath. "I didn't know where else you would go." She looked around at them all and joyously cried, "We have the most wondrous news. The Lord lives. He has risen, just as he said he would."

There was dead silence. Peter stared dumbly at her and John came over. "What are you saying? He is dead. We saw him die on the cross."

"Yes! Yes!" she cried. "But the angel told us he has risen when we went to the tomb to prepare his body. Susanna, Rebecca, and our Lord's mother were there. They saw him also."

Peter huffed. "An angel? You were seeing

348

things. It was dark, you just went to the wrong tomb."

Mary stood her ground. "Then if you won't believe me, come and see for yourselves."

Peter and John looked at each other and then hurried from the room and down the stairs, with Mary and Susanna right behind them.

John outran Peter and they both found the tomb still open with the stone rolled away. John rushed inside. Peter joined him and they stared at the linen cloths lying on the slab. John picked up the cloth that had been around the Lord's head, folded together in a place by itself.

Peter scratched his head. "He is gone. Where could they have taken him?"

Taken him? Mary stared at them. Then looking around the dark tomb, doubts began to creep into her mind. Could someone have taken the body? Could she and the other women have dreamed what they saw? She shook her head. There were four of them and they all saw the same being. Yet doubts persisted. Could the Jewish leaders be so cruel as to steal the body away?

Peter and John decided to return to the upper room and tell the others what they had seen, and Susanna went with them to share again with the other women. Mary, dispirited and near tears, remained at the tomb, her thoughts confused.

Where was the Lord? Would she never see him again?

A figure moved among the trees nearby, and at first she was frightened. She stood still, poised to run away. What was she thinking to remain here alone?

A voice said gently, "Woman, why are you weeping?"

Before she thought, she replied, "I don't know where they have taken my Lord."

The voice spoke again, as the figure moved closer and stepped out of the shadows. "Mary."

Only one person said her name like that. She gave a cry and fell on her knees before him. "Teacher!" Joy and amazement coursed through her body. Was it another dream? Did she want to see her Lord so badly that her mind was playing tricks on her?

He stepped back slightly. "Do not cling to me, Mary, for I have not yet ascended to my Father; but go to my brethren and tell them I am ascending to my Father and your Father, and to my God and your God."

She sat back on her heels and stared up at him. Yes, the dark wavy hair and heavy brows. The luminous eyes, filled with compassion. He looked the same, beard and all. Mary rose, and with joy filling her being, faced her Lord. "It is you."

He nodded and smiled at her in that familiar way before disappearing into the mist. *Go.*

Mary felt her feet weren't even touching the ground as she hurried back to the upper room.

She felt she would burst with the happiness inside.

"I have seen him. He has spoken with me." She told them what he had said to tell them, then without waiting to argue with Peter, Susanna joined her as she left them and hurried back through the streets that were now coming alive with merchants and their wares.

When they reached the home of Joanna and were admitted, the mother of Jesus, Rebecca, and Joanna rushed toward her.

"I have seen the Lord," she cried.

They clustered around her, and quickly she shared what had transpired in the garden. She turned to his mother. "Oh, my Lady, I have seen your son. I have seen our precious Lord."

His mother clasped her hands, glad tears running down her cheeks. "Oh, dear one, how blessed you have been. What a gift he has given you—the first to see him in his resurrected body. Then I shall see him also one day."

Mary gazed at her friends, beaming. "He told us, remember? He told us over and over and we didn't understand. We were looking for a conquering king, and the suffering Messiah had to come first. I remember from the scrolls. My father wanted me to learn the Torah and the Law. As his only child I was privileged to study the precious words of the Most High God, and the words of the prophets and the psalms. In the Twenty-second Psalm, I remember being puzzled as to what it meant, but it describes the death of our Lord and how he would die. I didn't understand until now."

The elder Mary smiled at her. "There is a reason in each thing that happens in our lives. The Most High will use your knowledge, Mary, to bring others into the kingdom."

Rebecca spoke up. "Mother, what should we do now?"

The elder Mary thought a moment. "I feel strongly that we should return to the upper room."

Mary nodded. "You are right, dear lady, I feel that is where we should go also. We must join the others to strengthen their faith and wait to see what the Lord will do next."

The women packed provisions in baskets to share with the other disciples, and when the baskets were filled and ready, they each took what they could carry and hurried to the upper room with light hearts.

Those in the upper room were relieved when the women arrived with the food. Many had not eaten in two days. As the day wore on, people murmured among themselves, discussing what they had heard from Mary and sharing the wonder of the story over and over. No one seemed tired of listening.

By the time two more days had passed, some were getting restless and wondering what to do next. The disciples disagreed on what to do. Peter insisted that they should stay one more night and then the next day slip out of the city in twos, for he feared the religious leaders were looking for them.

Mary looked around. "Where is Judas? He knows this place. You are not safe here either."

Peter scowled at her. "Judas is dead. He was found hanging from a tree in the potter's field. A just end for one who would betray the Lord."

Mary stood still, trying to understand what he was saying. "But why would he betray Jesus? He was one of you."

Andrew spoke up. "He was a zealot. Who knows what was in his mind."

John came forward. "At the Passover meal, when we asked who was going to betray him, the Lord told us plainly and gave the sop to Judas. We were just too blind to see."

Mary remembered the Lord's words. She too thought Judas had left them to do some errand for the Lord. John was right. Jesus knew he was going to be betrayed by Judas and told them.

Peter shook his head. "If we had realized, we might have stopped him."

Mary put a hand on his arm. "But could we have stopped him? Wasn't this what the Lord was telling us all along, that he would be arrested and killed, but that he would rise again? Judas must have felt remorse if he killed himself." She felt compassion for him. Judas had wanted so badly to conquer the hated Romans and saw Jesus as the means to do that. He must have been sorely disillusioned.

Evening came and the food the women had brought was running out. The group was subdued and continued to talk quietly among themselves. The disciples were more animated, still arguing over what to do next.

Then he was there, standing in their midst, just as he had appeared to Mary in the garden. "Peace be with you. As the Father has sent me, so I shall send you."

They sat immobile, staring at him as though he were a ghost and they were unable to speak. He smiled gently at them, as a father would look at beloved children. "Behold my hands and feet, that it is I myself. Handle me and see, for a spirit does not have flesh and bones as you see I have."

His mother rose and walked slowly to him, tears rolling down her cheeks. She slowly reached out and gently touched the wounded hands—hands that she held when he was a child. She looked up in his face for a long moment as the others sat, holding their breath. Then his mother bowed her head. "My Lord," she said softly. And they knew it was no longer her son who stood before her, but the Lord of them all.

Mary went slowly to his side also and was joined by Peter and the others as they crowded around him. Jesus held out his hands, plainly showing them the place where the nails had pierced them.

"Have you any food here?"

Susanna ran for some leftover broiled fish and a piece of honeycomb. He ate it in their presence and they marveled anew.

Still in awe, they settled down around him, realizing he was going to teach them again. "These are the words which I spoke to you while I was still with you, that all things must be fulfilled which were written in the Law of Moses and the Prophets and the Psalms concerning me." And he opened their understanding that they might this time comprehend what he had taught them. Scripture after Scripture came back to Mary's mind—things she had read long ago and not understood. Jesus made it all so clear.

"Thus it is written, and thus it was necessary for the Christ to suffer and to rise from the dead the third day, and that repentance and remission of sins should be preached in my name to all nations, beginning at Jerusalem. And you are witnesses of these things. I will soon send the Promise of my Father upon you; but tarry here in the City of Jerusalem until you are endued with power from on high."

He stayed the rest of the night with them, telling them the things they must know and emphasizing that they must remain in the city for this special anointing. Mary was puzzled as to what this might be, but she would wait with the others. She could not take her eyes off the Lord. He was the same and yet different. His garments were white like the being she'd seen at the tomb, yet light did not emanate from them. His face and body had been bruised and bloody when she'd seen him on the cross, but just as he'd appeared in the garden and now sat before them, he was without a trace of the marks of the whip he'd endured. She watched him gesture with his hands, and awe filled her again as she saw the jagged holes where the soldiers had driven the nails. The same jagged holes were in his feet, yet they did not bleed. The disciples needed proof that he was indeed the same, and the marks were blatantly visible for all of them to see.

Mary realized that what he'd told them about the resurrection was true, and one day she too would have a resurrected body. The thought amazed and delighted her. Then, out of nowhere, the thought came to her that she would see her Nathan again, just as she was seeing the Lord this night. She held the thought to her heart.

She listened to the words of her Lord and was filled with overwhelming joy. To think that she had lived to see the Messiah Israel had longed for through the centuries. Happiness bubbled up inside her and spilled out like an overflowing spring.

When dawn sent its golden streamers through the windows of the upper room, Mary gathered the women and the entire group left the upper room and walked through the Kidron Valley again to a familiar place, the Mount of Olives.

Mary clasped her hands. The five women waited anxiously for what he would do next. He raised his hands and blessed those gathered in front of him and then he began to rise into the air and disappeared. Mary watched, her eyes wide. Was he being taken up to heaven?

The entire company, their eyes still looking up, broke into words of praise and thanksgiving for the wonderful things they had seen and gave God the glory. They searched the clouds, not knowing what would happen next.

Suddenly Mary and the others were startled as two heavenly beings in white appeared before them. *Who are they?* Mary wondered. *Are they angels? Where did they come from?* She could only listen and stare.

Their voices resonating in the early morning air, the beings spoke to the gathered disciples. "Why do you stand still gazing up at the clouds? This same Jesus, who was taken up from you into heaven will so come in like manner as you saw him go into heaven." Then with a flash of light, the heavenly beings disappeared.

They were like the being she and the other women had seen in the tomb. Angels? They had to be—sent from the Most High God to remind them of the Scriptures.

Unable to speak, Mary clasped her hands. Joy rose up like a fountain within her. What wonders they had been privileged to see and experience.

Peter finally broke the stunned silence. "My friends and fellow believers, let us return to the upper room and wait as the Lord has commanded for the Promise of the Father. I do not know what that means, but he told us to wait for it and that is what we should do."

Mary observed Peter, standing tall before them. He had always been the bold one of the group. She smiled to herself. The big fisherman had come a long way and now was taking the place of leadership, and she was sure the Lord had known he would.

❈ 40 ❈

On the way back to the upper room behind the other disciples, Mary mulled over in her mind the amazing things that had happened in the last few weeks. She could scarce begin to put it all together. What a blessing to have been able to follow her Lord for these last two years. And as the Lord's mother pointed out, what a privilege she had been granted, of all the disciples, to be the first to see the resurrected Lord. Now that he was gone, she searched for her purpose and a direction.

Unconsciously thoughts of Magdala began to creep into her mind. There was nothing for her here in Jerusalem. Her headstrong nature had clashed with Peter more than once. Brash, impulsive Peter. He was still a little rough, but she realized Jesus had been grooming him for leadership, even from the beginning. Perhaps it was time for her to return home. A touch of homesickness assailed her, but she put it aside. First, she would wait on the Lord as he asked. He would show her his plan for her life.

Two days later, Mary was delighted that the disciples were joined by the entire family of Jesus. His brothers—James, Joses, Simon, and Judas—had heard of all the events and acknowledged who he truly was. Other believers joined them until there were over a hundred people in the room. The Lord's mother, Susanna, Joanna, Salome, Mary, wife of Cleopas, and other women were part of the group and helped Mary prepare and serve food to the others.

As other disciples and friends came and went, to Mary's relief, they brought additional food to share with the others.

When not serving, Mary sought a quiet corner of the room to pray. As she looked around, she saw that, though the believers were diverse, they were of one mind and heart in praising God and praying together.

One afternoon, as Mary was praying, she was interrupted by Peter, who stood up in their midst and said, "Men and brethren, this Scripture had to be fulfilled, which the Holy Spirit spoke before by the mouth of David concerning Judas, who became a guide for those who arrested Jesus; for he was numbered with us and obtained a part of this ministry. It is written in the book of Psalms, 'Let his dwelling place be desolate, and no one live in it. Let another take his office.' "

He looked around at the faces turned up to him. "Therefore, of these men who have accompanied us all the time that the Lord Jesus went in and out among us, beginning from the baptism of John to that day when he was taken up from us, one of these must become a witness with us of his resurrection."

Mary looked around the group, unsure of who might be the one to take the place of Judas. The group talked among themselves, and finally John stood and named two men who were proposed— Justus and Matthias.

She looked at the face of Matthias and then Justus. Both were good men.

The disciples bowed their heads and earnestly prayed for the Lord's guidance. Mary felt strongly for one of the two and when the lots were cast, she was pleased that it fell to Matthias. So he was numbered with the eleven apostles.

As the Day of Pentecost neared, some, including Mary, were tempted to leave, since nothing had happened for almost ten days. How long were they to wait?

Peter, always impatient, was ready to go fishing again, but Mary urged them all to stay a little longer. After some grumbling, the disciples finally agreed, and Mary suggested Peter lead them in a united fervent prayer for the Lord's leading.

While she gave herself to prayer, a sudden strange wind began to blow through the room. It was a wind they could feel, and yet the wicks in the lamps continued to burn steadily. The wind filled the whole house, and then above each of them appeared a tongue of fire. Mary gasped as the power filled her being. She felt rooted to where she was sitting, unable to move. Inexplicable joy began to flow through her body, and she raised her hands as the emotion coursed through her body. She began to cry out in a language she didn't know, but sensed she was praising HaShem. Then the entire group began speaking in strange languages, praising the Holy One and giving him glory. Unable to contain themselves, all those in the upper room spilled out into the street.

Mary was unaware of the number of people at first, so caught up was she in the language that flowed from her mouth and the joy that filled her. Some of the women, caught up in the power of the Spirit, were dancing in the street.

When she opened her eyes, those in the street in front of the house were pointing to her and the other disciples, murmuring among themselves. She couldn't blame them for being curious at this strange phenomenon. Some observers cried out, "I hear what they are saying in my language!" Others cried, "They are praising the Most High God and telling of his wonderful works!"

Mary looked around at the crowd and saw from the various styles of clothing that these men were from all parts of the Roman Empire: Parthians, Medes, Elamites, Egyptians, Libyans, Cretans, and Arabs. Each man seemed to be hearing his own language, telling of the wonderful works of God.

"What can this all mean?" cried a man from the crowd. Another laughed and shouted, "They are all full of new wine!" and the crowd laughed with him.

Then Peter found a table to stand on and began to speak. "Brethren, these are not drunk, as you suppose. As you know, it is only nine o'clock in the morning. But this is what was spoken by the prophet Joel. He told us, 'And it shall come to pass in the last days, says God, that I will pour out my Spirit on all flesh and your sons and your daughters shall prophesy' . . ." As he shared the prophecy from Joel, he then began to admonish them for seeing the miracles Jesus had done, and yet not believing. He spoke for nearly thirty minutes and then cried out, "Therefore, let all the house of Israel know assuredly that God has made this Jesus, whom you crucified, both Lord and Christ."

The people were beside themselves. Mary listened to the anguish they expressed at the truth they had just heard. The words of the Lord came back to her mind, something he had said once. "You shall know the truth and the truth shall set you free."

One after another, the people cried out, "Men and brethren, what shall we do?"

Peter answered, "Repent and let every one of you be baptized in the name of Jesus Christ for the remission of sins; and you shall receive the gift of the Holy Spirit. For the promise is to you and to your children, and to all who are afar off, as many as the Lord our God will call."

One by one the people agreed and Mary was amazed. Peter was only a poor fisherman, unlearned, and yet here he was, under the power of the Holy Spirit, speaking with knowledge and conviction to thousands.

Still filled with that wondrous joy, Mary felt almost giddy as she slowly climbed the stairs to the upper room with Susanna. Both women were wondering what they should do now.

Halfway up the stairs, someone called her

name, and Mary turned to see a familiar figure making his way toward her.

"Uncle Zerah, how good to see you! What are you doing here?"

"You forget, my dear Mary, I come for Pentecost. Amos and Daniel are with me. We had word the Lord was here in Jerusalem and planned to find you."

As the fervor of the people increased, he shook his head and spread an arm toward the crowd. "This is something I could not have believed. We have heard story after story since we got here, of the Lord's tragic death, and now this."

"Oh, Uncle, it has been such a time to remember, to walk and talk with the Lord, to see the miracles. The crucifixion was terrible to behold, and just when we had all despaired of seeing him again, he appeared to us, in his resurrected body. He even ate with us."

"I'm sure you have a great deal to share, Mary. Where are you staying?"

"At the house of Joanna, but her husband is King Herod's steward. With all that has happened, I'm not sure if I am to go back there."

He paused and studied her thoughtfully. "What will you do then?"

The thought came to her gently but firmly and she knew what she was to do. Peace flowed through her being and spilled out in a brilliant smile.

"Just let me get my things."

❊ 41 ❊

Mary was delighted. Her uncle could not have come at a better time. She wasn't sure she could have fully explained this outpouring of God's Spirit to Zerah. Amos and Daniel had experienced this great move of God for themselves.

As Mary walked with the three men toward the marketplace, Daniel was anxious to tell her about the new ship. "It is smaller in comparison to other merchant ships, but the largest one we have built, and sailing on its maiden voyage right now."

Mary glanced at Daniel and marveled. The young boy who had been so skinny when she left was now almost six feet tall and filled out from hard work in the boatyard.

"Oh Daniel, Nathan dreamed of building a boat like that one day. When will it be returning to Magdala so I can see it?"

He grinned. "About the time we reach home."

Mary walked beside the cart as Amos led the donkey by its bridle. At first Zerah wanted to sell the donkey and cart, then realized Mary still needed it to carry what she wanted to bring home. He went ahead of them to locate the other members of the Jewish community who had traveled to Jerusalem with them. They would meet at the northern gate of the city.

When they reached the Temple, Mary stopped a moment to observe the building, magnificent in its structure. "The Lord told us that there will come a day when not one stone would remain standing."

Daniel looked at the great blocks of stone. "How would any army throw one of those down?"

"I don't know, Daniel, but one thing I do know. When the Lord said something would happen, it happened. Perhaps it is not in our lifetime."

Mary thought of how many times she and the other women had stood in the shadows of the great pillars and listened to the Master teach the people. It was difficult leaving the women who had meant so much to her these last two years: Mary, the mother of her Lord; Joanna; Salome; and of course the one who had become as a sister to her, Susanna. How much they had experienced together on their travels with the Lord.

Mary had embraced each of them, and with tears in their eyes, they all promised to pray for each other. What a precious bond they had shared. Mary would never forget them.

The Lord's mother was returning to Nazareth with three of her sons and her daughter, Rebecca. They had much to share with their friends and neighbors. Her son James announced he would stay in Jerusalem and help Peter with the growing church. After Pentecost, they had over three thousand people to baptize.

Some of the disciples were returning to homes and families, but some were spreading out to other parts of Israel to spread the good news of the Gospel.

As Mary, Amos, and Daniel approached the gate, Zerah was waiting for them with other men from Magdala. Some nodded, acknowledging her, but the faces of the more orthodox Jews appeared cold and disapproving.

Amos had been quiet for some time, and as they began the road to Magdala, Mary finally asked him, "How are things with you, Amos? Is anything wrong?"

"My wife is having our first child at any time. I fear I shall not return home in time for the birth."

"Oh, Amos, I am so glad for you. The Lord loved the little children so. He blessed them whenever they came around him."

"When our child is old enough, he or she will know about Jesus. I pray my wife will understand what I've seen. She is not a believer yet."

"I will pray for you both, Amos. I know I have so much I want to share—with everyone. I will be glad to talk with her."

He nodded.

She listened to the sights and sounds of the

countryside around her as she had done so many times, walking with the Lord. This time her footsteps were bringing her back to Magdala. She could hardly wait to see the harbor again, and old friends. How was Huldah doing, and Merab? She thought of Keturah and her husband and the chubby baby she had held before she left. She listened to the birdcalls and passed fields of waving wheat, the golden kernels nearly ready for harvest. It saddened her that nearly all of her family was gone now, but still, Magdala, in spite of its dark secrets, and the Hippodrome—it was familiar and it was home.

How nice it would be to live in a house again —she'd spent so many nights sleeping under the stars, or in rainy weather, wherever they could find shelter. Yet she wouldn't trade those days following the Lord for the grandest house. She had walked with the Messiah, had seen the miracles, and had heard his teaching. She would never be the same again.

❋ 42 ❋

As each day passed, Mary could feel the excitement building. Home. It was like a magnet drawing her back. In the evenings after their meal, Mary shared about the Lord. Her uncle Zerah, Daniel, and Amos listened with drawn faces as she described the day of the crucifixion. They had all seen this particular form of Roman justice before and shook their heads in sorrow at the agony the Lord had endured. Then she told them about the morning she went to the tomb with the other women and watched their faces change to exultation at the Lord's promise to rise again, fulfilled. The orthodox Jews did not join them, but more than once she looked up to see some of them nearby, pretending to be occupied with something.

Daniel leaned forward. "What about Lazarus? Did Jesus really raise him from the dead? He was not just unconscious?"

"Daniel, he was in the tomb four days. When he came out, he was wrapped in graveclothes."

"Tell me again. What did Jesus do?"

"He just cried out for Lazarus to come forth. And he came."

Zerah listened thoughtfully. "If I had not seen the people he healed that day in Magdala, including you, Mary, I would not have believed. He only had to speak a word and years of suffering ended."

She looked into his face, sensing he was feeling again his part in her ordeal. "One thing I learned, walking with the Lord, is that there was a purpose in everything he did. I don't know why my suffering lasted so long, but my healing was in his time. And to think he allowed me the privilege of being the very first person to see him in his resurrected body."

As she repeated the joy of that magnificent morning, she felt the awe fill her heart again. When they camped, she found herself rising early in the morning as she'd seen the Lord do so many times, to spend time in prayer with HaShem, to praise him and trust him to lead her. Now she knew why Jesus had done that. It was the strength that moved his ministry.

While there were so many incidents to tell about, some things she kept in her heart. How could she share the memory of the Lord's rich, deep laughter, his pleasure at a story one of the disciples told? Or how could she ever see bread broken for a Passover meal without thinking of that night in the upper room when he explained how his body and blood were sacrificed for them? How he loved people, taking such delight in seeing them healed and whole. How the Lord had smiled at her when she gave him the robe she'd woven for Nathan. Then she remembered that same robe, stained with his blood, and the soldiers gambling for it at the cross. It was as if a knife pierced her heart.

When they at last came over the hills and the city was spread out before them, Mary caught her breath. She walked faster when she reached the street where her home was waiting. Daniel ran ahead to let the neighborhood know she was coming.

Neighbors waved and smiled at her when she passed. What a contrast, she thought, to the day she'd walked the street on her wedding day with Nathan. When she and Amos reached her home, her old friends were waiting. She smiled at Aaron and Samuel and embraced Huldah and Merab, women as dear as aunts to her.

Keturah, her husband Benjamin, and their two sons were waiting in the courtyard. Zerah greeted everyone cordially and then excused himself to return to his own home. He had seen his niece safely home and wished to wash off the dust of travel. Mary could hardly wait for a bath herself.

Amos unhitched the donkey for her and put the animal in the corner of the courtyard as Benjamin brought the animal some hay. Seeing there was nothing more he needed to do, Amos bade Mary a hasty farewell and hurried home.

"I will be anxious to hear news of the baby," she called after him.

Huldah beamed at her. "Mary, you've been gone so long. We want to know all that has happened to you."

Merab added, "We who believed in Jesus have been meeting together. Now you can tell us what it was like to walk with the Lord."

Mishma approached Mary, his eyes alight.

Mary put a hand on his shoulder. "You have grown tall in two years."

He grinned at her. "I am fourteen now."

A little boy peered out at her from behind Keturah. She smiled down at him. "Seth? Why, you aren't a baby anymore."

Benjamin observed his youngest son with pride. "He's three."

"Mimi?" Seth whispered, staring at her with wide eyes.

Mimi—Grandmother. Mary's heart was touched.

"Is that all right, Mary? He has no grandmother and I was trying to explain to him who you were."

"Oh Keturah, I cannot think of anything I would rather be called." She put out her hand and the little boy took it.

Benjamin nodded to her. "Welcome home,

Mary. We hope you find your house has had good care."

The women gathered around the cart and began to unload it. Mary let Keturah direct where items were to be placed. The small stove that had seen so many meals on the road was worn out, but Mary decided to sort the things later. She left her sleeping rug and traveling bag by the door of the house to take up to her room.

Benjamin proudly showed Mary some repairs he'd made to the house and the ten healthy goats in the pen. Keturah pointed out the pots of herbs in the corner of the courtyard.

She hesitated and then turned to Mary. "Where would you like to sleep tonight? We can move our things from the room where you and Nathan slept."

Mary had given that some thought on her way home. There was no need for her to live in that house alone. "If you are willing, let me just have my old room back, upstairs. If I am their Mimi, I need to get reacquainted with my grand-children."

The relief on Keturah's face was touching. "We had hoped—we wanted to stay. Thank you. We'd love to have you be part of our family."

Mishma stepped forward shyly. "Then I may call you Mimi also?"

"Oh Mishma, of course you may."

There was a knock at the gate, and to her

surprise, Zerah entered the courtyard with a woman. Tall and pleasant-faced, she still had traces of beauty. Mary liked her at once.

Zerah looked down at her and said with pride, "Mary, I wanted to surprise you so I said nothing until now, but I want you to meet my betrothed, Tabitha."

"Oh, Uncle, I'm so happy for you. You'll marry again at last. When is the wedding?"

"In two months," Tabitha responded softly, and looked up at Zerah.

It was obvious to Mary that she adored him. So HaShem had answered her prayers for her uncle. It would be a good marriage.

Mary looked around. There was one person she had not seen, her father-in-law, Beriah.

"Is the father of Nathan well?"

There was an instant pause in the conversation and Zerah shook his head. "He fell ill two months ago and was gone in two days. We did not know where to reach you, and as it turned out there was no time. I'm sorry, Mary."

"And Beulah?"

Merab spoke up. "She is not feeling well, but insists she will join us tomorrow."

Her dear father-in-law, who had been so patient with her during the years of her illness, was dead. She had looked forward to seeing that gentle, kind man again. Could the loss of his only son have hastened his end? She would never know.

Aaron and Samuel returned to the fields, and Zerah left Tabitha there and took Daniel to see to the boatyard. Keturah served the women fruit and cheese in the shade of the sycamore tree. Seth happily kept close to his Mimi, squatting down to watch a lizard scurry across the stones.

Mary felt her heart could burst with happiness. She looked again at the two women who had been like aunts to her as she was growing up and had helped care for her when she was ill. She smiled at Tabitha. Now she would have another aunt.

Huldah frowned. "Is tomorrow evening too soon for the believers to gather here, Mary? Surely you must be tired."

Mary shook her head. "I'm never too tired to share the wonderful things our Lord and Messiah has done. I will get settled today and tomorrow evening tell you all that occurred in Jerusalem."

Merab spoke up. "There are many here in our neighborhood who believed in Jesus because you were healed. They were there in the crowd and saw it all. We decided to start meeting together to encourage one another in our new faith."

"To the frustration of our rabbi," Huldah added.

"He does not believe?"

"He doesn't understand how we can follow this false Messiah, as he calls him, and still be Jews."

Listening to their concerns, Mary now knew why the Lord had sent her back to Magdala. There was much work for her to do here and others who needed to hear her story. She looked forward to the next evening with great anticipation.

When the women left, Mary felt the tiredness creep over her. When Keturah began preparations for the evening meal, Mary climbed the stairs toward her old room. She approached the door and hesitated. She and Nathan remained downstairs in her parents' room after she was healed. She had not been able to face the room that had been her prison for so long.

Now, so many memories assailed her mind as she reached for the handle. She slowly pushed open the door and saw that the room had been freshly whitewashed. Her bed had been restored with a new rug to cover it. A small table and an oil lamp were placed next to her bed. She reveled in the silence. No voices. Only peace. She thought of the madwoman who had occupied this room so long. It was as if that life belonged to someone else.

She put down her traveling bag and hung her cloak on a peg by the door. Slowly she sank to her knees on the small mat near her bed and thanked HaShem for bringing her safely home, for the prospect of her uncle's wedding, and for the joy of belonging to a family once again. She wondered if she would ever marry again, as did Nathan's father and now her uncle. Perhaps she was past the age of childbearing, but as she pondered the idea, she had peace. She would enjoy Mishma and his little brother, Seth. She would have grandchildren to sit on her knee to tell stories to. She would tell them about Jesus and how much he loved little children.

The latticework on the window had been replaced, but now she didn't look on it as a prison holding her in. As she looked out toward the sea, she remembered that there was something she wanted to do.

The next morning she helped Keturah mix the bread dough, noting with pleasure that Keturah was still using the ingredients Mary's mother had used. She looked around and made a mental note of some other repairs she wanted to have done to the house. She would speak to her uncle about the expense.

After Mishma had gone to Hebrew school, Seth was watching her as they ate a simple breakfast. It was as if he was waiting for something.

She smiled at him. "I am going for a walk, Seth. Our new boat might be coming in and I would like to see it. Would you like to come with me?"

He jumped up and put his chubby hand in hers, his face alight with anticipation.

Mary stood on the bluff above the Sea of Galilee and looked out at the fishing boats, their white sails like wings on the water. Seth stood solemnly by her side holding her hand, and she sensed a bond between them already.

"Mimi, will we see the new boat?"

"Yes, Seth, it will come. Look there at the point and you will see it soon."

"Is it a big boat?"

"Yes, it is a big boat."

She thought back to the time when she and her mother had stood on this same bluff, watching for a boat to come into the harbor—a boat bringing her father home. She wondered where Eliab was now. Had he made it home safely? Had he found any of his family? She had prayed for him and wished him well in his quest.

The little boy bent down and examined a bug crawling through the grasses. Mary lifted her head, breathing in the sharp, tangy smell of the sea, and listened to the gulls crying to one another above the fishing boats.

Suddenly Seth stood and pointed out over the water. "I see it, Mimi, I see it!" The merchant ship rounded the point, its sails billowing majestically as it headed into port. The finest ship her father's boatyard had ever built. It had returned safely from its maiden voyage.

She felt the wind in her face bringing a hint of

things far away. They watched the ship slowly glide up to the dock, and she reached for Seth's chubby hand. With a contented sigh, she led him back toward home.

"Are people coming to our house tonight, Mimi?"

"Yes, child, we will have a celebration, with music and lots of good things to eat."

"I will have a date cake," he announced happily.

"I think I will have one too."

He tightened his grip on her hand. "And will you tell us stories?"

She nodded. Yes, she had many stories to tell, wonderful stories of a Messiah, a Savior who had died on a Roman cross, that they might have life.

❋ Acknowledgments ❋

To the wonderful staff at Revell who have worked with me over the years; my editor, Lonnie Hull DuPont, for her sense of humor and encouragement; my agent, Joyce Hart, for her belief in my writing; my friend, Dr. Vicki Hesterman, for her encouragement and keen insights; and my San Diego critique group for their suggestions and help with chapter after chapter.

❊ About the Author ❊

Diana Wallis Taylor is an award-winning author, poet, and songwriter. *Journey to the Well* debuted in 2009, as did her Christian romance, *Smoke Before the Wind*. Her collection of poetry, *Wings of the Wind*, came out in 2007. A former teacher, she retired in 1990 as director of conference services for a private college. After their marriage in 1990, she and her husband moved to northern California where she fulfilled a dream of owning a bookshop/coffeehouse for writers' groups and poetry readings and was able to devote more time to her writing.

The Taylors have six grown children between them and ten grandchildren. They now live in the San Diego area, where between writing projects Diana participates in Christian Women's Fellowship, serves on the board of the San Diego Christian Writers Guild, and is active in the music ministry of her church. She enjoys teaching poetry and writing workshops, and sharing her heart with women of all ages.

Visit Diana's website at
www.dianawallistaylor.com.

Center Point Large Print
600 Brooks Road / PO Box 1
Thorndike ME 04986-0001 USA

(207) 568-3717

US & Canada:
1 800 929-9108
www.centerpointlargeprint.com